THE
SUSPECT

BOOKS BY KATHRYN CROFT

The Girl With No Past
The Girl You Lost
While You Were Sleeping
Silent Lies
The Warning

The Lying Wife
The Neighbour Upstairs
The Other Husband
The Mother's Secret

Kathryn Croft

THE
SUSPECT

bookouture

Published by Bookouture in 2023

An imprint of Storyfire Ltd.
Carmelite House
50 Victoria Embankment
London EC4Y 0DZ

www.bookouture.com

ISBN: 978-1-80314-861-8
eBook ISBN: 978-1-80314-860-1

For Ann and Derrick

PROLOGUE
APRIL 1993

The park is quiet this morning, multiple shades of green leaves glinting in the sunlight while tree branches dance in the pleasant breeze. Other than the warmth of the early April morning, nothing is out of the ordinary, and there's certainly nothing to suggest that the day won't progress just like any other.

It's seven fifteen, and Lori Gray has no reason to suspect that she will never see another sunrise, or watch her young daughter grow into a woman. That time is ticking towards something unfathomable. That she'll miss out on so many milestones, all those first times with her child, the happiness, sadness, joy and fear they'll experience together, because someone will decide that Lori shouldn't be here.

She lets the comforting rays of sun coat her skin. She hadn't expected it to be this bright so hadn't applied sun cream after her shower, but at least her toddler is protected under the hood of the buggy.

Her footsteps are light as she pushes her daughter through Clapham Common, and the nursery rhyme she sings accompanies the bird tweets above them. It's been too long since she's done this – never again will she let anything distract her. Lori looks down at her daughter. *It's just me and you now.*

She breathes in the scent of freshly mown grass, and it reminds her of being at school. She wishes she'd known then how much easier those days would be, when her life stretched before her, a vast unexplored landscape. She wouldn't have been in such a rush to grow up if she'd known all the things that would confront her in adutlhood. Still, all that's behind her now.

How wonderful to feel as though she and Jess are the only people in the world, right here in such a large city. She wishes she could bottle this feeling and take it with them, because this is something she always wants to remember.

It occurs to Lori that she forgot to have breakfast before they left. Coffee doesn't count, does it? She doesn't care, though; all that matters is her little girl, and the fact that now they are finally free to live their lives.

ONE

NOW

Jess

She knows someone is watching her, with the same certainty that she knows the sun will set this evening. It's not just her instinct pleading with her to be alert, it's because she notices things. Everything. Minuscule details that most people wouldn't register. A glimmering droplet of rain on a crisp autumn leaf, the anxious frown lines on a person's face as they walk by, the way someone's hair falls about their face. She sees all of this, because she's made it her life's work to notice things. Never again will Jess miss what's right in front of her.

It's stood her well, this ability to take in everything her eyes fall upon, and has helped ensure the success of her photography business, where she is one of thousands of others in London scrabbling to make a living from their art. Success, though, what is that? It should mean happiness, and that's a label she will never truly wear, like a perfectly fitting item of clothing. There will always be a wall around her, preventing her from being truly at peace. She's okay with that, though. It's surprising what she's learnt to live with, what she's had to endure.

It's Friday afternoon when it happens, unseasonably mild for February. The strength of the sun feels like a heavy blanket as she walks along Camden high street. Jess often takes an afternoon stroll; as much as she loves spending time in her studio, now and again she needs to come up for air, to remind herself the world still exists. And sometimes the walls threaten to suffocate her if she's inside for too long.

Only indoor photoshoots are booked in today, and even though she prefers the outdoor sessions – the ones which allow her creativity to flow – she will never turn down work.

As usual, Camden is full of life, bustling with Londoners going about their business, and this comforts Jess. Living somewhere secluded is not an option; the thought of that chills her bones. Paralyses her. Jess needs people around. Crowds. The constant noise of the living.

She notices the man heading towards her, how his eyes rest on her for just a fraction too long. She doesn't recognise him, yet she's sure she's seen him before. He appears to be in his late fifties or early sixties, so is unlikely to be one of her clients – they're usually younger. As he passes, she slowly turns and sees that he's stopped too and is turning back to face her, his dark eyes boring into her. The urge to run is overwhelming, her instinct screaming that something isn't right. High alert, she considers it. Yet surely she's safe here, on this busy London street? There would be a hundred witnesses if anything were to happen.

Paranoia often controls her judgement; the events of all those years ago haunt her still, even though Jess remembers nothing. All she knows are snippets of information that have accidentally been passed on by others. Everyone around her knows Jess can't allow herself to hear about it. Even now. But this second-hand information means the experience has never been hers to own, but is simply a family story filtering through generations. Perhaps this man has mistaken her for someone.

That's all it is. She scowls at him and turns away, tries to control her breathing.

'Jessica?'

Not a mistake, then. This man knows exactly who she is. Swivelling round, she takes in his features: the hazel eyes set slightly too close together, the thick mop of unruly dark hair, twisted into almost-enviable curls. The dark grey coat that looks too thin for the season, despite today's inexplicable warmth.

He's close to her now, his eyes still fixed on her, his hands in his pockets. There's time to run. Visions infiltrate her head: his thin arm pulling something out – is it a knife this time? – her bright red blood pooling onto the pavement, obscuring the grey concrete. People walking past them as if this is a perfectly normal occurrence. Jess forces the images away, wills them to leave her alone; she's come too far to let these intrusive thoughts control her. Those days are behind her. This man is just someone she can't yet remember, that's all that is happening here.

'Who's asking?' Jess's words are sharp and abrupt, almost drowned out by the bus shrieking to a halt across the road. Until she knows who he is, she'll show him that she's not someone to mess with. She will be in control of this situation.

Seconds tick by and the man continues to stare, saying nothing. It's not a hard or menacing stare, though. Rather, it seems as though he's struggling to get his words out as he takes in every inch of her.

Jess turns away; she doesn't have time for this.

'No, wait. Please.' He steps forwards, holding up his hand. It's shaking.

'Who are you and what do you want?' Her tone is even fiercer this time.

The man takes a deep breath. It's not just his hand shaking, but his whole arm. Drugs, possibly. Or alcohol. He must be some kind of addict. 'I'm... I... I knew your mother. Lori.' He pauses, waits for this information to sink in. 'Do you think we can talk?'

And that's when Jess knows exactly who he is, despite never being able to recall his face. They *have* met before. Her chest tightens, restricting her breathing. She is suffocating. 'Get the hell away from me.'

'Please.' He holds up his hand again. It's steadier now. 'All I'm asking is for five minutes of your time. We can talk right here in the street if that makes you feel safer? I promise I'm not here to scare you or cause any trouble.' He takes a step backwards, takes a deep breath. 'I just want you to hear the truth. Then I swear to you I'll leave you alone. You'll never see or hear from me again. I promise.'

In her pocket, Jess reaches for the alarm, cold and solid beneath her fingers. She could set it off now and wait for the piercing screech to shatter both their ear drums, to add to the already existing cacophony in the street. But there is something about this man standing before her, pitiful and shrunken, begging her to listen, something which stills her hand.

'Say what you've got to say,' she demands. 'But don't come any closer. Stay where you are.' At any moment her insides will collapse. She's never known this feeling to be so powerful; she's always shut away the things she doesn't want to address, locked them up so they have no chance of escape. Jess already has a plan, though: she will let this monster say his piece then she will put into practice what she's learnt in all those self-defence classes. A karate kick to the ground before he's had a chance to blink should do it. And seconds after he's on the ground, she'll be calling the police. She just needs to keep it together long enough for him to admit that he murdered her mother in the park that morning.

'I didn't do it,' he says, his voice so soft she barely hears him. 'I could never...' He looks frail. There are huge black bags under his eyes and his skin looks thin, as if it will tear if someone so much as touches it. His name is Nathaniel. Nathaniel French. He lived alone near the park. This is one of the only bits of information Jess has allowed herself to know.

She takes a deep breath. 'You've tracked me down in the street to tell me the same lie you spouted all those years ago? Twenty-eight years ago!'

'It's not a lie,' he pleads. 'I swear to you – I'm innocent. I could never have done such a... such a terrible thing.' He's visibly shaking, and for a fraction of a second she feels a morsel of pity for him.

Jess shakes her head, takes a step back. 'I'm calling the police. This is harassment.' She reaches into her pocket and pulls out her mobile.

'No, please wait! You have to know the truth. You need to hear it from me.'

A woman in a suit passes by, smiling at them as she strolls towards Camden station. She is oblivious to the flames engulfing Jess, to the significance of these two people speaking to each other

'How did you find me?' she asks. 'Nobody knows who I am.' She's had to become a person who didn't exist before the age of two and a half, the erasing of those years the only way she could carry on.

He clears his throat. 'It's taken me a long time. Years. Finding you wasn't the biggest problem, though. It was finding enough nerve to face you.'

Now Jess wants to scream at him, grab him by the collar and shake him until his bones rattle, demand to know why he ended her mother's life. Lori had never done anything to him – they were strangers to each other. The case never made it to court but everyone believed he'd done it. Innocent until proven guilty, people claim, but there are a thousand shades in between black and white. Sometimes you just *know*.

'What could you possibly have to say to me?' Jess

demands. Has he noticed that her hands are also shaking? Despite appearances, she's out of her depth, numb with shock. This man is the last person Jess will reveal that to, though.

'I didn't do it,' he repeats. 'I know you were only young, but surely you must know that? Maybe... all these years have helped you to somehow... remember?'

Disgusted, she shakes her head. 'I was two and a half. I don't remember a thing. Then or now.' *He wants to find out what I know, it has to be that. He's worried that I'll go to the police and he'll be arrested, that this time it will finally catch up with him. Nobody can hide forever.*

'You'd remember me, though, wouldn't you? There'd be a flash of recognition or *something*? Look at my face.' He steps closer. 'Really look at me. You know it wasn't me, don't you?' He's begging now. Desperate.

'Back off.' Even though she wants to tell him that he's wrong, that she does feel as though he's familiar, she felt it when he walked past her moments ago, she will save this information for the police. And say as little as possible to this man. 'And no. I don't know it wasn't you,' she insists.

He takes another step closer. 'You'll know my name's Nathaniel. It's so important to me that you believe me, Jessica. I've hidden away for too long and now I need to clear my name, if not to other people then at least to you. You're the only one who matters.'

Bile burns her throat and she takes a step back.

He slowly nods. 'You're afraid of me. I can understand that. The papers painted me as a monster.' He snorts. 'I suppose that was their job. Every day I thank God that social media didn't exist then – I'd have had no place to run. I'd probably be dead. Someone would have killed me too.'

'But they didn't! And at least you're alive!' Jess shouts, incredulous.

He hangs his head. 'I know. I can't complain about my life. You've had it so much worse. And your mum... Lori...'

'I don't want your pity,' she hisses. 'I've made a life for myself, despite what you did.' He has destroyed too many lives, and Jess has been hell-bent on making sure he doesn't take any more of hers.

Nathaniel French shakes his head. 'I'm trying to tell you that I didn't do anything. It wasn't me. Please, you have to believe me.'

Tears of anger fight to escape, and it takes all her strength to hold them back. 'You were in that park. Everyone knew that. You admitted it.'

Again, his words are spoken softly. 'Yes, I was in Clapham Common that morning. I've never denied that, but I was nowhere near Lori.'

'Why, then? If you're innocent, which I don't believe for one second, then why were you there? Were you just waiting for a stranger to prey on? Is that it?' Her raised voice is attracting attention from passers-by. An elderly woman turns to stare. She is frowning, but eventually shrugs and continues towards the bus stop.

Nathaniel shakes his head. 'I... um... this is hard...'

Jess has heard enough now. 'You're a murderer.' Summoning all her courage, she takes a step towards him. There are so many people milling around; she will be okay. *There is strength in numbers.*

'Wait,' Nathaniel says, louder than she's heard him speak so far. 'I need to show you something that should help convince you.'

'There's nothing—'

'Please just look at this.' He digs his hand in his pocket and thrusts something towards her. It's a photograph, discoloured with age. Jess stares at it and even though it's impossible, she's looking at herself. At her own dark, wavy hair, hazel eyes.

Yet it's not her. The woman in the photo is her mother, her arms wrapped around the neck of a younger version of the man who's standing before Jess, her pink lipsticked mouth kissing his cheek. It's one of those passport-booth photos that often make people look like they're posing for a police mug shot.

Not these two, though. No, their eyes shine as they gaze at each other, and no amount of photo editing can alter the truth of what's in someone's eyes.

'I don't understand. What is this?'

Nathaniel's shoulders drop. 'Jessica, this is exactly what it looks like. A photo of me and your mother, Lori Gray. The woman I loved.'

TWO

JULY 1992

Lori

Lori is distracted tonight, even though she wants to be present here with Danny. His job as a sales manager takes him all over the country, but he's assured her it won't be forever – his plan is to start up his own consultancy business. Lori's not sure exactly what that would involve – he only ever discusses work in vague terms, as if he assumes she won't be interested. She is, though, and she wishes he would see that. He'll do it, of course, achieve his goals. Danny is one of those people who always get what they want.

This evening they're at Lori's flat in Clapham, the whole evening just for the three of them. Little Jess is asleep, so now it's just the two of them eating dinner, and although Lori tries to focus on what Danny is saying, her mind keeps drifting. He's saying something about how quickly Jess is growing, how she takes him by surprise every time he sees her. 'She knows her own mind, doesn't she?' Danny remarks, as if he's talking about someone else's child. If he spent more time with her, he'd know her like Lori does. Anyway, Lori's glad about Jess's forceful character. She's proud of her spirit, and will do everything she can to make sure it's never extinguished. She is determined that her daughter will have none of Lori's flaws.

'Nobody's perfect,' Danny laughs, whenever she mentions anything she's not happy with about herself. 'We wouldn't be human if we were. Let's embrace our imperfections.' Lori loves it when he says things like this; it makes her feel that even though they're not married, he is invested in this as much as she is. That he believes they are a family, a tight unit that will never break apart. That's not the case, though, and as much as she doesn't want to face it, tonight the truth – whatever it is – will rear its ugly head, she's sure of that.

Danny's cooked for them – spaghetti bolognese, which she has to admit is better than her own – and he's even put Jess to bed, read her favourite story about the tiger coming to tea that elicited loud giggles from their daughter. From the kitchen, Lori could hear them, and happiness swelled within her, as though someone had flicked a switch and lit her up. She can't remember the last time Danny was here to read Jess a story. It's always work, work, work. This important client or that urgent meeting. He works hard, and he provides for his daughter, she's just grateful for that. Even if it means time together is so limited. He's vastly different to the other men she's dated; at thirty-five, not only is he older, with a more mature mind, but none of the others had the dreams and aspirations Danny has. This is what she loves about him. It's also the reason she felt so guilty when she fell pregnant.

Lori had been on the pill; it shouldn't have happened, but then she remembered that she'd been sick for a few days, unable to keep water down, let alone food, so that could have been why it hadn't worked that month. Or maybe it wasn't that at all, and it would have happened anyway. Either way, she will never regret little Jessica being here. And Danny had taken it well, told her it was a blessing and he couldn't be happier, even though they weren't even living together.

She had expected him to have reservations, but there had been no hesitation in his response, just a huge smile that made his dark eyes sparkle. And then he had proposed to her, told her that they should wait for the baby to arrive, give themselves a chance to settle into life as parents, and then have an amazing wedding with their little girl by their sides.

'Aren't you hungry?' Danny asks now, frowning. 'You normally love bolognese. That's why I made it.' He twists some spaghetti around his fork, making it look effortless. She finds it easier to cut hers into smaller strands.

'Can we talk?' It's now or never; she has to take this opportunity while he's here and Jess is asleep; there's only a small window of time before she'll wake up and need a cuddle. Lori doesn't mind this at all – she's only two so she's bound to need her mum in the night. Tonight, though, she needs as much uninterrupted time as possible.

Danny places his fork down and smiles. 'Course we can. I'm all yours for the whole night. What's on your mind?'

Here goes. 'I've been thinking a lot about my life, and... I want to make some changes. I'll be thirty in a few years and—'

Danny chuckles. 'You're only twenty-six, Lori. There's a while to go before thirty.'

She ignores his comment, as true as it might be. 'Jess is two now and she's so much more aware of things. I think it would be nice for her if you were... here a bit more?' She pauses to study his expression. She's normally good at reading him, but now it's impossible to tell what thoughts are flitting through his mind.

'I know,' Danny says, a smile spreading across his face. 'You're right. I do probably need to take a bit of a step back from work. It's just so hard right now and I really need this promotion. That will be good for all of us, won't it? Maybe we can even go on holiday this year? I've always fancied Portugal – how about you? But not the touristy places. I want to experience the culture, not just sit around on a beach all day. That's just not me, is it? What do you think?'

This is the thing about Danny – once he starts talking, Lori always loses her train of thought. She gets lost in him. Sucked into whatever he's talking about because he speaks with such passion. But she won't let that happen this time. This is far too important. She nods. 'Yeah, that sounds good, but that wasn't really what I was talking about.'

His eyes widen. Then he frowns. 'Oh, what is it, then?'

'Do I really have to spell it out to you, Danny?' Lori's voice is too loud; she needs to be careful not to wake Jess.

The frown remains on Danny's face. She hates it when those deep lines crease his skin, the disappointment that's aimed directly at her. 'I think you're going to have to,' he replies.

'Move in with us.' Now it's out in the ether she won't stop until she's said her piece. 'I don't see what's stopping you – when you're not working you're never at your flat anyway. Why not just give it up? Surely it's a waste of money? Before Jess was born you said it might be something we could do, then you never mentioned it again.'

He's shaking his head now, staring at his half-eaten plate of food. The spaghetti will be stone-cold by now. 'I knew this would come up again,' he says. 'I was just hoping you were happy with the way things are.' He puts down his fork, shakes his head. 'Aren't you happy, Lori? Don't we love each other? Isn't that all that matters? And that we're good parents to our little girl?'

So many questions – they spin around her head, crashing against the sides of her skull, because ultimately Lori knows that beneath whatever Danny says lies the fact that he doesn't want to live with her. He never has. And now she's sure he never will.

For several moments she stares at him, unsure how she should deal with this. If she accepts what he's saying then nothing will ever change and she deserves more than that. She needs to fight back, to stand up for what she wants; after all, isn't that exactly what she wants to teach Jess?

'Okay,' she says, her voice a whisper. 'What you're saying is that you don't want to move in with me and your daughter? You're happy for us to live apart for the rest of her life? You do remember that we're engaged? You're the one who suggested getting married. And Jess has your surname.'

'Yes. I meant in the future, once things were more settled for me at work and we'd got used to being parents. It's just that right now I'm happy living on my own.' He pauses, reaches across the table for her hand. 'I'm sorry that upsets you. I do love you, Lori. Both of you. And we will get married and live together. I just... I also love living alone at the moment. Having my own space. When I'm there at least. I'm happy and I don't want anything to change right now. It doesn't mean I don't love you.'

Lori snatches her hand away. She knows she's being childish, sulking even, but she feels like she's about to spiral out of control. Like everything is being decided for her and none of it's what she wants. Without a word she stands and picks up her plate of untouched food. She heads to the bin and empties it all in, scraping the plate long after there's nothing left on it.

'Five years we've been together!' she says. 'We have a daughter, yet you won't even think about moving in?'

'Calm down, Lori. Jess will wake up.'

'She's fine!' She's shouting again now, and she glances at the baby monitor, relieved to find that Jess hasn't moved.

'I think I should go,' Danny says. 'Give you some space. I don't know what's going on but... you're not yourself right now.'

Before she's even had a chance to work out how she feels about him leaving, Danny grabs his coat and disappears through the front door, closing it quietly behind him.

From behind a veil of tears Lori stands at the window and

watches him cross the road to his car. He glances up at her and seems to freeze. Maybe he'll change his mind and come back. But then he unlocks the car door and climbs in. The spasms of pain she feels are like nothing she's experienced before. Yes, there have been a couple of other men in her past, but neither of those relationships had such an impact on her life. Even before they had a child together, she felt inextricably linked to Danny; when she's with him she feels truly at home, at peace, right where she's meant to be. What does it mean that he's now walking away from her, refusing to even contemplate the idea of living together, of being the family she wants them to be for Jess's sake as well as her own?

It's only when Danny's Volvo disappears from view that she walks away from the window and crosses the narrow hallway to Jess's room. Before she goes in, she looks around the flat and tries to see it through Danny's eyes. Yes, it's lacking in space, but it's warm and cosy, and they wouldn't have to stay here. She should have told him that. They could go anywhere they want to.

She remembers her grandmother always telling her never to go to bed on an angry word. What has she done? She needs to apologise to Danny.

In Jess's room, she crouches down at her daughter's cot. Her little girl looks so at peace as she sleeps, soft snores escaping from her mouth, and this makes Lori even more determined to fight for her relationship. If it's at all within her power, she won't have Jess growing up in a broken home. She wants a healthy family life for her daughter – something she no longer has.

'Come on, little one,' Lori whispers, reaching into the cot. 'We need to go and find Daddy. There are some things I need to say to him that can't wait.'

Jess is such a heavy sleeper that she barely stirs while Lori transfers her into the car. Even if she does wake up, the motion of the car will soon lull her back to sleep, and Lori will just explain that they're going on an adventure to find Daddy. She'll make it into a game, and everything will be okay.

Driving through the streets of London towards Wimbledon in the early night calms Jess. With daylight fading, there's less traffic on the roads and the car moves freely. She's done this drive so many times, and she tells herself she's just visiting Danny as normal, that the equilibrium in their relationship hasn't been destabilised. Still, the tightness in her stomach exposes the lie she's telling herself.

Now she's reaching Danny's street, anxiety strikes her; the feeling that this won't end well courses through her body. After her outburst, she wouldn't blame Danny for having doubts about her. The Lori he witnessed tonight isn't the easy-going young woman he met at the video shop where she works part-time.

Jess is still sleeping in the back as Lori parks up. She'll probably wake up now, but that's okay. Once they're inside Lori can place her down on Danny's bed while they talk in the living room.

The parking space she's found is across the road. The usually bright royal blue of Danny's front door looks dull in the darkness. Everything feels different at night, she thinks, steeling herself for the inevitable confrontation. What she's not expecting is to see Danny coming out of his front door carrying a gym bag and walking quickly to his car. He looks so intent, his eyes fixed on his car, that he doesn't notice Lori's white Peugeot is right across from him.

Confusion grips her. Where would he be going this late at night? It can't be work related – this was a rare night off for him. He must be coming back to see her, to apologise and tell her that of course they should live together. It can't be anything else. She's about to get out and prevent him making the unnecessary journey back to hers – she and Jess can stay the night at Danny's – but Jess wakes up, emitting an ear-shattering cry.

'Oh, sweetheart,' Lori says, leaning back to comfort her. 'We're at Daddy's now, nothing to worry about.' Jess's cries begin to subside. 'Just hang on a minute.' Lori lowers the window to shout out to Danny, but it's too late – he's already starting the engine, pulling out and driving away, without even a glance around him.

There's no choice now other than to follow him, so of course she does, and as she drives, she comforts herself with the thought that he's coming back to them.

How wrong she is.

It's not long before Lori realises that Danny isn't going to her flat in Clapham; he's driving straight through Wandsworth towards Putney, continuing on through Hammersmith towards the North Circular.

And there it is again: the feeling that this won't end well. That somehow, this is the beginning of the end.

They're in Chiswick now, a place she's unfamiliar with, and it unsettles her. A quick glance in the rear-view mirror shows her that Jess is once again sleeping, her head leaning back against the seat, her tiny mouth forming an O.

It's several more minutes before Danny pulls into a residential street. Lori parks further away, making sure she can't be seen. But Danny is oblivious, too caught up in his own world to notice her, a world which is unfamiliar to Lori.

She doesn't need to get out of the car. No, what she witnesses next is enough to tell her that she does not know this man at all, that she never has. That he shouldn't be the father of her child.

And most of all, that she's made a terrible mistake.

THREE

NOW

Jess

Jess stands outside the police station, frozen, while the hustle of life carries on around her. Police officers walk past her with barely a glance, nobody stopping to wonder what she's doing. She takes deep breaths to calm herself. It's what she's taught herself to do whenever a panic attack rears its head – something she's not had to deal with for years. Then she stares at the steps leading up to the door, counting them to ground her, to take the focus from the rising anxiety.

Then she closes her eyes and pictures herself striding inside the building, telling whoever will listen that she has new evidence in her mother's case. Demanding that they listen. That they do something. Unlike most people, Jess's faith in the police is minimal. She knows they're only human, just like everyone else, and sometimes they just aren't able to find answers, like they couldn't for her mother.

Jess has always been a problem solver – someone who won't stop until she's worked out whatever the issue is, but this... it's something else entirely. It troubles her that Nathaniel French tracked her down to show her that photograph. If he is guilty, then what could he hope to gain by that? She hadn't stopped to ask him; the urge to run was too powerful, so that's what she did. Not once glancing back. Before that, though, he'd found a second to shove a crumpled business card into her hand, and while she'd let it drop to the ground, she went back after he'd disappeared.

She reaches into her bag to check it's there; it disgusts her yet she can't bring herself to throw it away.

Just in case.

Her phone rings and she snatches it from her pocket, desperate for someone's – anyone's – voice to ground her.

'Jessica? It's Eliza Clark. I'm at your studio but nobody's answering. I hope I haven't got the wrong time? Didn't we say twelve?'

Silently she curses. Eliza is her next appointment, and even if Jess runs she's at least ten minutes away from home. 'I'm so sorry, I had to pop out quickly and got caught up. At the bank.' A small lie that makes her cringe. 'I'm on my way now. And I'll give you ten per cent off for the inconvenience.'

Jess glances back at the police station entrance then steels herself for the sprint home.

With back-to-back appointments for the rest of the afternoon, Jess is too distracted to pay attention to her increasing anxiety. But when five o'clock comes, and her last client has left, the weight of it crushes her. She rushes from the house and heads to the Tube station, her heart rate only slowing as she merges into the sea of bodies crammed onto the platform. She stands among them, with barely a centimetre of space around her, and finally her breathing slows. Here, she is at peace. She remains on the platform as several trains stop and leave; as each one carries away a herd of people, they are quickly replaced with a flood of new commuters.

It's over an hour later before Jess heads home, and now her mind has calmed enough to turn her thoughts to the encounter with Nathaniel French. It's been constantly there, though, whirring away like an extractor fan. Sitting on the sofa with a glass of wine, she replays the conversation, searching for anything she may have missed. There's got to be something – some kind of clue that will reveal the reason he's tracked her down – yet Jess is unable to grasp it.

Unless he's telling the truth.

She closes her eyes and sees her mother kissing his cheek. How happy they both looked as they smiled, not for the camera, but for each other. What does it prove, though? Perhaps it's even more compelling evidence that the man is guilty. If they were having some sort of relationship, that could mean he had a reason to want her dead. Aren't the majority of murder victims killed by someone they know? The main reason no charges were brought against him was because the police couldn't tie him in any way to her mother. And there was nothing in his history to suggest he was mentally disturbed. In fact, there was nothing other than the fact that he was known to the police for something else he'd done. Violence towards another man. Something different. Jess can't make sense of any of this. She needs to speak to her father.

Her mobile vibrates and Zara's name flashes on the screen. Her younger sister is always the person Jess turns to when she needs to talk about anything, but this time she hesitates to answer. She won't burden Zara with anything to do with this, even though she knows her sister would listen.

Jess has grown up with Carolina, Zara's mother, and has always felt like a daughter to her, no different to Zara. Even now, though she's no longer with Danny, Carolina remains kind and loving towards her. Neither she nor Zara deserve the past to be raked up, muddying everything they've tried to build for themselves. Jess understands this only too well; erasing that early part of her life is exactly what she's done, until now. It's the only way she's been able to cope with her invisible scars.

Yet always lurking is the threat that it would reappear. And now it has.

'Jess! Are you excited?' Zara's voice, upbeat and loud, fills her ears. 'Please tell me you are – Gabriel's been desperate to meet you.'

Gabriel. The friend of Zara and Ryan who Jess agreed to go on a blind date with. Until now, she'd forgotten all about it.

'Oh, Zara, I, um—'

'Please don't tell me you've changed your mind.' Zara sighs. 'Ryan and I are both convinced you two will hit it off. You just have to trust me. I know this is right.'

She is touched by the disappointment in her sister's voice. Zara has put a lot of thought into finding someone who she considers to be a good match for her. Her sister fought hard against Jess's reluctance, determined to find someone for her after her relationship with Harrison ended months ago. 'It's time,' Zara had insisted. 'Things ended with Harrison ages ago and you're too young and amazing to spend so much time on your own. At least get out there and have some fun. It doesn't have to be anything heavy. Just enjoy yourself.'

It was for Zara's sake that Jess had given in. Her sister had already tried – and failed – to get her on Tinder, so this was a compromise. 'No, it's not that. I still want to meet him. It's just that tonight's not looking good any more.'

'Why, what's going on?'

This is the perfect opening for Jess to share what's happened, yet she sticks to her resolution not to burden her sister. 'I've been swamped this afternoon and I need to edit the photos from today. I also need to see Dad.'

'Why? Is he okay? What's going on?' Sometimes the speed

with which Zara talks is endearing, other times, like now, Jess can't keep up with it.

It's true that their father struggles to see Zara as a grown woman, but this takes nothing away from the strong bond Jess shares with him. It's something unique to them. They are two members of a club that, thankfully, not many people can understand, and this is the cement on which their relationship has been built. Jess has often wondered how different their bond might be if her mother had lived.

'Dad's fine,' Jess assures her sister. 'I just haven't seen him for a while and wanted to pop over for a chat. Can you let Gabriel know? Tell him I really am sorry. We'll make it another time, though.'

Zara sighs. 'Okay. You're just lucky he's so laid-back and won't take it personally.' She laughs. 'I wish Ryan could be a bit more like that. I don't know how the two of them are such good friends.' She chuckles again. 'You know I'm joking? Ryan will kill me for saying that.'

'I know you love him just how he is,' Jess reassures her. She'd been thrilled when Zara had met Ryan. Kind and patient, if a bit quiet and unadventurous, he clearly puts Zara on a pedestal. The two of them couldn't be more dissimilar, yet somehow it works, and has done for two years.

'That's true. I do love him. Bless him. Anyway, I'll let you know when Gabriel's free.'

Jess is on edge as she sits on her father's beige leather sofa, her mind a jumble of incoherent thoughts. Once again it strikes her how strange it feels to be among her father's things without any hint of her stepmother Carolina's belongings. Since their divorce, he has created a home for himself that is modern and minimal, a stark contrast to Carolina's fondness for ornaments and decorative items squeezed into every available space.

Danny hands her a mug of coffee and smiles. He's always happy to see her, and doesn't seem perturbed by her turning up unannounced. As usual, she doesn't have the heart to tell him that his coffee tastes foul; out of politeness she swallows it down without tasting it.

'So, how's life treating you, Jess?' he asks. 'Business good?'

She nods, forces a smile. 'Yep, everything's fine. It's always a bit slow at the beginning of the year but I've still been busy.'

He smiles. Sometimes Jess struggles to believe he's almost sixty-two – if she didn't know him, she'd guess he was nearer to fifty. 'That's my girl. Just like me, you are. Do you know, your face lights up whenever you talk about work? That makes me happy. I always say that if you can at least love what you do, then that can get you through anything life throws at you.'

Jess realises she's lucky to feel so passionately about her photography, and make a decent enough living from it. 'That's not always possible for everyone, though, is it, Dad?'

'No, it's not. I wish it was.'

As much as small talk is easier to deal with, Jess needs to get to the point. 'Dad, I need to talk to you, and... what I'm about to say might be a bit of a shock.'

He frowns, places his mug on the coffee table. 'You're scaring me now. Please tell me you're not ill?'

'No, no, it's nothing like that.'

'Not Zara?'

'No, she's fine. Everyone's fine.' Jess takes a deep breath, prepares for the inevitable impact her words will have. 'Someone approached me in Camden High Street this afternoon. A man. He knew my name and at first I didn't know who he was. Until he said he knew my mother.' She pauses. 'Dad, it was... Nathaniel French.'

Her father's skin pales, his face stricken. It takes him a moment to speak. 'What?'

'It was him, Dad.' She repeats his name, and it feels like

knives in her throat. 'He said he'd been searching for me for a long time, and that he wanted to tell me he was innocent.'

The shock and confusion on her father's face is instantly replaced with rage, his skin quickly turning puce. This anger is something she's never witnessed before. He stares at her for a moment before finally speaking. 'Are you okay? He didn't try to hurt you? Or threaten you? You should have run away. He's a dangerous man!'

Jess assures him she was fine. 'He didn't come near me.'

Danny sighs. 'Okay. Tell me everything that man said to you. And please don't leave anything out.'

Jess repeats Nathaniel French's words, all the time conscious of her father's immutable gaze. This will be difficult for him to hear; he doesn't need a reminder of what happened to her mother. She should have given him some warning.

When she's finished, she waits for him to speak. In this interlude she plans what will happen next: she'll tell him she's going straight to the police, and he'll insist on coming with her.

Danny composes himself then shakes his head and grabs her hand. 'I knew it was only a matter of time. Worms can crawl back into the woodwork, but they always resurface. Are you okay? I could tell something was wrong the second you walked in. I know you, Jessie.'

With a nod, she assures him that she's fine, that it will take more than Nathaniel French to shake her up, and every word she utters is the truth.

'That bastard,' he mutters. 'As if he hasn't already done enough.'

'There's more, Dad. He, um...'

'What, Jess? Tell me.'

She has to tell her father everything. Full disclosure, and then he can help make sense of it. There's bound to be an explanation; her mother must have been with Nathaniel before she met her dad.

'He had a photograph. It was of him and Mum. Together.'

A frown appears on Danny's face, increasing his age in an instant. 'I don't understand. What photo? From a newspaper?'

Jess, usually outspoken, struggles to form her next words. 'No, it was of him and Mum. Together. Like a couple.' She describes the photo in detail, so clear in her mind she could be looking at it right now. An image that will never fade.

Heavy silence floods the room.

Finally, her father responds, shaking his head. 'No. Lori didn't know that man, there's no way. That would have come out in the investigation.'

'I saw it, Dad. As clear as anything. It wasn't fake. I'd be able to tell.' Of course, her father doesn't want to believe this.

'It must be. You can do all sorts with all those photo editing apps.'

'Dad. It was a genuine old photograph. Somehow, Mum knew Nathaniel French. Do you think they could have been... having an affair?'

There is no hesitation in her father's answer. 'No. Definitely not.'

'Well, they definitely knew each other. Don't you see? This is new evidence but I don't know why he showed it to me – it does nothing to prove his innocence. He's made a huge mistake by coming to me.' Even as she says this, once again she wonders why Nathaniel French would have come to her if he truly was guilty, and risk opening himself up to more investigation? He'd got away with it, at least in the eyes of the law, and had never spent more than a few days in a prison cell. Jess forces this away. Given time, she'll figure out the reason. 'We need to go to the police, Dad. I'm planning to go right now, I just wanted to tell you all first. I'm happy going alone but I'm sure you'll want to come?'

He stares at her then shakes his head. 'No.'

The word – simple and unambiguous – knocks her off

balance. She'd been convinced her father would come. Perhaps it is too difficult. 'Okay, I understand. It's too painful. Well, I'll call you after and let you know what they say.'

'No, Jess. What I mean is neither of us is going.'

'What? But why?'

'They couldn't put him away for it before, what makes you think they'll be able to now? I know they wanted to, but the CPS said they had no case. I can't bear the thought of it all being dragged up again.' He stands up. 'I don't want him in our lives, Jess. He's already done enough damage. I've put it to rest, and I think you should do the same. He's a dangerous man, Jess.'

Later, she sits in her car outside her sister's flat in Kingston. Zara's at a gym class but it finishes soon and is only at the leisure centre around the corner. Jess could go in – Ryan is home and would be more than happy for her to wait inside if he knew she was out here – but she needs to be alone with her thoughts, to try to make sense of the day until she can talk it through with her sister.

It's her father's reluctance to get answers, despite asserting that Nathaniel is a dangerous man, that has drawn Jess to confide in Zara. He's her father too, so even if it happened long before Zara was born, this is in some ways her business too.

Jess has never seen him give up on things; usually he prides himself on seeing things through until the end. Still, she needs to try and understand it from his point of view: it destroyed him when her mother was killed, and it's understandable that he doesn't want that deep wound opened up.

Someone taps on the window, making her jump. She really is on edge.

Zara's face peers in, smiling. She's still in her gym clothes, a headband keeping her long hair off her face. 'What are you doing in the car? Didn't Ryan answer? He never said he was going out.' She frowns, pulls out her phone.

'No, I didn't knock. Didn't want to disturb him.'

Zara rolls her eyes. 'From what? His Xbox? You'd be doing him a favour.' She laughs, and this slice of reality is just what Jess needs to hear in the midst of this nightmare.

'Come in, you clown,' her sister urges. 'I don't like the thought of you sitting out here. It's bucketing down too.'

Jess doesn't have the energy to point out that she's hardly getting wet in the car. Instead, she lets Zara pull her out of her Golf. 'Come on,' her sister says. 'I can fill you in on what Gabriel said.' She frowns. 'I'm surprised you haven't asked, actually. Wait. You do still want to meet him, don't you? You said you'd postpone, not call it off.'

'Okay, now I really am getting soaked,' Jess says. 'This is not about Gabriel. Can we just go inside?'

She usually loves being in Zara's flat. It exudes warmth from every corner, and the soft feminine touches leave little space for anything of Ryan's, other than his Xbox. There are too many artificial flowers for Jess's liking, too much pink, but she admires her sister's eye for design, all the effort she's put in to making it a home. Tonight, though, Jess is too on edge to feel comfortable here.

After offering to make them coffee, Ryan explains that he's on his way out. 'Hope you don't think I'm being rude rushing off? I'm running a bit late as it is.'

'He's got a squash court booked,' Zara says.

Jess is relieved; it will be easier to talk to Zara if they're alone.

'So, did you see Dad?' her sister asks, once Ryan's left. 'Please promise me he's not ill. You would tell me, wouldn't you? No secrets, ever, remember?'

Jess nods. 'I promise you this isn't about Dad's health. He's fine.' At least physically, she wants to add. 'Look, I wasn't going to burden you with all this – at least not yet – but something happened today and I'm a bit worried about Dad's reaction.'

'Go on.' Lines crease Zara's forehead now, and instantly Jess regrets bringing it up. It takes a lot to dampen Zara's light-hearted approach to life. Maybe Jess doesn't need to say anything; she can handle it by herself. That's what she always does. But Zara would never forgive Jess for keeping her in the dark, when it's all going to come out. *No secrets.*

She launches straight into her encounter with Nathaniel French, fully aware of the horror scrawled across Zara's face as she listens. Several times her sister opens her mouth to speak, but each time she reconsiders, staying silent to let Jess finish.

'That's why I went to see Dad this evening,' she explains. 'I thought he'd want to come to the police with me. He knows so much more about the case than I do.'

'You were just a small child,' Zara says. 'We all understood why you've never wanted to read anything about the case. It was for your own mental health. So, what did Dad say? When are you going to the police?'

'That's just it. We're not. At least *he's* not. He told me to leave it alone. He laid down the law about it and said we're not going to the police or having anything to do with Nathaniel French.'

Zara's mouth falls open. 'I don't understand. Why would he say that? It doesn't make any sense. He should want to make sure that man's brought to justice.'

'That's why I wanted to talk to you tonight, Zara. It's so out of character. I know I've never asked this before, but does Dad ever talk to you about my mum?'

Zara frowns before shaking her head. 'He hasn't mentioned Lori for a long time. And even when he has it's never much, really. I've never liked to ask. He might have just mentioned her name in passing – you know, something like, "Oh, Lori would have loved that painting." Things like that. He's definitely never talked about what happened that morning. Sorry, Jess. I think it's just his way of dealing with it.'

Her frustration grows. 'What about to your mum? I know they divorced a few years ago but they're still good friends, aren't they? They still talk and see each other.'

'Yeah, but I've never really talked to Mum about Lori so I'm not sure.'

It occurs to Jess that hers is a family of silence. Close in so many ways, yet none of them feel able to talk about something so important. That needs to change; they need to be in this together. Now more than ever.

'Do you want me to ask Mum?' Zara suggests. 'We could call her now?'

She's grateful for her sister's offer, but Jess needs to talk to Carolina alone. 'Do you mind if I speak to her myself? I'll give her a call and see if we can meet up.'

'Okay.' Zara's reply is quiet, almost a whisper.

'I just don't want to drag you into all of this,' Jess explains.

'It's okay, Jess. I understand. Anyway, I suppose this is why you wanted to cancel your date with Gabriel?'

Gabriel. Jess can't keep avoiding this date indefinitely, not when she's promised her sister she'll give it a chance. Clearly, though, she's not as invested in it as she should be. 'Maybe we should just forget about it?' Jess suggests.

Zara's eyes widen. 'Don't say that, sis. He really wants to meet you. I've been trying to organise this for weeks. I messaged him this afternoon and he wanted to know if you could make tomorrow instead?'

'I really don't think that's a good idea. Not with everything that's happened today. I just don't have the headspace for meeting someone new right now.'

There's a brief pause. 'Okay, I get it.' Zara sighs. 'I'll let him know. But just remember, he might be new to you but Ryan's known him for ages so he's not a complete stranger.'

Disappointing her sister after everything she's done for her is the last thing Jess wants to do, and she's seconds away from changing her mind. She can't commit to it, though, it wouldn't be fair to Gabriel or Zara. 'Maybe if he's still free in a couple of months? Things might look different for me then.' They will. She's determined to put this Nathaniel French business to rest, as quickly as he's blasted into her life.

Later, as she lies in bed, Jess struggles to remove the image of Nathaniel French from her head. What presses on her mind even more, though, is her father's forceful determination that they shouldn't go to the police. Something isn't right, and she needs to find out what that is.

FOUR

SEPTEMBER 1992

Lori

For months now, Lori has managed to avoid seeing her family. Even though her mother's house in Clapham is only a short drive from Lori's flat, and her sister is close by in Balham, this avoidance hasn't been difficult – they're all leading busy lives. Important lives. She is too; she's bringing up her daughter who one day will contribute to this world – what's more important than that? But they won't see it that way.

Talking on the phone is something she can deal with, where they can't see the lie in her eyes whenever Danny is mentioned. She can't bear to tell them the truth, to face their disappointment that she couldn't even keep the relationship going with her child's father. So Lori has stayed silent about it whenever she's spoken to either of them, avoiding any topic that could lead to deeper questions about Danny.

It was bad enough when she'd had to tell them she was pregnant without being married. *'How can you look after a baby when you haven't even got yourself sorted? You don't even know what you want to do with your life. I do worry about you, Lori.'*

Her mother's words had stung, at a time when all Lori needed was someone to tell her she'd be fine. But at least they had loved baby Jess enough to sweep that under the carpet. And despite no one believing she would be, Lori had proven herself to be a more than capable mother.

This, though, they won't accept so easily. She invited Danny into their lives. Made him part of the family. Somehow, it will all be her fault.

Lori refuses to let them see how badly she has failed. How she couldn't see what was right in front of her. It's what they expect of her, so she will make sure she shocks them all. That she turns her life around and then, only then, will she explain the truth about Danny.

Her father's birthday has crept up on her, though, and today she needs to show her face at her mother's house. Ever since he died, they have marked this day by getting together to remember him, to celebrate his life, to make sure he is never forgotten. Lori will never be the one who doesn't show up. Her father meant everything to her. She's fully aware that her sister feels differently – that every year Mionie is desperate to say she can't make it. That's the thing, though – she comes for their mother, while Lori comes for her dad.

She will keep this visit brief, leave before they can extract the truth from her; Mionie has a way of making people talk. At least little Jess will distract everyone, and no matter how her family treats Lori, they at least love her daughter.

Mionie is already there when she arrives, sitting on the sofa with a glass of wine in her hand. 'We didn't think you were coming,' Mionie says, placing her glass down and rushing over. 'It's so lovely to see you. We don't get the chance often, do we?' She kisses the air next to Lori's cheek before reaching for Jess. She scoops her up and twirls her around, then plants a kiss firmly on her niece's cheek. 'We've missed you.'

Jess giggles. 'Play' she says, wriggling to get down.

'Of course, little princess,' Mionie says. 'What shall we play?'

Lori bristles; she loathes it when anyone automatically assumes Jess will want to be a princess just because she's a girl. She hates all the connotations of this label. Instead, she wants Jess to think of herself as a warrior.

As an afterthought, Mionie turns and gives Lori the briefest of hugs. One day Lori will grab her fiercely and force her sister to embrace her properly, just to make her feel uncomfortable, which is exactly how she makes Lori feel every time she's in her presence. Lori has realised this lately. It's how someone makes you *feel* that counts, more so than the words they're speaking. 'And where's Danny?' Mionie asks.

Lori takes a deep breath. 'Working.'

Mionie stares at her, so intensely that Lori's sure she can see through her lie.

'No Neil, then?' Lori quickly asks.

'He'll be here soon. He's just finishing a shift at the hospital. It's his eighth day in a row and he's utterly exhausted, but you try pulling him away from his patients.'

Lori always wonders how Mionie and Neil make their relationship work when they're both A & E doctors. When one is on a night shift the other is usually working days, so she can't understand how they have any time for each other. Perhaps they prefer it this way – knowing they've got each other but happy not to have to spend too much time together. A relationship of convenience. Lori likes Neil – he's always been kind to her – but she couldn't live like that. For Lori it's all or nothing; she won't be in a relationship unless she's fully invested.

More fool her.

Lori watches Mionie take Jess's hand and sing to her. It's not just their

personalities that are worlds apart – Mionie's light brown hair and blue eyes are the contrast to Lori's dark waves and dark eyes. *I'm just like Dad, and you are the image of Mum. You're even tall like Mum, while I'm barely average height.*

'You tell your daddy that we'd all like to see him soon, okay, Jess?' Mionie says, midway through 'Baa, Baa, Black Sheep'. 'If we didn't know better, we'd swear he doesn't even exist.'

When Jess giggles it occurs to Lori that Jess might actually let something slip about Danny. She hasn't seen him for two months. Thankfully, she's used to him working away so much, so it doesn't seemed to have registered yet that this has been a longer gap between visits than usual. Still, Jess's grasp of language is quite advanced for a two-year-old, so Lori will need to be ready to step in at any moment.

She reaches for her daughter and grabs her hand. 'Come on, Jess, shall we go and see Scout?'

'Woof woof,' Jess says, smiling.

'The neighbour's kids have taken him for a walk,' Mionie declares. 'To help Mum out.'

'Well, let's go and see Grandma in the kitchen while we wait.' Lori turns towards the door.

'She'll be busy getting the food ready – why don't you go and help her and Jess can stay in here and play with her aunt?' Mionie narrows her eyes. It's more of a demand than a suggestion, but in front of Jess at least she's trying to keep her tone neutral.

Lori's about to reject this idea but thinks better of it. If she protests too much, her sister will know something is wrong. And if Jess does happen to say anything, she'll have to explain it away as nonsensical toddler talk.

At the kitchen door, she stands and watches her mother preparing vegetables. She's so engrossed in peeling carrots that she doesn't notice Lori's presence until she clears her throat.

'Hello, Lori. So glad you could come.' Her mother walks over and gives her a light hug. Fleeting. Gone before it's fully registered.

'Let me help.' Lori heads to the kitchen island and reaches into the drawer for another peeler. There'll be one in here somewhere. Her mother has a collection of them and never throws anything away. 'Mionie seems happy to see Jess,' she says.

Her mother turns to her. 'She's happy to see both of you. Why wouldn't she be?'

Many times before Lori's tried to talk to her mum about Mionie, but Meredith never seems to understand what she's saying. Or prefers not to. 'She doesn't like me much, does she?' Lori ventures.

Her mother puts down the carrot she's just peeled. 'Oh, Lori, you always did tend to be a bit overdramatic. I've never heard her say anything unkind to you. Even after...' She turns away, picks up the carrot and begins chopping.

'After Dad left me all the money.'

Her mother chops faster, and Lori winces. If she was chopping through a carrot that quickly, she would have sliced through her finger by now. 'Well, I have to say, that wasn't exactly fair, was it? Of course Mionie's bound to have been a bit... upset by it.'

Lori understands this, and she offered to share the money, but Mionie wouldn't take it. The damage had been done. So she'd put it all in an account for Jess, and has never touched a penny. Her sister knows this, but it makes no difference.

'You know why he did it, don't you?' Meredith says. 'Because he knew Mionie could look after herself. She's always been independent. Sorry to say this, Lori, but he felt sorry for you. And that wasn't fair. But she's your sister – she loves you and Jess.'

'So, because we're family there's automatically love there? The world doesn't work like that, Mum.'

'Why do you always feel as though the world is against you?'

'I don't at all!'

'To be honest, Lori, it's all a bit tiring. It's your dad's birthday, and it would be nice if we could all just have a lovely meal and remember him. Can we just enjoy a family lunch together, darling? It's what he would have wanted.'

The guilt trip. Her mother always does this when Lori dares to mention her sister's treatment of her. Meredith knows this will force Lori to stay silent.

They carry on preparing the food in silence, Lori already too exhausted for a battle with her mother.

'No Danny, then?' Her mother asks eventually. 'Is he working again? I thought after not making it last year he'd put a note in his calendar to keep this day free? Such a shame.'

'Remember I said on the phone he wouldn't be able to come?' Lori had hoped this would put a stop to too much mention of Danny once she was here.

'Yes, you did. I just thought he might have still made it.'

Before Lori can respond, Mionie appears, Jess resting on her hip. 'We've come to see what Grandma's doing, haven't we, princess?'

Meredith rushes to Jess, who revels in the attention, and Lori stands back, as she usually does, withering away.

When the doorbell rings, it's Lori's chance to escape. 'I'll get it,' she calls, already rushing out.

Neil, Mionie's fiancé, is standing at the door, smiling. He swoops her up in a hug. He's still wearing his scrubs, and the strong smell of disinfectant makes her cut short the embrace. 'Hi, Lori,' he says. 'How's everything going?' He steps inside and puts down his backpack. But he watches her the whole time, showing Lori that he's not just making polite conversation but actually wants to know how she is.

A lump forms in her throat, his kindness somehow fuelling her sadness. 'Everything's great,' she says.

'I'm glad to hear that. Is Danny here?'

It's the kindness in his smile that breaks her. Tears roll down her cheeks.

'Hey, what is it?' He puts his arm around her. 'Shall I get someone? Meredith?'

'No,' she manages to say. 'I'm okay.'

Neil reaches into his pocket and pulls out a tissue. 'I promise it's clean,' he says, handing it to her. 'Look, I'm here if you want to talk. About anything.' He glances at the living room door, lowers his voice. 'I just want you to know that I see what goes on. And I'm here for you.'

Lori crumples the damp tissue in her hand. 'Thanks, Neil.' She needs to pull herself together. Even though she trusts him, he's still her sister's fiancé; his allegiance will be with Mionie. None of them can know about Danny.

'Where's Meredith?' Neil asks.

'In the kitchen.'

'Ah, and Mionie?'

Lori flicks her head towards the living room. 'In the kitchen too.'

'I'd better go and show my face, then.' He walks away, then turns back to her. 'Remember, I'm here if you want to chat.'

As soon as he's disappeared, Lori rushes to the downstairs toilet and locks herself in, sinking to the floor. She looks at her watch, focuses her attention on the second hand ticking away.

Sooner or later, Lori will have to face her family.

The lunch is surprisingly uneventful, all of them consumed with the roast dinner Lori's mother has prepared, and there's no more mention of Danny's absence. There is a moment, just before dessert, when it seems Mionie is about to bring it up, but Neil quickly shuts it down.

Lori glances at the bottle of wine on the table, almost tasting it just by looking, and then she remembers that she and Jess aren't staying the night. She reaches for her glass of water instead. She can live without the wine; having to get Jess home to bed will be the perfect excuse to leave early, and the thought of being in her own tiny flat, curled up on the sofa with Jess in her arms pulls Lori through the long afternoon.

'You look a million miles away,' Neil says, joining her on the sofa after lunch. Jess is napping upstairs in the spare room, while Lori's mother clears up in the kitchen. Lori had offered to help, had even started to load the dishwasher, but her mother had taken over and sent her out of the kitchen, insisting on doing it alone.

She has no idea where Mionie's got to. She thinks she heard her mention something about walking off all the food they've eaten.

'Do I?' she says to Neil. 'Sorry.'

Neil holds his hands up. 'Hey, please don't apologise to me. Look, I know it's not my place to say it, but have you and Danny had some sort of argument?'

Lori doesn't want to open up to Neil, or anyone else, but she needs to stop him asking more questions. 'Something like that,' she says. 'Please don't say anything to Mionie. Or Mum.'

'I won't. Do you want to talk about what happened?' Neil asks.

It hits her that, through Jess, she will always be inextricably linked to Danny. She hates the idea of this, needs to be free of him and his toxicity.

'I know one thing,' Neil says, when she doesn't respond. 'If you can just find a way to be at peace with each other, for Jess's sake, then nothing else matters.'

Lori stares at Neil, soaking up his words, wanting them to be absorbed so deeply within her that she is able to believe them. Neil doesn't know Danny, though, what he's capable of, and neither does she. He's not a good man, she wants to say, and for just a fleeting moment the words are there at the edge of her mouth, willing her to set them free.

'You're right,' is all she says. 'We'll be fine. It's just a stupid disagreement.'

Neil pats her arm. 'Course it will be fine. And even if it's not, you're strong, Lori, don't ever stop believing that.' He glances at the door, carries on when he is sure they're alone. 'You're a good mother to Jess and you have a great future ahead of you. You're only twenty-six, your family need to cut you some slack. I don't know why they can't see all this.'

Lori is so shocked to hear this that she's momentarily speechless. 'I'm really trying to get my life together. To plan for the future.' She tells him how she's enrolled on a degree course at university, starting next September. 'I'll be studying law. And until then I'll keep working at the video shop to save up as much money as I can.'

'That's great, Lori. Do you know, your eyes lit up when you were telling me that.'

'I've finally found the thing I was meant to do,' she says. 'Criminal law. I want to help protect victims of crime. I've always thought about it, I just got a bit... sidetracked. And then my beautiful Jess came along.'

'And you'll do it,' Neil says. 'Getting sidetracked happens to the best of us.'

Lori raises her eyebrows. 'I'm guessing not you. You're a doctor, you must have always been on track.'

'You'd be surprised. I actually took a year out before med school to go travelling. And when I was in Thailand I nearly changed my mind about studying medicine. I even considered not coming back to the UK. I just wanted to be a free spirit.' He pauses, stares into space. 'I guess it was just a wobble and my true calling really is medicine.'

Lori wants to tell him that he's too good for her sister,

too... nice. Ultimately, though, she realises that she's happy Mionie has found someone like Neil, even though she thinks their relationship is bizarre. Neil is laid-back and at ease with himself, while Mionie is always uptight.

'This time next year I'll be your brother-in-law,' Neil says, as if he's just read Lori's thoughts. 'Then you'll know you've always got someone in the family who's on your team. Maybe I can even change how things are for you.'

She's not sure what makes her do it but Lori leans over and wraps him in a hug, catching him off-guard.

'Oh, wow. What did I do to deserve that?' He chuckles, his cheeks turning crimson.

Lori's about to answer when she catches sight of someone standing in the doorway, watching them.

Mionie.

Her sister glares at her before turning and walking away without a word, but she'd stayed long enough for Lori to catch the disgust in her eyes.

FIVE

NOW

Jess

Ever since her mother was killed, she's avoided parks. The beauty of these places has been forever tarnished, the world made smaller and claustrophobic by the act of another. Even spaces that have the remotest of connections to parks are places Jess cannot bring herself to enter. Despite having no memory of what happened that morning, just the thought of being in a park cuts off her breath. Jess knows she would see her mother everywhere, visualise the attack as if it were happening right then, despite never recalling the details.

All of this means it's taken every bit of strength she can summon to meet her stepmother Carolina at the canal in Islington. It's nothing like a park, she assures herself, even though if she closed her eyes, the sounds of bicycles whirring past and the birds fluttering above her head would make it feel like she were in one. Her body tenses. There are plenty of people around. Nothing can happen here. It's not eerily quiet like that April morning twenty-eight years ago.

Thankfully, Carolina is already here, waving at her as she approaches, Rocket on a lead by her side. The dog's name always makes Jess smile, his advanced age having forced him to slow down to anything but speedy.

'Hi, love,' Carolina says. She pulls Jess towards her, wrapping her in the bear hug she always gives to Jess and Zara. Her flowery scent reminds Jess of her late childhood, of the times when she'd sit cuddled up to Carolina, crying in her arms because even though she loved Carolina, she always felt guilty for thinking that it should have been her mum who read her bedtime stories. Her mum who slipped a pound coin under her pillow, replacing the teeth Jess left there.

'How are you, love? You didn't sound good on the phone earlier.'

Carolina has always been sharp and perceptive; Jess is sure that, along with her kindness, this is one of the reasons her father fell in love with her so quickly. Even though she and her father are no longer together, Jess knows nothing will destroy the friendship she has with Carolina.

It takes Jess a minute to order her thoughts. She doesn't want to sound irrational; she wants to show Carolina that she's handling this calmly and logically, not letting her emotions run away with her. That's the kind of person she always is, and Jess knows Carolina is similar.

'I know it might seem strange for me to ask this now, but did Dad ever talk about my mum when you were together?'

Carolina slows down to almost a standstill and turns to face her. She must be shocked that Jess has brought this up – she's rarely mentioned her mother before, and never in the context of her father. Mostly out of respect for the new life he had with Carolina and Zara, but also because it's too painful. 'Well, sometimes he did. Why do you ask?'

Once again, she recounts the details of Nathaniel

approaching her on Camden High Street, this time ending with how her father refuses to go to the police.

'Oh dear,' Carolina takes her arm. 'Are you okay? It must have been frightening to suddenly be confronted by that man. How strange that he'd track you down after all these years.'

They begin walking again, while not too far away Rocket gnaws at a stick he's commandeered.

'It just doesn't make sense, Carolina. I've been going over and over it, and if Nathaniel French is guilty, then why did he bother finding me? He got away with it, so wouldn't he want to hide away for the rest of his life? Yet he was adamant that he's innocent and wanted me to know that.'

Carolina's mouth twists. 'Hmm. I'm not sure. It's very bizarre. Unless... maybe he wanted to check *you* hadn't remembered anything?'

'But he'd know if I had because the police would be knocking on his door.'

'True.'

They resume walking. 'That photograph is hard to explain away,' Carolina says. 'I've never heard your dad mention any of Lori's previous relationships, but I always got the impression there was no one significant before Danny.'

Jess nods. 'The timings just don't add up, either. She was twenty-two when she got together with Dad, and in that photo she looked the same as she did in the ones just before she died. She definitely wasn't twenty-two in them. Besides, Nathaniel swore they had been together around the time she was... killed.' Even now, it's still hard for Jess to say this word out loud.

Carolina slows down, turns to face her. 'Could it have been a fake? Photoshopped?'

'That's what Dad suggested, but it wasn't, I could tell.'

'Yes, of course you'd know. Oh, Jess, I don't know what all this means. I wish I had some answers for you.'

In the distance, Rocket is getting too far ahead, despite his slow pace.

'What's even stranger,' Jess continues, 'is Dad's reaction. Why

wouldn't he want us to go straight to the police if Nathaniel is dangerous?'

There's a pause while Carolina considers this. 'I do agree with you, it seems very odd.' She turns to whistle at Rocket, who has wandered off. 'Come here, boy! Look, Jess, the only thing I can think of is that your dad doesn't want the past being raked up. Sleeping dogs and all that. He's worked hard to find a way to live with what happened. He really did love Lori, you know. She was his whole world.'

Jess nods. 'I know that.'

'Even when I came along, and that was three years later, he was still in love with your mum. That was fine with me, though. I loved him enough to realise I didn't need to compete with Lori. I know your dad loved me too – it was just a different kind of love.' She smiles. 'And I got a beautiful daughter from our marriage, so I don't regret a thing. And stepdaughter, of course. You know you mean the world to me, don't you, Jess?'

She does. Carolina has always been a mother to her, without ever trying to fill the empty space Lori's death left. 'It feels like you've always been there.'

'Ah, bless you.' Carolina whistles for Rocket again, who's still wrestling with his stick and ignoring her calls for him to come back.

Jess stares at the ground. 'There is one thing I've always wondered but never wanted to ask either of you.'

'Ask away, dear.'

'I'm just curious why Dad never married my mum, even though they had me.'

Carolina nods. 'And you probably want to know why on earth he married me so quickly?'

'Something like that, yes.'

'I don't blame you for asking. I'd want to know too, if I were you. That's all down to me, I'm afraid. As you know, I can be quite pushy. I know what I want, don't I? Well, as soon as I found out I was pregnant I told your dad we had to get married. Oh, he grumbled and moaned a bit, spouted stuff about us not needing a piece of paper to show our commitment, but he knew he'd end up losing me if he didn't agree.' She stops, frowning. 'Oh dear, I realise just how awful that sounds now I'm saying it out loud.'

'No, I understand.'

'As far as your mum's concerned, I think she was just probably too sweet, and let your dad get his own way too much.'

'Do you think?'

'Well, I can't be sure because I didn't know her, but they were together for a long time. Five years, wasn't it? And unless she didn't want to get married, then I can't see a reason why they didn't.'

In all her daydreams about the kind of woman her mother was, Jess has never considered the possibility that Lori didn't want to marry her dad. What was her reason for that? Does this give more credence to Nathaniel's claim?

'Listen, love,' Carolina says. 'Do you want me to speak to your dad? See if I can work out what's going on with him? I think he's always found it easier to talk to me about the more difficult things than he does you and Zara. He never wants to bother you with his issues.'

'I assumed the only issues he had were work related,' Jess says.

'It might appear that way, but I know he worries about you girls. He's terrified of anything happening to you. Of losing you like he did Lori. I know he never says anything to you and Zara but that's because he doesn't want you worrying about him.' She sighs. 'To be honest, his fixation on work is probably a good thing – it stops him dwelling on things he shouldn't be worrying about.'

This makes sense to Jess; she needs to stop being so hard on her father about how much he works. He needs it. Just as she needs her business to keep her mind healthy. She takes Carolina's arm. 'He's lucky to have you in his life. We all are.'

'Oh, Jess, that's lovely. But I'm not perfect. I make mistakes just like everyone else. I try hard to learn from them, though. Now, do you want me speak to your dad?'

Normally she'd decline this offer, but Carolina might have more luck getting through to her father, as stubborn as he is. 'Yes, I think it might be better coming from you. He needs to realise how important it is that we go to the police. I would never want to go behind his back and do it anyway, but if it comes to that, then I might have to.'

Carolina nods. 'Leave it with me. I'll sort Danny out. But in the meantime, Jess, you need to be careful. Nathaniel French is a dangerous man, and I don't like the fact that he's tracked you down. He could know where you live! Promise me you'll be careful?'

She assures Carolina that she will, but as they continue walking along the canal, all Jess can think about is that she needs to talk to Nathaniel French again. For years she's lived in fear, and having some answers might finally help her to heal. If her father won't go to the police, then Jess will get the truth out of that man herself.

Work is the only thing that distracts Jess in the afternoon, and with three photo sessions to edit, everything else has to wait. This is her livelihood, and she prides herself on meeting deadlines, keeping her customers happy.

With ear buds in and music blaring as she edits, Jess sits in her studio at the back of her garden, so engrossed in what she's doing that she doesn't notice there's someone standing at the door. It's only when the song stops that she finally registers the tap on the glass.

Immediately she is wary; she has no appointments this afternoon and her studio can only be accessed by the gate at the side of her house. Unless someone has an appointment, people don't normally walk into the garden unannounced.

Nathaniel French must know where she lives, and that's how he knew she would be on the high street yesterday. What else does he know about her? Has he been watching her? Following her?

But although it's a man standing in her garden, it's not Nathaniel. He's much younger, about the same age as Jess, holding his hand up in a tentative wave as he smiles at her. His hair is the dirty blonde colour that she loves to see in photographs because of the way the light reflects each separate tone, and she can tell that he's at least six feet tall.

With a frown on her face, she leaves her computer and heads to the door. 'Can I help you?'

'Hi, yeah, sorry to just turn up like this. I'm Gabriel.' He holds out his hand, his smile spreading as he does so. 'I know Zara said you were too busy to meet up, and that you work most weekends, so I thought, well, it's nearly lunchtime and maybe you might be hungry?' He holds up a brown paper bag.

Jess is taken aback that he's turned up like this, when she'd put him far out of her mind, and for a moment she struggles to respond. She's seen a photo of him on Zara's Instagram, but like most people, he looks different in person. 'Um...' Does she want him here? Part of her thinks it's nice that he's gone to this effort, but the sceptical side of her wants to dismiss him as too intense. They've never even met before. Zara and Ryan know him well, Jess reminds herself. That's got to count for something. Still,

Zara shouldn't have given out Jess's address without asking first. She'll try to let this go, though – Zara means well.

'I know it's a bit weird me just turning up like this,' Gabriel says. 'So you can tell me to go and I won't take offence. But we can get so caught up in our busy lives we forget to do what's important sometimes. Like connecting with people. And from everything Zara's said about you, well, I thought I'd take a chance and see if you can spare just an hour. But more importantly, these sandwiches are the best in the area. Freshly made just now from that bakery round the corner.' He shakes the bag.

'I, um... okay. I suppose I can take a short break.' And the sight of that bakery bag has made her stomach growl.

'I promise you, I ran this by Zara before I came and she said it's just what you need. Look at it this way – at least you won't have to sit through a three-course meal with me if you end up wanting to run away! It's a win–win, I reckon!'

Jess checks her watch; It's nearly one o'clock and she's ahead with her editing, so there's no reason she can't take an hour out to eat. And if it turns out that Gabriel is some kind of weirdo, then at least she'll have got this date out of the way. Proven to Zara that she is trying to get on with her life after Harrison. Besides, she'll never hear the end of it from her sister if she doesn't give this a chance.

'One hour then,' Jess agrees. She points to his padded coat. 'You're wrapped up warm so I'll grab my coat and we can sit in the garden.' Not only is it cold today, but slate grey clouds loom overhead, threatening to erupt in the sky. Still, she'll be more comfortable outside, where the garden is overlooked by houses on every side.

The sandwich Gabriel's bought is tuna mayo, which Zara must have told him she loves, not realising that lately Jess has gone off it. Out of politeness she takes a bite, hoping he won't notice if she doesn't finish it. 'So, how do you know Ryan?'

'I met him through his dad. Years ago. I'm a property developer with my dad and brother, and Ryan's dad did some work on a house I was doing up. It's a small world, isn't it?'

'It is,' she agrees. So small that Nathaniel French could track her down. 'Some people make it that way, though, don't they?'

Gabriel frowns. 'Um, I suppose so.'

'Oh, just ignore me. I often go off on a tangent. Sorry.'

Gabriel laughs. 'Well, I do have that effect on people. As well as being really forward and turning up unexpectedly at their homes.'

Jess finds herself reluctantly warming to him. Yet even if they do hit it off, she just can't get into anything right now. A flash of guilt washes over her. She's wasting his time. Wasting both of theirs. Still, the least she can do is try to be good company for the rest of this hour she's promised him. 'So, dish the dirt on Ryan, then,' Jess says. 'Does he have a secret wild side that none of us know about?'

By the end of the hour, Jess has almost forgotten whatever awaits her outside of this moment. She hasn't needed long to ascertain that Gabriel is interesting and intelligent, and more than anything he's somehow distracted her from everything, something only work has done up until now.

He checks his Apple Watch. 'Well, it's five to two. I guess my time's nearly up. He smiles. 'So, what's the verdict? Am I worth seeing again? I promise I'll only turn up when you invite me.'

'I want to, I really do,' Jess replies. 'It's just... my life's complicated at the moment.'

He nods. 'Zara told me you've come out of a long relationship. I thought that was a while ago, though?'

'It was. Over a year. It's...' She's about to explain that her reluctance is not just about Harrison, but she doesn't want to involve Gabriel in whatever is going on. Zara has assured her that he knows nothing about her past and she wants to keep it that way.

'We're still friends, so he's still in my life,' she admits. 'I know that can make things messy.' She doesn't add that it's been months since she saw Harrison, or that she's been ignoring his messages lately. That it's tricky to maintain a friendship when there are residual feelings.

'Okay,' Gabriel says. 'Let me just promise you that this doesn't have to be a big *thing*. We can just get to know each other and see what happens? No pressure. I like to just go with the flow anyway.'

This is exactly what Zara has told her. 'Oh,' Jess says, feigning disappointment. 'Does that mean you're not going to propose to me any time soon, then?'

'Definitely not. I'd need at least one more date before that happens.'

They both laugh, and Gabriel's sparkling green eyes make Jess realise she does want to see him again, despite her reservations. 'Okay, even though you turning up here like this is bordering on stalker behaviour, I'll let that go for now.'

'Great!'

'Just two more things,' she warns. 'Please don't propose to me next time, and also, I prefer cheese and salad in my sandwich.'

Things feel different in the evening, once darkness descends. Heavier. Everything tainted by shadows, no matter how many lights Jess turns on in the house. She's tried calling her father, only to be met with his voicemail message each time. She's even considered going over there again, but Carolina's promised to talk to him and Jess doesn't want to push him. Whatever his reasons for not wanting to pursue Nathaniel French, Jess has to believe that he's doing what he thinks is best.

It's nine forty-five when she picks up her mobile and presses in the number on the card she was given. Then she waits, holding her breath until a quiet husky voice answers.

She almost hangs up.

'It's Jessica Moore,' she says eventually.

'I was hoping it was you. Thank you. Thank you for calling.'

'I'm not calling for your sake so don't thank me.' She pauses. 'I want... to know more. And then I'll make up my mind what to do about you.'

There's a pause on his side this time, lasting so long she wonders if he's ended the call.

'Fair enough,' he says. 'I can understand that. You should be cautious. Can we meet somewhere? Today?'

The muscles in her stomach tighten. 'No. We can talk now, on the phone.' The thought of being face-to-face with him again unsettles her.

'I understand your reluctance, but this is better in person. Please believe me.'

Jess is about to refuse again when it occurs to her that it will be easier to detect his lies if she can look him in the eye. And body language never deceives.

'Okay. Not today, though. Tomorrow.' She pauses. 'Oxford Street, outside Oxford Circus station at two p.m.' The place will be crammed with bodies, even on a Sunday. She will feel as safe as is possible. As difficult as this will be, it will be worth it if she can reclaim the life she should have had. She will find out more from him, and then she will go to the police.

'I'll be there. And thank you again.'

Jess ends the call without another word. She won't grant that man any respect.

Sleep evades her after that, her mind too full of all the scenarios that could play out when she meets Nathaniel French tomorrow. Is he her mother's murderer? She needs to be sure. And she wants something more concrete to take to her father.

Something which will leave him no doubts about going to the police, and getting justice for Lori.

She finally drifts off and then wakes with a start, long before morning, her mind unable to escape the vision of Nathaniel French holding a glistening knife, slicing across her throat, a crimson pool fanning out around her.

SIX

OCTOBER 1992

Lori

She doesn't believe in fate. It's a cop-out, she reckons. Something to help people deal with life, because it would scare them too much to accept that everything is just random. Things don't happen for a reason; they happen because we make them. Because we want them to. Or they happen for no reason at all. It's as simple as that.

Lori isn't destined to go to university; she's starting next September because it's what she wants to do, and what she's planned to do, what she's living every day of her life working towards. There's been no divine intervention; the universe has nothing to do with it. Lori is in charge of her own life.

This is why, when she walks into the bustling bar in Islington, she does it with the knowledge that it could have been any bar that she and Belle chose to meet in. In fact, they'd even changed their minds at the last minute and decided against Covent Garden. Not for any particular reason. Just because.

There's no sign of Belle when she steps inside, even though Lori is ten minutes late. She smiles, despite feeling slight annoyance, because she's read that how you present yourself on the outside can impact how you feel inside. Besides, she should have expected this; she and Belle both work part time at Blockbuster in Wimbledon, and she can count on one hand the amount of times her friend has actually turned up the required ten minutes before her shift starts. Lori's never sure how Belle hasn't been disciplined for it, but she smiles to think that somehow she's wrapped Nigel – the manager – around her finger.

Lori can feel eyes on her as she heads to the bar; she doesn't turn to face anyone's gaze, though, instead keeping her focus on the female bartender. Her glossy black hair falls in perfect ringlets and it's mesmerising – it's now Lori's turn to stare. As Lori gets closer she notices there's a small diamond stud in her nose and a tattoo of a word Lori can't make out on her wrist.

The girl flashes her a bright red smile. 'What can I get you?'

Lori scans the room again, just to see if she needs to order one for Belle too, even though she has no idea what her friend would like – they're close at work, but this is the first time they've arranged to meet up outside of work. There's still no sign of her, so Lori orders for herself. This is a rare night to herself – Jess safely tucked up in bed at Lori's mum's house – so she should make the most of it. 'Gin and tonic please,' she says, folding her arms and leaning on the bar. Perhaps people will think she's used to doing this, when the truth is, it's only the second time she's ever been in a bar. They've never really interested her. Lori doesn't want to think about that first time, though. No, she's shoved anything to do with Danny far to the back of her mind, bolted that door, thrown away the key. At least this is what she has convinced herself.

'Coming right up,' the girl says, spinning around to grab a glass.

'Hurry up, Belle,' Lori mumbles. Even though she feels

comfortable here, the atmosphere friendly enough, Lori doesn't want to sit on her own for too long.

Yet this is exactly what happens, and three quarters of an hour later, Lori is still by herself, her third drink in front of her, her eyes darting to the door every time it opens. She's stopped hoping now, has given up expecting Belle to appear. The music is louder now, but she's glad of this – it makes her feel less alone.

'Can I buy you a drink?'

The voice comes from nowhere, startling Lori. She's been rummaging in her bag, trying to find her address book so she can call Belle from the payphone by the toilets. She looks up and there's a young guy in a suit standing by her table, smiling at her, lifting his own glass. There's a cigarette in his hand and he puts it to his mouth and blows smoke rings into the air.

'No, thanks,' she says, turning back to her bag.

'Ah, come on, let me get you one. I won't even sit with you – you can drink it by yourself while you wait for whoever it is you're waiting for.'

Lori tuts. 'How do you know I'm waiting for anyone? Can't a woman go to a bar by herself?'

He laughs. 'Yeah, course. But you've been checking that door every few seconds.'

She has to admit he's got her there. 'And clearly you've been checking me every few seconds.'

He laughs, stubs out his cigarette in an ashtray on the table next to them. The people sitting at it don't seem to mind, or even notice. 'Don't worry, I'm sure he's on his way,' the guy says when she doesn't reply.

Lori rolls her eyes. She should let him believe she's meeting a man, her boyfriend perhaps, or a first date, and then this guy might actually leave her alone, but she hates to let him think he's right. Then she spots the gold band on his finger. She's made assumptions about him when maybe he's simply being friendly. 'Actually, I'm waiting for a female friend.'

'Well, in that case, how about I keep you company until she gets here?'

It's a split-second decision, nothing to do with fate, just a whim. 'Okay,' she agrees. 'Gin and tonic for me, then.' She watches as he makes his way to the bar. Belle hasn't turned up, but she can still have some company while she has one more drink before going home.

When he returns, he sits in the seat that Belle should be in. Lori can't help glancing at the door, hoping once more that her friend will flounce through it bursting with apologies, but no one new has entered in the last few minutes. She turns back to her new acquaintance, who's watching her and grinning.

'What's so amusing?' Lori asks, reaching for the drink he's bought her.

'Nothing at all, I just finding you intriguing. Like no one I've ever met before.'

Lori sniggers. 'Well, that's bordering on the worst chat-up line I've ever heard. You met me a few seconds ago. What could you possibly know about me?'

To his credit, he doesn't seem to take offence. 'Hey, that's a bit presumptuous, isn't it? What makes you think I'm chatting you up?'

'Actually, I don't.' She points to his hand. 'Not with that beauty on your finger.'

For a second he looks flustered, but quickly recovers. 'Ah, let me explain. I'm actually separated and I can't get this off.' He pulls at it, as if this will be the proof Lori needs to believe him. How many times has he uttered those words to women in bars?

She studies him, takes in his appearance. He's attractive enough. He has an interesting face, one with character. A mouth she can imagine kissing.

'I'm sorry to hear that,' she says.

'Don't be,' he says. 'I'm not.'

They both raise their glasses simultaneously.

'Hey, I don't even know your name. I'm Shane.'

'Lizzi,' she says, smiling at him. She's not going to give this man her real name when she knows nothing about him.

He holds out his hand, even though they are way past this stage. 'Nice to meet you, Lizzi.'

For the rest of the evening, Lori no longer glances at the door. In fact, she barely even registers that her friend hasn't turned up. She's got something more important to focus on now.

Jess, of course, is never far from her thoughts. This is why she is here, sitting with Shane. This is just the beginning. Everything she does, she does for her daughter.

And later, as she leaves the bar with Shane, letting him put his arm around her, murmur into her ear all the things he wants to do to her, she laughs silently. Perhaps she does believe in fate after all.

Because this is definitely meant to be.

SEVEN

NOW

Jess

Even here, in the middle of an Oxford Street teeming with bodies, anxiety floods through her veins. She tries to reassure herself that Nathaniel French can't hurt her, not here in front of all these witnesses, yet how can she be sure of this when, in all likelihood, he is the one who so savagely attacked her mother? It might have been early morning then, while most of London still slept, but he was undeterred by the bright glare of the sun. She needs to do this, though. For too long she's lived with the threat of her mother's murderer being out there. She wants to put an end to this, to find a way to prove he is guilty.

If it *was* him.

Jess is twenty minutes early; she can't help it – there's no way she'll run the risk of him assuming she isn't coming, or thinking she might have called the police. She can't let him disappear now. For some reason he's infiltrated her life, and she wants answers. Whatever they may be.

A hand presses firmly on her shoulder, forcing her to spin around at the same time as her stomach somersaults. 'What the hell?' she demands, before she's even registered that it's Nathaniel French.

'Sorry, Jessica! You just seemed a thousand miles away. I didn't mean to startle you.'

Had she been distracted? Jess prides herself on being alert. 'You didn't startle me,' she snaps. 'I just wasn't expecting you to be so early.' She can't help being defensive, it's born of her resentment that this man acts as though they have some kind of friendship, as though it's the most natural thing in the world that she's talking to him.

'I couldn't risk being late and you thinking I wasn't coming. I'm so grateful you called, and you're willing to hear me out,' Nathaniel says.

He looks different today, less nervous, more together. His face seems to have more colour than last time, and he's shaved too, which makes him look younger. Jess pictures the young man from the photo, and for just a flicker of a second, she can understand why – if it's true – her mother might have found him attractive. And as she stares at him, she struggles to connect what she sees with the heinous act that was carried out in the park.

The monsters are always the ones who look harmless. Kind, attractive even. She's not about to fall victim to the fallacy that evil can be seen. No, evil is camouflaged, insidious, and that's how it catches us unawares.

'I told you on the phone not to thank me,' Jess tells him. 'I'm not doing this for you.'

He nods. 'Of course. You're doing it for Lori. And for yourself, of course. I can only imagine how difficult it's been for you.'

Hearing her mother's name leave his mouth turns her cold. This is a dangerous game she's playing.

'Actually, we have a lot in common,' Nathaniel continues. 'We've both had our lives torn apart by what happened. We're both vicitms here. And it's time to put it right.'

'Let's walk,' she demands. 'And you and I are nothing alike.'

'Actually, would you mind if we find somewhere to sit? I injured my knee while I was running years ago, and sometimes it's still painful putting pressure on it.'

Jess glances at his jean-clad legs. Of course, there's no way to know if he's telling the truth. 'I suppose. There's a coffee shop down the next side road, with tables outside. Don't expect me to buy you one.'

'I wouldn't dream of it,' he says, as they head off.

She notices his limp. Is it all just part of his act?

Outside the coffee shop, Jess selects a table while Nathaniel heads inside to order something. She's refused his offer of a drink; just the thought of it is too... normal. This situation is so far from that, there is no way she will have coffee with him. It's bad enough that they'll be sharing a table. She imagines her father's horror if he knew what she was doing at this moment, and guilt overwhelms her. It's not too late to change her mind; she could run now, while Nathaniel's still inside. Or she could ignore her dad's wishes; her phone is in her coat pocket, she could be speaking to the police within seconds. Nathaniel would sit there, oblivious, sipping his coffee while the police make their way here.

But she doesn't move. She's already gone too far to turn back now.

'Start talking, then,' she demands, folding her arms. 'And say everything you've got to say now because this will be the last time we meet. Do you understand?'

There's a slight movement of his head and it's hard to discern whether it's a nod or a shake. 'I met your mum in 1993,' he begins. 'The year she—'

'No, that's impossible. She was with my dad then. You must have known her before they met.' Yet Jess knows this can't be true – that the photo shows her mother as a twenty-six-year-old woman, not a teenager.

Nathaniel shakes his head, throws her a look that shows pity, something she hates anyone feeling for her. 'I'm afraid not. We met in January '93. In a coffee shop. I'd only gone in there that day because my usual café was closed for refurbishments.' He rolls his eyes. 'Turns out stepping inside that place was the best and worst thing I ever did. If I'd never met Lori, then...' He shakes his head again, slides his coffee cup towards him and wraps both hands around it. 'But I can never regret having her in my life. Even with everything I had to go through after I was wrongly accused. She was... a special person.'

A scream grows in Jess's throat. He needs to stop talking about her mother. He has no right. But if she stops him, she'll never understand what he's doing, and why he's so determined to talk to her.

'She was captivating,' he continues. 'Different from any of the other women I'd ever met. I can't explain it but I was drawn to her. I just had to know who she was, even if nothing ever came of it. She used to come in and sit with her textbooks spread out on the table. Engrossed in her studies. She was about to start university that year – I guess you already know that.'

Jess doesn't respond. She knows her mother had plans to become a lawyer. It just makes her murder even harder to comprehend. Lori was about to start a new life, have all the experiences that young people should have. And it was all snatched away from her in an instant. Jess feels the familiar stab of pain and tries to turn it to anger towards the man sitting in front of her.

'Anyway, that's how it started,' he is saying.

'So, you're telling me she was cheating on my father? That's despicable. She would never—'

'Hey, hang on. I didn't say that. Look, I didn't even know about your dad until the police arrested me. Lori told me she was single. That she was no longer involved with your dad. I knew about you, of course – she talked about you all the time.'

He smiles. 'Her face used to glow whenever she mentioned you. You really were the person she loved most in the world. The love she might have felt for anyone else just couldn't compare. You were her whole world.'

Despite these words coming from this man, they are like a warm blanket spreading over her body. Jess has no memories of her mum; over the years she's created a picture made up of other people's impressions. Opinions she is unable to judge for herself. She'd give anything to have a concrete memory of Lori, some words of encouragement whispered to Jess to help her navigate life, a lesson passed on. Instead, there is nothing but a gaping hole, which she's filled with photos and words she's no longer sure she can rely on. Jess doesn't want this any more. She wants reality, whatever it is. Has she been wrong about her mother all along? Jess refuses to believe this just because Nathaniel French has crashed into her life.

'She loved my dad,' Jess says, fixing her eyes on Nathaniel, daring him to contradict her.

Nathaniel nods. 'Maybe she did. Life's complicated, isn't it? Look, I don't know what happened, but as far as I knew she was single and we were in a relationship. A good one. We were happy.'

Jess shakes her head. 'Everyone argues.'

'Maybe, but it was a new relationship. Early stages. We were only together a few months before... it happened. And actually—'

'Why didn't you tell the police? You let them believe you were a stranger to her. Why would you deny your relationship, if what you've said is true and she meant that much to you?'

Nathaniel French falls silent. She's got him now. Seconds tick by until he finally opens his mouth to speak.

'Because I was scared. Of many things. Looking back now I see that I was just a coward. I thought if I told the police, it would be like handing them the key to lock me away. And I was innocent. I didn't think it mattered whether I told them because I didn't do it. I could never have hurt a single hair on Lori's body. It was easier just to say nothing. Half the time the police just want to pin the crime on anyone, just so they can close it.'

Jess is incredulous. 'That's not true! You sound like a conspiracy theorist. And you were in the park that morning! There was a witness who saw you. You were running away and she said you were sweating and there was blood on you.'

'Yes, yes I was there. I've never denied that. There was no blood, though. That woman was lying. Or mistaken.'

'That witness knew you. She said you were always hanging around the park and she knew where you lived.'

'That woman was someone I'd had an argument with in the park once. About her dog. She wasn't cleaning up after him so I pointed it out to her, asked her to clean it up. She didn't like that. I used to see her all the time in the park and she'd swear at me. The police didn't listen to that, though. They didn't want to believe that she had it in for me. And I was always in the park because it was my local park. Lori's too. We both lived nearby. I kept myself healthy – I was a runner in those days.'

'And you seriously expect me to believe that you were just there by chance, the same early morning that my mum decided to take me for a walk there?'

'No,' he says. 'It wasn't by chance.' He sighs. 'I've never told anyone this before but I was there because I'd gone to Lori's flat early that morning. There was no answer so I assumed she was staying at her mum's. I knew where her mum lived – it wasn't far – so I went there and that's when I saw her leave with you in that buggy thing. I... I followed her to the park.'

Jess's body feels as though it will explode, the anger she feels is so overwhelming. 'What? You were stalking her?' She reached inside her pocket and felt for her phone. 'If you were together, why would you have needed to do that? Why didn't you just go up to her and say something?'

'No! No, it wasn't like that. I just wanted to meet you. You see, she hadn't introduced me to you. I know you were only young, but it bothered me that she'd kept me a secret from you. And when you were so important to her. I'd just gone round there hoping she'd invite me in. We had... some things to talk about.'

'You said you had a healthy relationship! What was it you needed to talk about?'

'I just wanted to tell her how much I loved her. I wanted to be sure that she knew.' There's a tear in his eye, but Jess remains unmoved by his story.

Nathaniel stares into his cup. 'Anyway, I admit that when I saw her leaving the house with you, I should have gone straight home. I just wanted to see her with you, to feel part of your lives in some small way.'

'By stalking.'

'I'm not proud of myself,' Nathaniel insists. 'But what I regret the most is that I didn't go up to Lori, either outside her mother's house or in the park. If I had, then she'd still be alive today, and you'd have your mother here. The person who did that to her wouldn't have done it if I'd been with her. There isn't a second that goes by when I don't blame myself for that.'

'If you were there at the same time, then surely you would have seen something? If it was quiet there, how did you not notice anyone?'

Nathaniel lowers his head. 'I ask myself that all the time. I don't know how I missed them, but I didn't see anyone. If I had, everything would be different.'

'Why were you running?' Jess demands. 'How can you explain that? You weren't dressed for a jog.'

'I was running because I thought she'd spotted me and I changed my mind. I didn't want her to think I was forcing her to do something she wasn't ready to do. I fled so that if she ever confronted me and told me she'd seen me, I could deny it was me. Mistaken identity. It happens.'

She shakes her head. 'Do you realise how far-fetched that sounds? You can't seriously expect me to believe that! And clearly you have a history of lying because you never told the police that you knew my mother.'

He holds up his hands. 'I know how this sounds. But answer me this: what possible reason would I have for searching for you and telling you all this?'

'Because you're insane? Playing some sick game? Why don't *you* tell *me*?'

'Like I said on Friday – I want my name cleared. I've lived with this huge shadow hanging over me for too long and I'm finally doing something about it. I want justice. For Lori and for myself.'

'Why now?' Jess hisses. 'It's been years and you've waited all this time.'

'For years I tried to bury what happened. Not that I ever forgot Lori, I just forced myself to push away everything surrounding her death. But then my partner left me, and—'

'Oh, hand me a tissue.'

His eyes widen. 'I'm not after sympathy, I'm just trying to explain what's led me to be here now.'

Nathaniel once again stares at his coffee cup, holding his hand over the top so the steam warms his hands. It's cold out here, and she can see why it might comfort him.

After Lori died, I spent so many years drifting. I lost everything. My home. My job. My whole life. I'd never lived anywhere other than London before, but I was forced to go up north to Manchester, just to get away from all the media attention. It was in the papers for months. All over them. The police might not have charged me but everyone in the country still believed I'd done it. You wouldn't believe the harassment I got. The death threats. The abuse. There was no social media back then, but there is now, and people still talk about it. My name is the name of a murderer. I've lived in fear of my life for years. What if someone recognises me and decides to take the law into their own hands? I can't live like that any longer.'

'You were known to the police, weren't you? That's why they paid so much attention to you in the first place. You'd already been arrested for assault a few months earlier.'

Nathaniel lowers his eyes. 'Yes, and I'm not proud of that. I had my reasons.'

'Like what?'

He sighs. 'Jessica, I will tell you anything you want to know, but I really can't talk about that. It was nothing to do with this. I'm not proud of it, but it doesn't make me a murderer.'

'It speaks to your character, though, doesn't it?' Jess says. 'Loud and clear.'

'I'm sorry you think that. But I'll have to live with it. I just hope you'll believe that it had nothing to do with anything, and it's not who I was, or am.'

Jess shakes her head. 'Not being charged doesn't make you innocent. It just means there wasn't enough evidence. I bet people get away with crimes all the time because of that.'

He nods. 'Yes, that may well be true. Anyway, please let me finish. It was around ten years later that I met Elsbeth. I hadn't really been interested in any woman after Lori, but there was something about Elsbeth. She was the only person I'd met who could make me forget who I was, and what I'd run from. I needed that. But I did a terrible thing to her. A truly awful thing. Unforgivable.'

Jess almost forgets to breathe. *What is this man about to admit to?*

'I lied to her, and let her fall in love with the person she believed I was, not the man who'd been accused of murder. The man who had lied to the police about knowing Lori.' He sighs. 'Ten years had passed so I just wanted to leave it behind me.

Not that I really could, unless I was with Elsbeth. Anyway, long story short – she found out around a year ago. She found an old newspaper clipping I'd kept and that was the end of us. Everything was out in the open. It nearly destroyed me. Once again, I was back to that pitiful loner I'd become after Lori. Only this time I decided I wasn't going to stand for it. I was going to clear my name by any means necessary.'

He glares at Jess as he says this, and for a flash she sees a different person altogether. It is a reminder to keep her guard up. 'Lies always come back to haunt people in the end,' she says. 'Anyway, what exactly is it you want me to do? And what makes you think I won't go straight to the police with what you've just told me?'

The smile on his face appears slowly. 'Oh, Jessica, if there's one thing I can be sure of it's that you won't go to the police.'

'And why is that?' Again, her hand reaches into her pocket, her fingers tracing the cool glass of her phone screen.

'Because you want the truth and I think you know I won't talk to the police.'

'They'll find out. They'll investigate and realise you knew my mum.'

'It was twenty-eight years ago. We didn't have mobile phones or email then so there's nothing for them to find. Lori hadn't introduced me to any of her friends or family, either. We hadn't had the chance to do any of that.'

Something occurs to Jess and she's surprised she didn't think of it before. 'Someone took that photo of you two, so someone knew you were together.'

'That was just a passer-by on the street, I'm afraid. Nobody who would have even remembered us at the time, let alone now. They never came forward after it happened.'

Anger boils inside her again and she stands, scraping her chair aside. 'The police will work it out.' She turns away from him, then quickly changes her mind. 'There is one thing. If it wasn't you, and you loved my mum, wouldn't you have wanted to find out who did that to her? Wouldn't you have been worried, even?'

Nathaniel rises too and grabs her arm. 'That's just it, Jessica. I know exactly who did that to her. And when you know too, you'll realise that you're not safe. You never have been.'

EIGHT

NOW

Jess

Nathaniel's words ring in Jess's ears as she makes her way through the throng, heading towards the Tube. *'You're not safe. You never have been.'* She'd demanded more from him, answers to all the questions burning in her throat. *'I know exactly who did that to her.'*

But as soon as he'd said it, Nathaniel's phone had rung and he'd insisted he had to go and help his neighbour with something. He'd begged Jess to trust him, assured her that he would meet her again and explain everything. He just needed more time.

And now, as she steps onto the Tube that will take her back to Camden, all she feels is confusion. He had to be playing a game. Yet the fear on his face was real; unless he was a professional actor she doubts he could have faked that. Jess is usually a good judge of character; it's rare that people can fool her.

But Nathaniel French, she can't seem to get the measure of.

· · ·

At home, Jess has no choice but to focus on work, shutting out all other thoughts, forcing them away when they attempt to creep in. But the moment she's finished, everything crashes down on her. She tries to call Nathaniel, hoping to pin him down to another meeting, but all she gets is his voicemail.

With intrusive thoughts trapped in her mind, Jess is desperate to talk it over with someone. There's no way she can tell her father she initiated a meeting with Nathaniel, and that she's been exploring the possibility that he's telling the truth. Telling Zara isn't an option; expecting her sister to keep secrets from their father isn't fair. There's Carolina, but she can't drag her into this. Jess is alone with these thoughts.

In the evening Carolina calls, immediately explaining that she has bad news. 'I'm sorry, love. I really tried hard, but your dad just shut down. He wouldn't even entertain the notion of talking about it. He said the past is best left in the past and I didn't want to push him. You know what he's like. Stubborn as anything. It's where you and Zara both get it from.' She gives a small chuckle. 'As much as it infuriates me, I'm glad you both know your own minds.'

Her dad doesn't give in easily, but she'd hoped that Carolina might have got through to him. 'Thanks for trying.'

'What will you do now? Are you going to the police?'

'He wasn't proven guilty,' Jess says, surprising herself that she's jumping to Nathaniel's defence, that she's wavering.

'That's true, love, but the police were still convinced it was him, weren't they? I don't think we can ignore that. Anyway, if you haven't heard from him since Friday, then maybe he'll leave you alone?'

'I'd better go, Carolina. Thanks again for trying.'

'Okay. You just let me know if you need anything at all, okay? And one more thing. You need to be careful, Jess, and keep yourself safe. Who knows if he'll turn up again?'

· · ·

The tap on the living room window takes Jess by surprise, immobilises her so that she can't work out what to do. Her senses are already heightened; she's stepped into a place that feels unfamiliar, and she isn't sure how to respond. Before now, any threat had only ever been imagined – now it is real.

Reaching for her phone, she tentatively rises from the sofa, leaving her laptop on the coffee table. With a deep breath, she pulls up the blind, her mouth falling opening when she sees who's standing there. He's smiling, but it's a smile of uncertainty. He's being careful not to give too much away.

'You look shocked to see me,' he says, when she opens the door.

'I am. It's been a while.'

'I know, I'm sorry. I just needed time.'

She silently calculates. It must be three months since she's seen Harrison. He looks different tonight, half stranger and half someone she knows intimately. They were able to remain friends for a while, until it got too difficult. Jess isn't sure who it was harder for – him because she was the one who ended things, or her because she felt his pain as though it were her own. She tried not to, but that's not how she operates. She's been blessed, or cursed, with too much empathy.

'How come you're here?' she asks. 'Not that I mind,' she's quick to add. 'It's good to see you.'

Harrison smiles, a more confident one this time. 'Really? You didn't look too happy to see me at the window.'

She assures him it's not him, only the shock of him standing there, when she'd expected... who? Nathaniel? There's nothing to stop *him* turning up. Why does that worry her when she's keeping an open mind that the man could be telling the truth?

'Come in.' She opens the door wider. As soon as Harrison steps inside, though, she wonders if she's making a mistake. Taking a step backwards into dangerous territory. Things still feel raw between them – a wound that might look healed but can gape open at any moment. Still, she won't leave him standing on the doorstep.

'So, how have you been, Jess? I haven't heard from you for a while.'

'I've been... you know... I've just thrown myself into work. You know how I like to do that.' She appraises him, notices his hands are in his pockets, his gaze fixed on her. There's no way to know his thoughts, but he's here to say something, that much is clear.

She shouldn't have let him in. There are any number of excuses she could have made. It's easier when she doesn't see him.

'I've missed you,' Harrison says, still watching her intently. 'I just wanted to tell you that. You don't have to say anything, and I know nothing's going to change. I just want you to know that I still care. As a friend. We should have tried harder to keep that going at least, shouldn't we?'

Perhaps he is right. After all, there aren't many people other than her family who know the whole history, who really understand why Jess is the way she is. And she's always been able to talk to Harrison.

His question, though, cannot be answered so instead she offers him something to drink. 'I have a bottle of wine already opened.'

They sit together on the sofa, in between them a space wide enough for two more people. She's relieved about this; having him too close could be dangerous. Lack of passion was never a problem in their relationship.

'So, are you going to tell me what's bothering you, Jess?' he asks, before taking a sip of his wine.

'Nothing. I'm fine. Just busy with work.'

'You're forgetting that I know you. I can tell something's wrong and I'm pretty sure it's not about me being here. Come on, you know you can talk to me. At least I hope you can. I'm still the same person, and we were always good at talking, weren't we?'

Under any other circumstances Jess would be discomfited by Harrison bringing up their relationship when she's trying to put it behind her. Right now, though, she's too consumed with thoughts of her mother and Nathaniel, and her dad's strange behaviour. With no forethought, she finds herself opening up to Harrison, telling him everything that's happened since Friday.

He listens without interrupting, and she's grateful for this. If he stopped her mid-flow, she's not convinced she'd be able to continue.

'Wait, are you saying you believe this man?' Harrison asks, when she's finished.

Jess sighs. She can't just dismiss what he's said, or the photograph she's seen. 'I don't know. I just can't think of any reason why he'd track me down to lie about it when it's been so long. He was free. Why would he bring it all up again if he's guilty?'

Harrison shakes his head. 'I don't know, Jess. People do strange things. This just doesn't sound right. What if he—'

'What? Wants to hurt me? Why would he when I could never identify him as the man who attacked my mum? He's got nothing to worry about there. It's not like I'm suddenly going to remember nearly thirty years later, is it?'

'But if he's... disturbed? He won't be thinking straight. And for someone to do that to your mum – well, they have to be a twisted person, don't they?'

He has a point. 'I need to watch him. Find out how he lives his life and what he does every day. I need to get a sense of what kind of person he his.' Jess says this aloud, but it's more to herself than Harrison. 'He got really freaked out at the end of our conversation. Scared. I don't know why, but he really didn't want to keep talking to me. He was on edge too. Looking around all the time as if he was expecting something to happen.'

'He might have thought you'd called the police.'

'Perhaps,' Jess says, yet silently she doesn't believe it. She and Nathaniel both knew she wouldn't. She hates to admit it, but it was as if something had bonded them together. 'Whatever the case, I'm going to follow him.' This is what Jess does when she's fearful – she turns things around so she won't be the victim. Besides, it is only what he did to her mother. 'I've got his address from his business card so that will be my starting point.'

'I really don't think that's a good idea,' Harrison insists. 'It's not safe.'

'What choice do I have? I need to find out if he's telling the truth, or if he really is the monster who killed my mum. I'm not going to sit around waiting for something to happen, I need to be one step ahead.'

Harrison stares at her for a moment, resting his chin on his hands. 'Let me do it. He doesn't know me, so even if he looks straight at me, he'll never know I'm watching him.'

Jess is about to answer with a resounding no until it occurs to her that this does make more sense. Besides, she's got clients she can't let down so she'd only be able to follow Nathaniel in the evenings. The chances are he probably doesn't even leave his house at night.

'You've got work, though, Harrison.'

'Actually, I'm on annual leave for the next few days and have no plans.'

'Does my dad know that?'

'Yep. He signed it off himself.'

It will always feel strange to Jess that Harrison works in the IT department at her dad's company. 'Please don't mention any of this to him?'

'Course not. I imagine this would be hard for him to deal with.'

Not hard, Jess thinks. Almost too easy.

'So that's settled, then,' Harrison says. 'What's his address?'

The two of them talk long into the night, neither of them

aware of night merging into the early hours of the morning. Jess always found it easy to be around Harrison, effortless, like waves folding across an ocean. That's how she always used to think of them, as though they were at one with each other, at one with nature together. Until everything had to change.

'It's past midnight,' she says, glancing at her phone.

'Really?' Harrison checks his own phone. 'I probably should have gone hours ago but I don't want to move. I wish we could just stay like this. Like we used to.'

She turns away, can't look him in the eye. 'Stop, please don't do that. We need to move forwards now. We agreed.'

'I know.' He reaches for her hand. How easy it would be to fall into old habits, to let him stay. She won't, though. She can't. Jess has worked too hard to get over him to take a single step backwards. 'I wasn't going to ask you this, but I have to,' Harrison continues. 'Have you... met someone else? It's been long enough – I wouldn't blame you if you had. In fact, I'm sure you must have. I didn't want to know until now, but I think I'm ready to hear it. *I* haven't, by the way, in case you were wondering.'

'I don't think we should talk about this.' Jess looks away. She never thought there'd be a time when she and Harrison would be discussing relationships with other people.

He smiles sadly. 'Ah, so that means yes, then.'

'Not exactly.' She forces herself to look at him.

Seconds of silence follow, both of them lost in their own thoughts. Jess prepares herself to answer Harrison's questions in more detail; after all, if he had met someone, she'd definitely want to know more about the woman, as unhealthy as that may be.

'Well, I hope he's a good person, Jess. I hope he makes you happy. I mean that.' He stands, picking up her empty glass from the floor. 'I'll take these to the kitchen, then I'd better go. I'll let you know what happens with my surveillance.'

She's so consumed with Nathaniel French that she doesn't realise until later what she's feeling. Disappointment that Harrison didn't ask her any more about Gabriel.

And it's even later when she questions why someone else in her life is acting out of character.

NINE

NOVEMBER 1992

Lori

Occasionally Lori asks herself whether she's doing the right thing. It's questionable; she knows this deep in her gut, but she can't, and won't, stop.

This evening she is skittish, darting to the window every time she hears a car pull up outside. Danny has been calling her nearly every day, demanding to see Jess on his own, to take her to his home, and it will be difficult to hold him off much longer. She knows Danny well enough to know that he'll take matters into his own hands soon enough. And he always gets his own way.

Well, he can come tonight, she thinks. Jess isn't here, and he would never dare to knock on her mother's door. No, he doesn't want her family finding out what he's done.

Outside, another car pulls up. This time, without looking she knows it's him; she can tell the noise of his car engine from any other. She leaves her flat and rushes outside before he can make a scene in front of the neighbours. She likes the elderly woman opposite and doesn't want to scare her.

'Where's Jess?' Danny demands. 'I haven't seen her for months now. You can't do this, Lori.' His eyes narrow as he stares at her.

There's a chill in the air, and Lori pulls her cardigan tighter around her body, folding her arms. 'You have seen her. We met you in the park the other week.'

'That's not good enough. I want her to stay with me. To have her at weekends.'

'That's never going to happen, Danny. Not without me there.' As much as she loathes being around him now, she knows Jess needs to spend time with him.

He moves towards her and shoves his head so close to hers that she can feel his breath. 'Don't fuck with me, Lori. You're making a big mistake.'

'Go away, Danny. Do you want me to call the police?'

Danny continues glaring at her. 'Guess who I bumped into the other day?'

'I'm not going to guess, Danny – I really don't care.'

'Your sister.'

Lori freezes. Mionie and their mother believe that she and Danny are together, that everything is okay.

'Funny thing,' he continues. 'I was expecting her to rage war on me, but d'you know what she said instead?' He doesn't wait for a reply. 'She said, "you all must come over for lunch. We haven't had a get-together for such a long time. Sorry we missed you at our dad's birthday." Something like that at least.'

Lori almost doesn't want to ask what his reply was, but she needs to know, then she can deal with it. 'What did you say?'

He smiles. 'I said, of course we will, and told her to let us know some dates when she and Neil are both off.'

Lori is momentarily stunned into silence. When she recovers, she lets out a deep breath. 'Why would you do that?'

He shrugs then smiles at her; it's not from kindness, though, more the knowledge that he's got one up on her. Now she owes him something. Even after what he's done. 'Now,' he says, 'are you going to tell me why they don't know you left me months ago?'

'I would, but it's not really any of your business what I tell my family, is it?'

Danny glances up at the window of her flat. 'I want to see Jess. Tonight. On my own. Unless you want me to tell them the truth?'

'You won't, though, will you? Because you care too much what people think of you. And you know that, because of Jess, you're linked to my family whether you like it or not. And she's not here, Danny.'

He hesitates for a moment before turning back to the car. 'Just so you know – I won't let you do this.'

And then he is driving away, leaving Lori staring after him.

Inside, she calls Mionie. They haven't spoken since their father's birthday two months ago, despite Lori's attempts to call her. Mionie always has an excuse why she can't talk. It's always a bad time. Paranoia floods through Lori. Does Mionie think she's after Neil? Surely not, when all Lori and Neil were doing that afternoon was talking. Does her sister think that little of her? Despite all of her academic achievements and career success, deep down her sister is afraid of her relationship failing. It's not Neil she really cares about, Lori is convinced of that, it's how it would look to everyone else if they never made it to their wedding day.

The phone rings three times before Mionie answers. 'Oh good, you're home,' Lori begins. She's nervous, but she wants to put things right. She misses her sister.

'I can't really talk now, Lori. Sorry. I'm about to leave for work. How's little Jess? I miss her terribly. I'll call you when I have a chance, okay?' The line goes dead.

That's when it hits Lori how truly alone she is. 'We'll be

okay, Jess, I promise,' she says, her voice echoing around the empty room.

Later, as she's scrambling eggs for dinner, all she can think about is how Danny shouldn't get away with what he's done. Nobody should.

Leaving the eggs untouched, she picks up the phone and dials Shane's work number. They've talked several times since they met in the bar when Belle didn't turn up, but now Lori is ready for more. He'll be finishing for the day soon, but hopefully she'll catch him.

'Hello?' he says. He sounds tired. Ready to leave after a gruelling day. He works in advertising, she has learnt. Long hours. Pressure she could never imagine, he tells her.

'It's Lizzi.'

'Hey!' He perks up. 'Funny thing, I was just thinking about you.'

'Let's meet up tonight. Go for a drink.' Lori feels like a different person saying this, an actress immersed in her script.

'Say when and where and I'll be there,' he says.

Just as she knew he would.

TEN

NOW

Jess

It's nearly midday and she stands outside Charing Cross Hospital, staring up at the large edifice, people swarming in and out of the main doors like ants. Jess has never visited her aunt here before. On the phone last night, Mionie had been surprised to hear from her, but she'd readily agreed to meet this lunchtime, never once asking what was so important.

The urgent questions Jess needs to ask burn within her, questions she's never wanted to know the answers to before. Now, though, it's imperative that she finds out everything she can about her mother. It's the only way she'll know what to make of Nathaniel's story. Whether or not she is safe.

She spots Mionie the moment she steps inside, sitting on a seat in the foyer, exactly where she said she'd be. She's tapping something into her phone but looks up as Jess approaches.

'Jessica! How lovely to see you!' Her aunt stands and waves, striding over to her. It's hard to believe Mionie is in her sixties, when from a distance she can easily pass for twenty years younger. She looks after herself, makes sure she never has a fleck of grey hair, even though that must be a lot of maintenance.

'Hi, Mionie. Shall we walk? I can buy you lunch somewhere?'

'Actually, I'm afraid I don't have a lot of time. Do you mind if we just grab a quick coffee here? They do a lovely espresso and a caffeine fix is just what I need.'

Jess scans the hospital foyer. As much as she prefers crowded places, it's too noisy in here; she needs a more private space to talk to Mionie. 'Maybe we could go to your office instead?'

When they get there, Jess waits until they're both seated. 'I know this is going to sound a bit strange, but I need to talk to you about Mum.'

'Oh. Okay.' Mionie frowns, her eyes narrowing. There's a pause. 'Have you come all this way to ask me about Lori?'

It's important that Jess keeps this vague. 'She's just been on my mind lately. And I know you've told me some things about her before, but I was a lot younger then, and I wondered if you'd ever... tried to shelter me from anything? Anything I might not want to hear?'

Mionie reaches for her hand. Hers is cold and dry. 'I have to admit, this is a bit of a surprise. You coming all this way to ask about your mum. You haven't mentioned her since you were a child. What's going on, Jessica? Are you sure nothing's happened?'

'No. It's just that I'm thirty now, and I'm ready for answers. I need to hear things people might have tried to shield me from. I know up until now I've just wanted to cling to my idea of Mum, the one where she's close to perfect. To me, she was an angel, my protector. I suppose I've been scared that my illusions would be shattered. So, I've just held on to my childhood stories. Until now.'

'What's changed?' Mionie lets go of Jess's hand.

'Sooner or later we realise that nobody is perfect. Not a single one of us. And I want to know the real person my mum was. Who better to tell me than her sister?'

Mionie smiles. 'I'm more than happy to talk to you, Jessica. What's your dad said about her?'

'It's hard for him to talk about her, even now. Besides, you and Grandma knew her as a child too.'

Mionie sighs. 'Yes, that's true. Look, Jess, are you sure you're ready for the truth? Once words are spoken they can't be taken back.'

Jess nods, her chest tightening.

'Your mum was the thread that held this family together. We loved her very much. When she died we seemed to... drift apart. Mum and I didn't know how to live with what had happened.' Again Mionie takes Jess's hand. 'I'm sorry if that meant we weren't there for you as much as we should have been. I was already working such long hours in A & E, and throwing myself even further into work was the way I coped with it all. I should have been there for your dad as well.'

'He chose to move away, though. That's not your fault – it's the only way he could cope with everything.' Jess has so few memories of the years following her mother's death. All she can really remember is playing on the beach in Portugal with her father. He had taken her there straight after Lori died, and it became their home for a couple of years, until he decided to take Jess back to London to start school. Then Danny had met Carolina and they became a family, the only one Jess remembers. Having no memory of her mother has made Jess feel like a traitor for most of her life.

'Still,' Mionie says, 'I'll always feel guilty for not being more involved. How is your dad, by the way?'

Jess tells her he's fine. She's usually outspoken, and she could take this opportunity to also tell Mionie that yes, it did upset her that Lori's side of the family all seemed to drift away when she was growing up. Looking at Mionie now, though, aware that there's a blanket of guilt wrapped around her aunt, she keeps quiet. 'Do you think Mum would have ever... cheated on my dad?'

Mionie's eyes widen. 'What makes you ask that?'

'Nothing in particular. I just wondered.' She knows her aunt is unlikely to believe this. But Jess refuses to drag anyone else into the murky business with Nathaniel French.

'No. Lori absolutely adored your dad. She would never have done anything like that. They were solid. Nothing except what happened could have torn them apart.'

These words hang in the air until their meaning sinks in and they plummet to the ground. Her mum might have died because someone didn't want her to be with her father. Mionie might insist that Lori would never have cheated on her father, but Jess has seen evidence.

And there can only be one person who wouldn't have been happy about her relationship with Jess's dad.

'I have to go,' she announces, standing.

'Already? Okay, well, I promise I'll give you a call and we can meet up for dinner or something? We can go and visit Mum. She gets lonely on her own. It's only a matter of time before she can't live by herself any more. And it's difficult for me to see her, with work and everything. She can tell you her memories of Lori.'

Jess is only half listening as she nods, giving Mionie a hug before hurrying out of her office. It's time now. She needs to go straight to the police.

Back in the hospital foyer, her eyes focus only on the door, so when an arm reaches for her, she screams.

It's a man. A familiar face, but one it takes Jess a moment to place. 'Sorry – I didn't mean to scare you.'

'Uncle Neil, sorry, I didn't realise it was you.'

'No, it's my fault. What brings you here?'

Her heart pounds, unable to calm itself. 'I came to see Aunt Mionie.'

He bites his lip. 'Oh, that's a nice surprise. Me too. I thought I'd pop in and take her for lunch.' He lowers his voice, and amid the gentle cacophony that fills the lobby, Jess can barely hear him. 'I keep telling her it's time to retire, like I have, and enjoy herself while she's still youngish but she won't listen to me. This work's stressful enough for a younger person and it's not doing her any good.' He pauses. 'I know I shouldn't be saying this, but there's no one else I can talk to. Please don't tell her I said this but I hardly recognise her any more.'

All of this information feels too personal – something her uncle should be discussing with Mionie herself, not Jess. She likes him, though, he's always been kind to her, and ordinarily she'd be happy to listen to his woes. But the longer she stands there, the more chance there is of Nathaniel trying to prevent her from going to the police. And there's every possibility that he's following every move she makes.

'I'm sorry to hear that, Uncle Neil.' She edges closer to the door.

He nods. 'Oh, don't be. It's been happening for years. I should be used to it by now. Anyway, how are you doing? Forgive me for saying this, but you don't look okay. Has Mionie said something to upset you. I know she can be—'

'No, not at all. I'm just in a bit of a rush. It was nice to see her, we were just talking about Mum. I've finally got to that point where I need to hear about her from the people who loved her and knew her the best.' She glances at the main door.

Something changes in her uncle's demeanour when she says this. She can't put her finger on it, but it's there, the tiniest hint of discomfort. His eyes narrow. 'Are you sure she didn't upset you? Because she's probably not the best person to talk to about your mum.'

Stunned, Jess focuses her attention on him. 'What do you mean? They were sisters. They were close.'

For a moment Neil stares at her, seeming to grapple with his words. 'Oh, Jess.' He glances around the foyer. 'Look, have you got a minute to spare? I think there are some things you need to know.' Another heavy pause. 'Mionie wasn't even speaking to your mum when she died.'

ELEVEN

DECEMBER 1992

Lori

She's scared.

Now that she's done it – put in motion events which can never be taken back – she's left with the overwhelming fear that this could get out of control. It's bound to; she's playing with fire after all.

Lori won't stop, though. She's doing this for Jess, so that she can have a better life, far different from the one Lori's had so far.

Even her own life will change because of this, for the better. She's starting university in September and this will all be a distant memory. For now, though, she will carry on, despite her reservations.

Today is Sunday, and she knows, from something her mum let slip on the phone, that Neil is at home and Mionie's on shift at the hospital. This is why Lori is sitting on a bus with Jess sleeping on her lap, staring out of the window and wishing her family could change. Lori has never fit in with her mother and sister, even as a young child; she's always been someone who could have disappeared with it making little difference to them. It was different with her dad; he loved her unconditionally. Holding back tears, she looks down at Jess and silently promises that it will never be like that for her.

It feels strange walking along the path to Mionie's door, when Lori already knows that her sister isn't there. It is a betrayal of sorts, especially given that Mionie barely seems to want to talk to her. Still, she walks to the door and presses the bell, smiling down at Jess in her buggy as she does so. 'We're here to see Uncle Neil,' she says. 'And then we can go for a walk – won't that be fun?' The December air is bitter today, but the sun has found a way to shine through the clouds, offering brief respite from the icy chill.

Jess nods, and her smile fills Lori with warmth, securing her with the knowledge that there is so much love between her and her little girl, enough to make up for Danny, and nothing can change that.

It takes Neil a while to answer the door, and when he does he's still dressed in his pyjamas, his hair ruffled from sleep. 'Lori?' He peers past her. 'Mionie's at work.'

'I know. It's you I came to see.'

He frowns. 'Oh. I... um, you'd better come in then. Sorry about these.' He tugs at his pyjamas.'

'It's my fault for coming so early. I got you out of bed.' Since she had Jess, Lori is always up early, ready to start the day.

'Don't worry, I wasn't sleeping. Just enjoying a rare moment reading in bed. I can't remember the last time I could lie in for this long.' He looks across the road. 'Come in, though – the neighbours will wonder why I'm leaving you standing on the doorstep.'

Lori's discomfort increases as she crosses the threshold. How would Mionie react if she came home now? Judging by the look of disgust on Mionie's face when Lori was simply hugging Neil, her sister would no doubt be appalled that Lori is here, alone with him. Her sister has always been possessive in her relationships – Lori should have been careful.

Inside, while Neil changes upstairs, she sits on the floor while Jess roots through the box of toys Mionie keeps in the living room. Her sister's house is a Victorian terrace – spacious but cold and dark. Not somewhere Lori would like to end up.

When Neil returns, she wastes no time getting to the point. 'I feel like Mionie's avoiding me. She hasn't seen Jess for months now, and she always likes seeing her. Is there something going on?'

Neil's cheeks flush. 'I don't... um, she's been busy at work.'

Lori stands. 'Neil, please don't lie to me. I know something's wrong.'

He sighs and sits on the sofa, clasping his hands together. 'You're not the only one she's avoiding,' he begins. 'In fact, we've hardly even seen each other.'

This doesn't sound out of the ordinary, given their shift patterns. But the frown on Neil's face suggests otherwise. 'Why?' she asks. She knows, though. This is to do with that hug.

'Oh, this is awkward. She's barely spoken to me for months. She, um... maybe thinks there's something going on between us.'

Lori stares at him, her insides suddenly on fire. 'Why would she think that? It doesn't make sense. All I did was hug you.'

He sighs. 'She said that when we were together for your dad's birthday, she could tell.'

Lori is enraged. She would never do anything like that to her sister. 'You did put her straight, though, didn't you?'

Neil remains silent, staring at his bare feet. She notices there's a loose thread hanging from the bottom of his pyjamas. 'Neil? Say something!'

'I tried to explain to her, but I can't lie, Lori. I don't like being deceitful. I had no choice but to tell her.'

Beside the toy box, Jess begins to fuss as she struggles to reach something buried at the bottom. Lori rushes over and helps her pull out a toy keyboard. 'Here you go, Jess. Is this what you want?' She turns back to Neil. 'Let's go out there.'

In the hall, she demands to know everything Neil has told Mionie.

'When she saw us talking alone that afternoon, she said she could sense there was something between us, even though she has no evidence.'

'But why would she think that?'

Again, Neil falls silent, the only sound in the house coming from the musical notes Jess is tapping on the keyboard.

'I'm so sorry, Lori,' Neil finally says. 'I... Oh God, I never wanted to say all this to anyone... but she's right, at least on my part.'

Lori's stomach churns. 'What are you talking about, Neil?'

'I've had feelings for you for a long time now, Lori. It just crept up on me. I tried to bury it, of course I did, but... well, Mionie knows me better than I know myself, I think.'

Lori tries to make sense of what he's saying. Neil's always been friendly to her, yes, but she's never suspected he felt this way. He's never given her a reason to.

'I'm sorry, Lori. You must hate me,' Neil says. 'I don't blame you. I'm engaged to your sister and here I am confessing all this to you. It makes me a despicable human being.'

'So, Mionie knows you feel this way. But surely she must realise it's not me? This is all you. It's not my fault. I didn't even know any of this until this second!'

'I tried to tell her. I assured her that you had no idea, and that you've never so much as suggested you feel anything for me. It fell on deaf ears, though. She kept insisting that she knows what she saw.'

'She saw us talking, Neil! Nothing more. We only hugged because I was upset – did you tell her that?'

He nods. 'Of course I did. Several times. She won't listen.'

Lori clasps her head in her hand. 'I have to put Mionie

straight. She can't go on thinking this. And what about Jess? She hasn't had one of her special days out with Mionie for months now. My little girl's going to lose out on seeing her aunty because of this... this...' She has no idea what to label it. 'I need to talk to her right now.'

He offers a tired smile. 'You can try. I hope she listens, for both our sakes.'

'I have to go, Neil. I can't be here alone with you. This is wrong.'

She can feel him watching her as she tidies away the toys and ushers Jess out of the living room.

TWELVE

NOW

Jess

'You can't tell your aunt any of this. Please promise me.' Neil, usually so confident and assured, seems to have diminished right before Jess's eyes. 'It's messy. And I don't want to open up old wounds. They've healed and I'd like to keep it that way.'

Jess pulls him away from the door, towards a quieter part of the hospital foyer. 'What exactly are you telling me?' she demands, making no promise to keep quiet.

And that's when he tells her. Things he's previously only discussed with Mionie and Lori, words which now they have been passed on to Jess will have no choice but to ravage lives.

'I'm sorry, Jess. You should never have had to hear this, but I can't bear Mionie continuing her lies to you. She was never kind to Lori. On the surface she seemed to be a caring enough sister, but behind closed doors she would moan and bitch about Lori. I think it stemmed from jealousy that your grandfather loved her so much. She was his little angel. Maybe he didn't realise what was going on – I think Mionie was good at being on her best behaviour when he was around. And then of course when he died, she had free rein to treat Lori with contempt. Unless of course Danny was around. He wouldn't have seen it, either. She loved you, of course, and doted on you, but Lori, well, she was just... the black sheep of the family.'

It's not often that Jess struggles to speak, but Neil's revelation has paralysed her, rendered her unable to articulate a clear thought.

'I think that's why I fell for her. I wanted to protect her, to help her, even though she didn't need it. She was such a strong woman, your mum. Mionie never gave her credit for that. And even Meredith often couldn't see the good in her, only the mistakes she made.'

'What mistakes?' Her voice sounds strange, as if it's not her own.

'I don't know. They never talked about it, and certainly didn't let me in on their family secrets. Your grandmother wasn't happy that Lori didn't go straight to university after school, when that's what she'd wanted both her daughters to do. She saw it as letting the family down. And Meredith was always one for keeping up appearances. Even now, at eighty-five, she wants people to think the best of her. All she cared about was how things looked to the outside world. And then Lori getting pregnant without being married was something else to add to the list. Poor Lori had to live up to successful Mionie, who anyone, except your grandmother, could see was far from perfect.'

Jess takes a moment to digest this information. It feels as though Neil is talking about someone else's family, not her own. Strangers. 'And my dad definitely didn't know all this?'

'Danny was hardly ever at family events. And as I said, when he was there, they were careful what they said to Lori.' He sighs. 'I just wish I'd done something about it at the time. Then maybe things would have been different.'

'Did you love her?' Jess needs to know this. It changes everything.

Neil hesitates. 'There was nothing between us, nothing physical at least. And doesn't love have to be reciprocated to exist?'

He's avoiding her question, but she's heard enough.

'I have to go,' Jess says. She can't even look at him. So many lies about her family have come to light that she no longer knows who she can trust.

Neil reaches for her arm. 'I know what I said before about keeping quiet, but I take it back. You'll have questions for Mionie, and Meredith, and I won't try and stop you speaking to them. It's about time all of this came out in the open. I don't care what happens to my marriage, I really don't. I only ask one thing – that you give me some warning before you approach either of them. Please?'

Jess nods. Is it a promise she'll be able to keep?

Outside the hospital, she turns and stares back through the glass doors. Mionie is walking towards Neil, shaking her head. And Jess watches them long enough to suspect that discordant words pass between them.

Nothing she's planned to do is happening. Before bumping into Neil, Jess was intent on going straight to the police, and telling them all about Nathaniel French, yet now everything has changed. So much of what she believed about her family are lies, and she needs to find out why. To dig deeper and uncover the truth at all costs; that's what matters. If he is indeed lying, Nathaniel isn't the only one. And it's even worse that the rest of them are her own flesh and blood.

Going to the police can wait; her fear of Nathaniel is slowly depleting. He's had every chance to harm her, if that is his wish. It's her father she needs to speak to first.

Sitting at her kitchen table, Jess calls him, tapping her fingers on the table as she waits. With a client due in fifteen minutes, she doesn't have long to speak.

'Where have you been, Dad?' she asks, when he picks up the phone. 'I've been trying to call you.'

'Sorry, love. I've had a lot going on with work. Getting a bit fed up of it all to be honest. Think it's about time I take a step back.'

Jess knows he won't. Even at sixty-four, work is far too important to her father for him to consider stopping now.

'Okay, Dad. Well, can we talk? Today?'

'Of course. Just not right now, though. I've got a situation to deal with but I should be free later. How does that sound?'

'I'll come over after work,' Jess says.

'Or how about I come to you instead? It's been a while since I've seen your place. It will have to be quite late, though – I really do have a lot to sort out.'

She has no choice but to agree.

'Jess? Please tell me this has nothing to do with that man. I hope he hasn't turned up again.'

After assuring him she hasn't seen Nathaniel French, Jess ends the call. It still makes her uneasy that her father isn't hankering to go to the police.

Later, when her last session is finished and she's done enough editing, Jess realises she hasn't eaten since breakfast. As much as there are bigger things to worry about than food, her stomach grumbles, a warning to refuel. But when she checks the fridge, it's empty, and she can't bear the thought of traipsing to the supermarket. Jam on toast will have to do.

She's barely taken a bite when her phone rings, Gabriel's name showing on the screen.

'Hey.' Jess can't tell whether she's irritated that he's called, or whether it's a relief to hear from someone who has nothing to do with her mum, or any of her family issues.

When Gabriel asks how she is, she plays things down; she is fine. Just busy with work. He is still a stranger to her so she will be cautious.

'I know it's a bit last minute,' Gabriel says, 'but I was supposed to have a work meeting and it's just been cancelled – if you haven't already eaten, how about we grab some dinner? No pressure.'

Jess glances at the barely eaten toast on her plate, which grows colder by the second. She's tempted by his offer; it will allow her some escape, albeit temporary. Yet the timing of whatever this is with Gabriel is terrible. How can she get involved with someone – even if nothing comes of it in the end – when everything she thought she knew is being turned upside down?

'How about Italian?' Gabriel continues. 'Zara might have let slip that it's one of your favourites.' He laughs. 'Oh God, I really do sound like a stalker again, don't I?'

Jess can't help but smile. She would usually find this sort of behaviour too pushy, but there is something about Gabriel that she likes. Besides, he is a friend of Ryan's and that offers her comfort.

'Okay.' She pushes aside her plate. She needs this; something to distract her for a couple of hours. 'Where shall we meet?'

As she had hoped, sitting in the restaurant with Gabriel offers Jess an escape. She focuses only on him, forcing aside everything else that's happened since Friday. Two things will come from this evening: either she'll want to see him again, or she won't and she can put an end to it now. At least Zara will know Jess gave it a chance.

'It feels strange, doesn't it?' Gabriel says, after they've

ordered. 'When someone you know fixes you up with someone. It's like there's more pressure, an expectation. Kind of like you owe it to them to make it work.'

'I know what you mean,' Jess agrees. 'But believe me, I'll have no qualms about telling Zara she couldn't have got it more wrong.'

He laughs. 'Wow, you're tough. Hmm, no pressure on me, then.'

'In all honesty, though,' Jess says, 'I've never done this before, but I can only say please just be yourself. That's all I ask of anyone. Don't try to put on a show for me, and I won't for you. What you see is what you get with me.'

'I like that,' he says. He tugs at his tie. 'Now might be a good time to tell you, then, that I hate wearing suits. Give me a pair of jeans over a suit any day. Don't think that would go down well in meetings, though.'

Jess smiles. 'Well, if it's any consolation, you look pretty good in a suit. There. Make the most of that compliment because I don't dish them out often. Anyway, if you're a property developer, you probably don't have to wear them often?'

'That's true. It's just that today was a meeting with a possible investor.' Gabriel takes a sip of his wine. 'Enough about me. Tell me something about you. The real Jess. Unedited.'

Hearing words like this is what she dreads about meeting someone new; it's a large part of why she hasn't wanted to get into another relationship after Harrison. It had been different with him – working for her father meant he already knew what had happened. People at the company talked, used her father's past to offer excuses for his managerial style. The perfectionism he insisted upon from not only himself but from every employee. Jess had never had to prove to Harrison that she is more than that tragic nameless child whose story was plastered over every newspaper in the country for months. But starting something with Gabriel will mean that's exactly what she'd have to do.

Now is not the time to tell Gabriel any of her story.

Jess's phone pings with a WhatsApp message from her father. 'Sorry, it's my dad,' she tells Gabriel. 'I just need to read this.'

'Of course.' Gabriel smiles.

As she reads her father's words, she sighs and shakes her head. He's been held up and won't be able to see her tonight after all. Tomorrow, he offers as a consolation. But tomorrow is just too long for her to wait.

Jess shoves her phone in her bag and turns her attention back to Gabriel. 'Right, what were we talking about?'

'Is something wrong?' he asks.

'No, it's just my dad. I was supposed to see him later and he cancelled. Anyway, what were we talking about?'

'You were about to tell me all about you.'

'You'll have to be more specific. What exactly do you want to know?' She holds her breath while she waits for an awkward question to hit her.

'Hmm. Let's see.' He pauses. 'What's the most embarrassing thing you've ever done?'

Finally, Jess exhales, searching her mind for a humorous anecdote.

She's in the ladies' toilets, reapplying lip gloss. Her reflection stares back at her, and she's surprised by how relaxed she looks. Being with Gabriel this evening really has been escapism, and the lasagne was divine. They've still got dessert to come, but already Jess is disappointed that the night is coming to an end. Is she developing feelings for Gabriel? She still knows so little about him, but she's at ease in his presence and is already entertaining the idea of seeing him again.

Her phone vibrates in her pocket, and for a second she's tempted to ignore it, to leave it unchecked, until she remembers her life outside this restaurant.

Only the number shows up on the screen, and she presses the phone to her ear, waiting.

'Jessica? It's Nathaniel.'

She lets go of the breath she hadn't realised she'd been holding in. 'Finally! I've been trying to call you. What number are you calling from?'

'My landline. I'm sorry, I know you've been calling. I... it's been...'

Jess might not know this man but she can tell something is wrong. 'What's going on? Are you all right?'

'No, no, I'm not. I think someone's been following me.'

Harrison. He'd promised he would track Nathaniel, to see if he could get a picture of the man's life. 'I'm sure you're just—'

'Imagining it? No, definitely not. It's no coincidence that this has happened right after I've spoken to you. And after I told you I know who's responsible for what happened to your mother. And now...'

'You need to stop this and tell me what exactly you think you know. Now.'

There's a long pause. 'I... can't do that on the phone. You'll understand why after I've told you.'

'If you know who did it, then why don't you tell the police?'

'How can I? I lied to them all those years ago – that's all they'll care about. They won't care about what I say.'

'You need to tell me,' Jess says. 'If it wasn't you, then I want to know who you're claiming it was. Now. And I've just learnt some things about my family and I need to talk to you.'

His reply is immediate. 'We need to meet tonight. I can't bear this burden any more. You need to know. Meet me in an hour at The Shakespeare pub in Stoke Newington.'

Jess doesn't know it but she'll find it. 'I'll be there.'

'Just be ready, Jessica, because nothing's going to be the same after we've talked. Look, I have to go. I'm not safe where I am, but I'll see you in an hour.' He ends the call before she can say another word.

Back at the table, Gabriel is smiling as she sits down. He'll be certain that the evening is going well, and now she's about to break the news that she has to cut it short. He'll think she's not interested in him, but that's a risk she'll have to take. 'I've just had a phone call. Family emergency. Sorry but I'll need to go.' Jess hates being dishonest, but at least what she's telling him is partly true – this *is* to do with her family.

Gabriel reaches for his wallet. 'Sorry to hear that. Is everyone okay?'

Only now, when it's too late, Jess realises she shouldn't have mentioned family. Gabriel is bound to mention it to Zara or Ryan. 'Yeah, it's fine, just my aunt. I need to go and see her.' This will be easy to explain to Zara if it comes to that; her sister never sees anyone on Lori's side of the family.

'I didn't bring my car,' Gabriel says, 'but I'll come with you to make sure you get there okay. It's quite late.'

'No, no, I'll be fine. I'll jump in an Uber. Thanks, though. Sorry about cutting this short. I'll call you.' She's not sure what makes her do it, but she leans in and kisses his cheek. His face reddens as she pulls away, but he's smiling.

Jess is lying to Gabriel already and they haven't even started a relationship yet. Yet. There it is: that small word that has huge significance in her life. She likes him, even though she doesn't want to acknowledge it.

'Okay, let me just pay the bill and I'll wait with you outside,' Gabriel says.

'No, stay. Finish your drink. I'll message you later.'

Outside, Jess glances back to make sure Gabriel isn't watching, then rushes to the Tube. It will be quicker than navigating London traffic in an Uber, and she needs to keep moving.

. . .

The pub is small, with only a few people scattered around, lots of them on their own, staring into their glasses. It's not a pub where large groups come to socialise – at least not on a Monday night – and she imagines it's a refuge for anyone wanting to escape their homes for a while, to have some peace.

It's been an hour and a half since Nathaniel's phone call, and with every passing minute, her frustration increases. He has to turn up; she's counting on him, and as well as needing to hear what he claims to know, she wants to ask him if he knows anything about her uncle Neil. Another man who had feelings for her mother.

Jess expected Nathaniel to be early, just like last time she met him, so she's not prepared for this uncertainty. Meeting here tonight had been his idea – it's not as though she'd pushed him into it. Why, then, isn't he here? It also makes her uneasy that he's picked somewhere so far from either of their homes.

With her eyes fixed on the door, she calls Harrison. It rings for so long that she's about to end the call when he picks up. 'Hi, Jess.' He sounds out of breath.

'Have you seen him?'

There's a pause before he answers. 'Yeah, I'm fine, thanks for asking.'

'Sorry. It's just... urgent. Have you seen Nathaniel French?'

'Has something happened? Is he harassing you again?'

Jess stares around the pub, hoping that somehow she might have missed him, that if she looks again he'll be standing at the bar right now ordering a drink. 'No.'

'I'm sorry, Jess,' Harrison says. 'But I haven't had a chance to follow him yet. I got an urgent call from work and they needed me in today so I had to give up one of my days off.'

It wouldn't be fair to argue with this. Besides, Harrison's

news brings up another more important issue. 'So, you haven't seen him at all? You haven't been to his house?'

'No. I can start following him tomorrow, though.'

Nathaniel had told her someone was following him. 'Sorry, I have to go.' She ends the call.

After another scan of the pub, Jess calls Nathaniel one more time, willing him to pick up, to have an explanation for why he isn't yet here. It goes straight to his voicemail, his gravelly voice telling the caller to leave a message.

Leaving her coat on the chair, she heads to the bar. She'll order one more drink – a tonic water; she's already shared a bottle of wine with Gabriel tonight – and give it half an hour longer. That's it.

Back at the table, her mind replays the conversation with Nathaniel. He'd been worried, repeated again that he knows who killed her mother. She wants to believe this, but she can't ignore the possibility that he's playing some sick game with her. Still, no matter how she pulls it apart and attempts to reassemble it, there's no reason she can identify for him to do this. For fun? Psychopaths do things like that. Yet, no matter how much she might want to believe he is her mother's murderer, how much easier that would be to swallow, she's sure she's missing something monumental here.

Time ticks away, one of the few things humans are power-less to stop. And then it's time for her to leave.

She will go to Nathaniel French's house. And put an end to whatever it is he's doing.

THIRTEEN

DECEMBER 1992

Lori

Sometimes when she's sitting beside Jess's bed, stroking her back to help her fall asleep, Lori likes to play a game. She pretends she's taken a different path, and plays out how her life might be now. It's just for fun – she would never change anything, never be without her darling girl.

Tonight, as she sits bathed in the warm yellow glow of Jess's night light, her thoughts have turned to Neil. His declaration yesterday has knocked the wind from her. Shocked her to her core. It's also forcing her think about him when she doesn't want to. Like now, as she sits back with her eyes closed imagining an alternative scenario. In it, she met Neil before he met Mionie, and now they are together. Maybe they're married, maybe just living together – it doesn't matter. What matters is that they are unbreakable. Connected. Physically and mentally.

Jess stirs and Lori's eyes snap open. It sickens her that she's thinking of her sister's fiancé like this. It's a line never to be crossed. She looks at her daughter, who has finally drifted off. For over an hour Lori has sat here with Jess, but she doesn't care. It's part of being a mother, and she does whatever she has to, however hard it is at times being a single parent. 'Goodnight, sweetheart,' Lori whispers. Slowly she leaves the room, shutting Jess's door behind her.

In the living room, Lori sits by the low window, watching the street outside. There's a small playground across the road, and she's grateful to have something more interesting than blocks of flats to look at on nights like these. It's also somewhere she'll be able to take Jess when she's a little older.

Again, Lori thinks of Neil. Her sister's fiancé. A man who has confessed that he has feelings for her. What kind of person is he? She needs to know. The cordless phone is on the windowsill, and she reaches for it now, dialling the number of the hospital. She leaves a message with the operator and waits, silently staring out of the window, this time imagining Jess as an older child, the two of them having fun in the playground together. A different life. One that's more secure than the life she's living now.

Seven minutes later, her phone rings. She snatches it up and whispers a greeting.

'It's me. Neil. You left a message? Is everything okay?'

'Can I see you?' she says, still keeping her voice low.

There's a fraction of a pause. 'When?'

'Now?'

'Is everything okay?'

She explains that she just needs to see him, and this is all it takes. He's finishing his shift in half an hour and will come straight to her place afterwards.

Lori hangs up the phone. She needs to assess her feelings now that she has set this in motion. She's not elated, but neither does she feel regret. Not yet at least. So far, it is all innocent.

She's still sitting by the window when he pulls up outside. Rising, she watches him lock his car, taking deep breaths to calm herself. She's nervous, unsure how this will all go. She thinks of Mionie, wonders what her sister is doing at this moment.

There's a frown on Neil's face when Lori answers the door, and he's breathless; he must have raced up the steps to her flat. 'Is everything okay? Are you alone? Where's Jess?'

'Everything's fine and Jess is asleep so we need to be quiet.'

He steps inside. 'I'm a bit surprised that you've called. I thought after we last spoke... you said we shouldn't be alone together.'

'Neil, can you at least come in so I can shut the door?'

He steps inside. It's clear to Lori that he's nervous; all of this feels forbidden.

She tells him they should go in the kitchen. It's a tiny space but it's further away from Jess's room, and she doesn't want to wake her daughter. Especially not with this. 'What you said yesterday shocked me,' she begins, 'and I didn't know what to do with that information.' Lori avoids looking at him, instead staring at the kitchen table. 'Sometimes it takes me a while to process things like this. I need to sit with things for a while before I know what to do or how to feel.'

He nods. 'I understand. I dropped a bomb on you.'

Lori looks him in the eye. 'Do you love my sister?'

'I did.' He sighs. 'I want to still. It would be so much easier. It's just... these feelings I have are messing me up. When I first met her, I didn't notice her negativity. I only saw the good in Mionie. How hard she works, how driven she is, how intelligent. And later, that clouded everything else.'

'She's all those things and much more,' Lori says; the urge to defend her sister, in spite of everything, is second nature to Lori. Mionie may not do same for her, but she isn't like them.

'I know that,' Neil says. 'But there's an ugly side to her, and the longer we've been together, the more I've noticed it. Now I can't stop seeing it, and I can't find that love I felt in the beginning. It's just... gone.'

Lori sympathises with Neil – he's clearly struggling with this. 'I think you're confused. Maybe you've built up these feelings in your head for me that aren't real, they're just a diversion so you don't have to address the real issues.' She reaches out to take hold of his hand but then pulls back, folding her arms.

'I don't know what it is, Lori. I only know how I feel about you. It's grown slowly and I tried to bury it, but now...'

'Let me ask you something, Neil. What do you want to happen now?'

He stays silent, shaking his head. 'I don't exactly know.'

'Are you going to leave Mionie? If you don't love her, then it's not fair to stay with her, is it?'

He doesn't say anything.

'Neil?'

'We had a long talk last night and she finally believes that nothing has happened between us. She said that she won't end our relationship when I haven't actually done anything.'

Lori is surprised to hear this. She thought Mionie wouldn't tolerate Neil admitting he has feelings for someone else. Especially her own sister.

'She said she can make allowances for the fact that I was honest with her,' Neil continues, 'and told her how I was feeling. She said she's grateful for that.'

But there will be a price to pay, Lori knows it. 'What else did she say?'

Neil clears his throat. 'She, um, she said... Oh, I'm sorry, Lori.' He lowers his voice. 'She said she thinks it's your fault for making me confused. Flirting. I'm sorry. I tried to put her straight again. I told her it's absolutely not your fault, that you've never done anything inappropriate.' He stares at his shoes. 'What she was saying shocked me. She told me that you know exactly what you're doing, even if it doesn't seem obvious to anyone else.' Finally he looks at Lori. 'I'm so sorry. She said she needed to cut you out of her life.'

Lori's chest tightens, and bile rises to her throat. She and Mionie have had their issues but she didn't see this coming. What about their mother? Will she be forced to take sides? And where does this leave Jess?

'I think you should go,' Lori says. 'Now.'

Neil frowns. 'But, I...'

'Just go. You being here will just make things worse.'

'No, wait, you don't understand. I came here to tell you that I'm not staying with her. Not after all of this.'

Without another word, Lori walks to the front door, pulling it open and shuddering at the chilling breeze that swarms in. 'Just go.'

Neil does as she asks but stops at the door, pushing against it so Lori can't close it. 'I thought you and me... why are you doing this? And what would Danny think if he knew?'

The mention of Danny is too much. She pushes Neil out and slams the door shut.

Neither of them will ever know what might have happened if their conversation had gone a different way. Too many paths, too many choices. And none of it means anything.

FOURTEEN

NOW

Jess

She reaches into her pocket, yet again checking her alarm as she walks towards Maitland Road in Sydenham. A week ago, she would never have believed she'd be traipsing the streets of London late at night, alone, but here she is. The street lights do little to ease her anxiety as she makes her way to Nathaniel's home. Or at least the place he is claiming is his home. Several times she's tried his phone again, only to be met each time with the same message.

Jess regrets not going home to change first; her jeans are fine, but her shoes are too high for her to run fast in if it comes to that. She is out of her comfort zone here; even without the shroud of darkness, this area is far too quiet. It could be a trap; maybe Nathaniel wanted to lure her here. Yet there's no way he could have been certain she would come when he didn't show up at the pub.

The address on his business card turns out to be a flat in a small three-storey building. Thankfully, there's no entry system, and she walks straight in, scanning the numbers on the doors as she passes each one. Nathaniel's is number six, which she assumes is on the top floor as there seem to be only two flats on the ground floor.

Ignoring the lift, she heads for the staircase on her right, and she's barely reached it when there's a crash behind her. She spins around, her hand already clasping her alarm.

It's only the door slamming shut behind her, but still Jess's heart pounds.

When she reaches the top floor, she's relieved to hear music coming from somewhere. Signs of life. Outside number six she raps on the door, folding her arms as she stands back to wait.

There's nothing but silence from within the flat, and no light streaming through the gap under the door.

'He isn't there.'

The voice catches Jess off-guard and she turns to see a woman in her late fifties standing in the doorway of the flat next door. With dark hair cut into a neat bob, she reminds Jess of Carolina.

'Hi, I don't suppose you know where Nathaniel is?'

The woman shakes her head. 'I wish I did. He was coming over this evening to help me with something in the flat. He never showed.'

'Oh, sorry. I was meant to be meeting him tonight. A couple of hours ago.'

The woman's forehead creases. 'That's strange. He's usually so reliable. He's never done anything like this before, and he's always helping me out.' She frowns. 'My husband died a couple a years ago and it's hard for me to manage everything on my own. Nathaniel's been so kind to me. Something must be wrong. He would have let me know that he couldn't come.'

Jess takes a step towards her. 'When was the last time you spoke to him?'

The woman rubs her chin. 'Musta been around lunchtime, I reckon. He said he'd be over for five. I've tried calling but his phone's off. Who switches their phone off these days? I mean, we need to be contactable, don't we? What's the point of a mobile otherwise?'

Jess nods. 'So, you know Nathaniel well, then? Do you have any idea where he might be? Where he normally goes in the evening?'

She shrugs. 'I dunno. He sometimes goes to the pub by himself or he comes here for coffee. Other than that, I really can't say. He's not one for socialising. Keeps himself to himself.' Her eyes narrow and she stares at Jess. 'And how do *you* know Nathaniel?'

'He was an old friend of my mother's. I've... come here with bad news.' Jess leaves it vague, hoping this neighbour will jump to her own conclusions and not probe any further.

'Oh, right. I'm sorry about your mum. Look, why don't you come in? We can try calling again?'

Jess should refuse; this woman is a stranger to her. So is Nathaniel French. But the need to find out more about Nathaniel is greater than any threat, and she has the security of her alarm.

'Maybe just for a minute,' she agrees. 'I'm worried that he didn't turn up when we'd only just arranged to meet an hour before. It doesn't make sense.'

'No, it don't. I'm Kim, by the way,' the woman says, leading her inside.

'Jessica.'

'Come through, let's see if we can find out what's going on.'

The flat is warm and neat, family pictures adorning the walls. Children, grandchildren. This woman is certainly not a loner.

'Have a seat and we'll try calling again,' Kim says, gesturing to the sofa. She pulls out her phone and dials. 'I'll put it on speakerphone.' The ringtone sounds out into the room before the voicemail message that Jess can recite word for word kicks in.

'I don't understand.' Kim bites her lip. 'I wouldn't normally be worried but lately Nathaniel's been a bit anxious. Not himself. He told me he thought he was being followed the other day, and asked if I'd keep an eye out and call the police if I saw anything unusual.'

'When was this?'

'Couple a days ago. He seemed a bit on edge so I asked him what was wrong. He didn't wanna talk about it at first but I insisted. Stubborn as a mule, I am. Besides, he's always been so kind to me, I just wanted to see if I could help him for a change.'

Jess leans forwards. 'What did he say?'

Kim stares at her, narrowing her eyes. 'Not much. Only that he might be in trouble because of something that happened a long time ago. He said he's been living with this worry for years.'

'I see,' Jess says, as she digests this information. What does it mean? She struggles to make sense of it all; there are too many possibilities. Nathaniel could be mentally unstable, or he could genuinely have something to fear. She needs to find out which it is, and the more she looks, the more it seems to be tied up with her family.

'Kim, do you know any of Nathaniel's friends or family? Maybe we could contact them?'

'No, I don't, otherwise I would've already called 'em. I think I'll give it till morning then I'll 'ave to report him missing to the police. I'll call round the hospitals too. Just in case he's had an accident. If he can't talk or something, then they wouldn't think to call me, would they? I'm just his neighbour.'

Jess wants to ask more questions but that would only arouse suspicion. 'I'd better get going, but can I give you this?' She stands up and rummages in her bag for a business card. 'Will you call me when you hear from him? Or even if you don't. Whatever happens.'

Kim reaches for the card, taking a moment to read it before flipping it over. 'Course. I really hope he's okay. This just don't feel right to me. So was your mum a good friend of his?'

'Um, yeah, they were... close.'

Kim nods. 'He don't talk much about his past. I'm sorry, anyway. You're too young to have lost a parent already.'

If only she knew.

At the door Kim says goodbye and promises again to call. As Jess thanks her and walks to the stairs, she can feel Kim's eyes on her, and she waits to hear the click of the front door. It doesn't come until Jess is already making her way downstairs.

This time, standing outside her father's front door, everything feels different. Something has shifted and Jess struggles to pinpoint what it is. All she knows is that everything she thought she knew about her family, and her mother's death, has been turned upside down. And it's time she had some answers.

Which is why she's here now, at nearly midnight, waiting for her father to answer the door. Unable to face walking the streets again so late, Jess got an Uber from Sydenham instead, spending the journey to Ealing formulating what to say to her dad.

She has her own key, but he's likely to be in bed and she can't risk him thinking someone has broken into the house.

There's a frown on her father's face as he answers the door, and even when it's replaced with a warmer greeting, it's still clear that he's not pleased to see her – something she's never experienced with him before.

'Jess, is everything okay? Has something happened with that man?'

'No,' she's quick to reassure him. 'I suppose he was just playing some twisted mind game.' As she says this, she thinks of

Kim, Nathaniel's neighbour, and how she only had good things to say about him.

'Well, whatever it is, come in.'

He leads Jess into the living room and she stares at his navy dressing gown, his light blue pyjamas flapping at his legs as he walks.

She doesn't wait until they're seated to begin. 'I went to see Aunt Mionie yesterday.'

Her father's eyes widen. 'Oh? And how is she?'

'Still busy working.'

'That sounds like Mionie.' He rolls his eyes. 'Although I'm the same so I can't talk, can I?'

'We talked about Mum.'

A pause. 'I see. And did you tell her about Nathaniel French approaching you?'

She shakes her head. 'I didn't want to go into all that. I only wanted to find out what kind of person Mum was.'

'You know you can always ask me. I know we haven't talked about your mum much but it's not that I haven't wanted to; you just stopped asking. And I never wanted to upset you.'

'Okay, well, I'm asking now. It just feels like I don't have the full picture of who she was. I have this childish image in my head, that she was some kind of superwoman, perfect or something. But nobody is, are they?'

It takes a moment for him to answer, and in that time Danny sits down and watches Jess closely. 'You're right, none of us are perfect. But that doesn't mean we're not good people. Trying our best.'

'Mionie painted this picture that they were one big happy family, with no issues or conflict. She even said that Mum was the one who held them all together.'

'Well, if that's what she told you... she knew your mum a lot longer than I did.'

'The thing is, Dad, then I bumped into Uncle Neil, and he

told me a completely different story. He said that Mionie treated her badly, even though she'd done nothing to deserve that. And it seems Grandma ignored it most of the time.'

He raises his eyebrows. 'Neil said that? That's odd.'

'Are you saying he's lying?'

'I... well, I didn't really see her family that often. I'm sorry to say this but I was so consumed with my career, I could rarely make get-togethers with Lori's family. When I did, though, Meredith and Mionie were always good to me. And to Lori.' He pats the sofa. 'Sit down, will you? You're making me nervous hovering over me like that. And why is this beginning to feel like I'm being interrogated by my own daughter?'

Jess sits down. She doesn't want to believe her father is lying. 'Why would Uncle Neil say that? Why would he contradict what his own wife had just told me? What possible reason could he have?'

For too long her father remains silent, his eyes fixed on her. She feels herself shrink underneath his gaze. It's not the first time she's been grateful to be his daughter rather than one of his employees. 'Unfortunately, I don't understand people's hidden motivations, love. Maybe he and Mionie are having problems in their marriage and he's trying to get at her? Or... maybe he just saw things differently. Even the truth has many versions, Jess, depending on who's telling it.' He stands up. 'Can I get you something to drink? I've got a feeling this will be a long conversation.'

'Coffee, please.' Desperate for a caffeine fix, Jess might actually drink it all this time.

She's ready with more questions when he returns, but he beats her to it. 'What do you remember about growing up?' he asks.

Jess takes a moment to consider his question. 'I, um, remember bits of when it was the two of us, but not much. I always felt safe with you, though.' She looks at him now, willing him to assure her that this will never change.

He clears his throat. 'I'm glad to hear that. I tried hard to make sure you were okay. That you were happy. You know, after your mum... died... you had night terrors every single night for months. At least I think they were night terrors. You'd always been a good sleeper, but after that day you just couldn't settle. Even being in my room didn't help, you'd still wake up several times a night. Screaming most of the time. That's when I decided I had to take you away somewhere. That all of this had affected you in ways you'd never be able to express, and we needed a new start somewhere far away from it all'

'Portugal,' Jess says.

'I'd always loved the Algarve for holidays, but had never considered living there. I just knew I had to bring you up in a different environment, somewhere the painful memories couldn't get to us as easily. It was for both our sakes.'

Jess has only hazy memories of living with her father in Portugal, but she knows, or *feels* at least, that she was happy there.

Her father smiles. 'You know, you cried when I said we had to move back to England to start school here.'

'Did I? You've never told me that.'

'Oh, you were fine once we got here and you made lots of friends at school, but it took a lot of convincing. I almost changed my mind about coming back.'

Jess nods. 'And then you met Carolina. I feel as though she was always with us.'

'Yes,' he agrees. 'She was. Until she left me.' He rolls his eyes. 'My own stupid fault for not being good enough for her. I'll regret that for the rest of my life.'

'Why did you ask me what I remember about growing up?'

He shrugs. 'I just want to know that you were happy. Or as happy as you could be. That I did right by you. I know I've been work-obsessed but please tell me I did something right in my life.'

Jess stands and walks over to him, placing her hand on is shoulder. 'Dad, of course you did. And you've been a brilliant dad to Zara too. She adores you. We both do.'

This time when he looks at Jess, his eyes are glistening. 'I'm proud of you both,' he says. 'I hope you know that? You're better people than I will ever be. But listen to me, Jess. All you need to know about your mum was how much she loved you. You were everything to her. You need to be happy to leave it at that, okay? This delving into the past isn't good for anyone. Now, finish up your coffee – you might be able to stay up all night but those days are way behind me, and I've got a breakfast meeting in the morning.'

Outside, Jess pauses and turns back to the house, tempted to knock on the door again and question her father further, more assertively. She came here for answers yet she's leaving with nothing. And now, even though she's wrapped up in double layers, a hat, scarf and gloves, she is numb and frozen.

FIFTEEN

JANUARY 1993

Lori

On the day she first meets him, she's sitting alone in a café, engrossed in a law textbook. Lori's itching to start her studies, but the months until September loom in front of her. Still, at least she's getting a head start, already working on her future. The university administrator had been more than happy to provide her with a reading list. It was based on last year's course, but she'd assured Lori the books wouldn't change. 'Good on you,' she had said. 'That commitment will get you far in life.' Lori had beamed at these words; she isn't used to getting compliments.

As she looks up to take a sip of her fruit smoothie, she notices someone at another table staring at her. A young man, around the same age as her, maybe slightly older.

He's attractive, in a rugged way, his almost-black hair falling across his face, but it's his smile that captures her attention. Warm and kind; she knows only too well that not everyone's is. She's learnt that the hard way. Still, she's not interested in smiling back at him – all she cares about is the book lying open in front of her. She needs this head start; Lori is all too aware that the others on her course will take more easily to studying. Most of them will be younger, straight out of school, no long gaps to decay their minds.

She gives the smiling man no more thought until a few minutes later, when she finds him standing by her table, speaking. She doesn't catch what he says, but he's looking right at her.

'Sorry, what was that?'

He smiles and points to her book. 'I just said it must be good. You've been in here longer than me and I've been here a while. Anyway, have a good day.' And then he is disappearing through the door, never once glancing back to see if Lori is watching.

It's a few weeks before she sees him again, in the same café one lunchtime. Once again, Lori doesn't notice he's there, but this time it's not because she's engrossed in a book; this time it's because she's just had an argument with her mum, when she'd come to take Jess out for the day.

'Mionie's very upset,' her mother had said. 'It's really not a good idea to get too close to your sister's fiancé, is it?'

For a moment Lori had stood staring at her mother, speechless. She couldn't believe Mionie had talked to their mum about this; Lori had been convinced she would keep her false allegations to herself, to save face.

'I haven't done anything,' Lori had protested, only to be told by her mother that she didn't want to be stuck in the middle, and that they needed to sort it out themselves.

'And you've got Danny,' her mother had said. 'Why on earth would you want to risk your relationship with him? Oh, Lori, what would your dad say?'

And then she'd gone, whisking Jess off in the car, leaving Lori shaken.

This is what Lori is thinking about as she sits in the café, immersing herself in the innocent hiss of the coffee machine and the soft clatter of cutlery. And perhaps because she is consumed with sadness, this is why she is grateful for the kind words of a stranger when they come.

'Whatever it is, things always work out in the end.'

She looks up, sees the attractive man from a few weeks ago who'd commented on her book. 'What?' she asks.

'I know that look because I've seen it on myself a fair few times. And I can tell you categorically that things absolutely always get better, if you give them a chance to, that is.'

Lori rolls her eyes. 'Are you a counsellor or something?'

He laughs. 'No. But I have lived, and I have learnt.'

Lori will never be able to pinpoint what exactly compels her to invite this stranger to sit with her. It's something to do with the words she's just exchanged with her mum, the gaping hole it's left in its wake, but it's more than that, she just can't say what. 'Have a seat,' she says. 'You spend half your time in this place staring at me so you may as well have an excuse to.'

He laughs again and slides out a chair. 'Nathaniel,' he says, holding out his hand.

The name Lizzi is ready to roll from her tongue, but she changes her mind without knowing why. 'Lori,' she says, taking hold of his hand. She's pleased to find it cold; there is nothing worse than shaking hands with someone who is warm and clammy.

'So, do you want to talk about it?' he asks.

'No. I don't even know you.'

'All the more reason. You don't have to care what I think, you never have to step inside this place again and see my face, so I reckon you've got nothing to lose.'

He is right; she doesn't have to see him again, and besides, who else does she have to talk to? 'It's just family stuff. With my sister. I'll be okay. I'm fine how I am and I've got a future to look forward to. So, actually, there's not much more to say.'

'Of course,' he agrees.

'What about you?' Lori asks.

'Me?'

'I've told you something about me so now it's your turn. That's only fair.'

He smiles and takes a sip of coffee before answering. 'Well, I can't argue with that. Hmm. Where do I start?'

Lori listens as he tells her he works for an insurance company, and that he lives on his own opposite Clapham Common. 'I often wonder if I need a change of scenery,' he says. 'There are a million beautiful places to live in this country. Trying somewhere new would be an adventure.'

'Why don't you, then?' She raises her eyebrows.

'Because, ultimately, I'm a Londoner through and through. It's in my blood. It wouldn't feel right to live anywhere else.'

'There's a whole world out there to explore,' she says, even though his sentiments echo her own.

'For sure. Don't worry, it's all on my bucket list. For now, though, I'm happy right here. Right where I am.'

Lori smiles. She likes his honesty. A lot of men might try and make themselves sound more worldly than they are. Nathaniel, though, seems comfortable in his own skin.

By the time he's finished talking, she's almost forgotten about the tension with her mother. Nothing else has been able to distract her.

Checking his watch, Nathaniel tells her he has to get back to work. 'I hadn't meant to be away this long.' He stands up and pulls on his coat. 'It's been nice chatting to you, Lori. I'll see you here soon, I'm sure,' he says. 'And remember, just keep focused on that future of yours.'

And as she watches him leave, Lori is pleased that he hasn't asked for her number. There is something different about this guy, and she likes it.

. . .

At home later, she feels calmer, lighter almost. Usually, she's on edge when Jess isn't with her, worry over whether she's safe causing Lori's body to tighten into knots, but somehow this afternoon she feels at peace. She is certain that, even though her family have their issues with her, they do love Jess. She is safe with them.

The phone rings when she's making lunch, and despite being okay that Jess is with her sister, she holds her breath when she answers, waiting to be assured that it's not bad news.

'Lori, it's me.'

Neil. She recognises his voice, but demands to know who's speaking. He shouldn't be so familiar with her, as if there's something going on between them. She supposes that in a way there is; neither of them has mentioned him coming over the other day, or their clandestine conversations. Isn't that enough?

'What do you want?' She grimaces; Lori hates being rude, yet doesn't know how else to deal with Neil, and she's acutely aware of how wrong talking to him feels.

'You didn't have to throw me out the other day, Lori. I hadn't even finished talking. Will you just hear me out?'

'There's nothing more to say. My sister isn't talking to me and I haven't done anything. This is your fault, Neil. Don't call me again.' Lori slams the phone down on the table, watching as it skids along the surface and drops to the floor. She makes no move to pick it up.

As the afternoon turns to evening, she forgets the phone is still on the floor until it rings again, shortly after nine o'clock. Once more, she prays it's not her mother telling her something's happened to Jess.

'Hello?'

Silence. All she can hear is static.

'Hello?' she tries again. 'Who is this?'

Still nothing, but there's someone there; the line hasn't been disconnected, she can hear someone's light breathing.

She's about to say Neil's name but thinks better of it; it might not be him on the other end, and if by any chance it's her sister and it's just a bad line, she doesn't want anyone wondering why she would think it's Neil.

Click. Now the ringtone pierces her ear.

She's puzzled for a moment, but doesn't give her silent caller much more thought until it happens again half an hour later. This time she hangs up as soon as she's greeted with silence. She won't let this person have the upper hand. She immediately calls her mother.

'Is Jess okay?'

'What? Yes, of course. She's asleep.'

'I just wanted to check.'

'You know you don't need to worry when she's with me. She's fine, Lori. I'll drop her home in the morning as planned. You really need to stop worrying so much – you're overreacting again, dear.'

Lori lets this wash over her; she's going to prove to her family that she's not the person they think she is.

She brushes her teeth and gets ready for bed.

Jess is safe. It's unlikely that the silent calls are coming from her sister, or Neil for that matter. So that only leaves one other option.

And she expected something like this to happen.

She's been playing with fire – it was inevitable that sooner or later it would begin to catch up with her.

SIXTEEN

NOW

Jess

'I want something arty. Not, you know, those awful cheesy photos with everyone facing the camera and fake smiling. Something tasteful.'

Jess attempts to focus on her client, to understand exactly what it is she's asking for – or demanding – with this photoshoot. 'I totally understand.'

'I know exactly what I want.' The woman – Melinda, according to Jess's appointment schedule – reaches into her oversized designer bag and pulls out a folder full of printed pictures. 'Like these.' She hands it across, and Jess takes it with a smile and flicks through the images.

She doesn't need to look at them all to get the idea. 'Yes,' she tells Melinda. 'As you can tell from my website, these are exactly the type of family images I like to capture.' Jess studies this woman's face: late thirties, flawless make-up, a woman who pays attention to every detail. Jess respects this – it mirrors her own philosophy when it comes to her work – but she doesn't have the headspace to handle a person who is so fixed and intent on what she wants that she won't listen to other opinions. Jess usually likes to talk things through with a client, make sure they understand how everything works before they make final decisions.

'How did you hear about me, again?' she asks, even though Melinda hasn't mentioned how she came to select her. There's no shortage of photographers in London.

'What? Oh, a Google search I think. Yes, that was it.'

Jess is on edge now, more than she already has been while talking to this client. 'Okay, well, let me just get a few more details and I'll—'

Her mobile blares out; she's forgotten to switch it to silent, something she's never done before. 'I'm sorry, I just need to take this. I'll be right back.'

Melinda rolls her eyes, but Jess ignores her; it might be Nathaniel so she needs to answer this call.

'Hello? Is that Jessica?'

'Kim?' She recognises her voice from last night.

'Nathaniel's still not home. This isn't good. In all the time I've been his neighbour he's never stayed away for a night. Not once. I've called all the hospitals round here and he's not in any of 'em.'

'Okay, um, let me think. Do you know where he works?'

'He's retired. But he does volunteer at the local care home, you know, keeping the elderly folk busy with activities. Playing scrabble with 'em. That type of thing. He's there most days. I was about to call 'em but then I thought it might be better if I just go down there and see if he's there for myself. Then if he's not, I can at least prove that I'm his neighbour. I'll show some ID and then they might actually talk to me?'

'Hopefully. I would come with you but I'm just with a client. Will you call me as soon as you know anything?'

Kim assures Jess that she will, and they end the call.

When she heads back into the studio, there's no sign of

Melinda. Her client has gone, leaving no trace that she was ever there.

It's three hours before Kim calls back, and in that time Jess has been trying to lose herself in editing photos. While she's usually able to focus her mind completely on work, her attention is evaporating, leaving in its wake a vast black hole of confusion and dread. Nathaniel French. Her father. Her aunt and uncle. And all the questions that have been thrown up about Jess's mother.

She snatches up her phone the second it rings. 'Have you found him? Is he at the care home?'

There's a heavy sigh. 'He didn't show up for work, and they haven't heard a thing from him. I knew it. I knew this was out of character. He would never mess the old folk around. I'm going to the police right now. There's no way he's disappeared on purpose.'

'The police will find him,' Jess offers. It's the only thing she can manage to say. 'I'm sorry, I know he's a good friend of yours.'

'Yeah, he is,' Kim agrees. 'And I don't like this at all. Not one bit.'

'Do you want me to come with you?' Her father's warning rings in her ears as she says this, but everything has changed now. Jess is still unsure whether Nathaniel has done this on purpose, even though she can't think of a single reason why he would just show up like that and then just as quickly disappear. Unless he's been telling the truth all along.

'No, it's fine.' Kim sounds deflated. Anyway, this isn't your problem, is it? You didn't even know him very well, did you? You just get back to your work and I'll let you know what they say.'

Kim is so wrong. As much as she doesn't want it to be, this *is* Jess's problem.

How strange it feels to be in her sister's flat knowing everything has changed, yet she can't speak of it. Zara is always the one Jess goes to, and it feels deceptive to sit there on her sofa, staying silent about the most important thing going on in her life.

'Are you okay?' Zara asks. 'You're being quiet. Have you heard from that monster again?'

'No. And I'm fine. Today's been a strange day, though.' Jess tells Zara about her disappearing client.

Zara's eyes widen. 'That's so rude. If she changed her mind about using you, then she should have at least had the decency to say so. What is wrong with people?'

Perhaps it's paranoia but Jess hasn't even considered this. After Melinda vanished, Jess spent the rest of the afternoon convinced she'd come to keep an eye on her for some reason, or check her out, when it could have simply been down to rude manners.

'You look like you need this,' Zara says, handing her a glass of wine. 'And you're staying for dinner, no arguments. I'm making lasagne and there'll be plenty of it.'

There'll be no argument from Jess. She pictures the inside of her fridge, still bare other than a bottle of milk, which must be curdling by now, and some butter. She really does need to go shopping. 'Thanks, sis.'

Zara takes a sip of wine. 'Have you seen Dad since we spoke last? You were a bit worried about him, weren't you?'

'Yeah, I saw him the other night. He seems to be okay, just working too much.' Jess looks away, hating that she's keeping something so important from her sister. She stares at the picture of Zara and Ryan hanging on the wall. It's from a photoshoot she did for them last year, and it always makes her happy to know how much it means to them, that it has pride of place on their wall.

On the table, her phone vibrates. She sees Harrison's name on the screen. She grabs it and places it in her pocket, praying for it to stop ringing.

'Everything okay?' Zara asks. 'Don't you want to answer that?'

Again, Jess avoids looking at her. 'It's Harrison. I'll call him back later.'

Zara frowns. 'Harrison? I didn't realise you were still talking?'

'Not really. It's been a while.'

Zara is staring at her, and Jess knows her well enough to guess what she's thinking. Her sister is wondering if she's back on that slippery slope, if Jess will get sucked back in just when she's come out the other side. Thankfully, she changes the subject. 'Hey, I heard you and Gabriel finally went out for dinner? I want all the details, please.' She sits back on the sofa and curls her legs under her.

Jess can't help but smile; she knows exactly what Zara is doing and she appreciates it more than Zara could know. 'It was... nice. We got on.'

'Nice? Is that code for he's boring and you don't want to see him again? Because I never would have labelled him dull!'

'No, it means... I guess I quite like him. He's interesting. Like I said, it's just really not great timing right now. It's hard to get my head fully into it.'

And even if they do end up liking each other, if it turns into something with longevity – what then? It will be the same thing as it was with Harrison all over again. It's easier if Jess stays away from relationships. She hasn't shared these fears with her sister, or anyone else. She doesn't even want to think about what it all means.

'Just go with it, Jess,' Zara says. 'There's never a perfect time for anything. You like him and I know he likes you, that's all that matters.'

They're interrupted by a key turning in the door, followed by voices in the hall. Zara calls out, 'We're in the living room.'

'Ah, hey, Jess, how's it going?' Ryan appears in the living room doorway, loosening his tie.

'Sorry, looks like I'm staying for dinner.' Jess shrugs an apology, even though there's no need; both Zara and Ryan have always been happy to have her here.

Ryan's eyes flick to Zara; it's such a fleeting gesture that most people wouldn't notice, but Jess does.

'I don't have to if you're—' She stops mid-sentence, aware that someone is now behind Ryan.

'Hi, Jess. Nice to see you again,' Gabriel says, smiling.

Zara stands and gives Ryan a kiss before she heads over to hug Gabriel. 'You're staying for dinner too, right?'

Gabriel glances at Jess, another fleeting gesture that would be easy to miss. 'Oh no, I can't. Need to get home. I just bumped into Ryan and I popped in to borrow a book he was telling me about.'

Zara shakes her head. 'That one about the junior doctor? Yeah, Ryan was raving about it. Anyway, now you're here you may as well stay. No, you're staying. Jess is here too, and there's plenty of lasagne for all of us, right Ryan?'

He nods. 'Sorry, guys – you know how pushy Zara is.'

She flicks his arm. 'Not pushy, just assertive. Now come on, you can help me get dinner sorted or we won't be eating until midnight.'

Zara and Ryan head to the kitchen, leaving Jess alone with Gabriel.

'Is everything okay with your aunt?' he asks, joining her on the sofa. 'I asked Ryan but he didn't know what had happened.'

Jess is confused, until she recalls the lie she told Gabriel when she cut their dinner short. 'She's, um, doing okay, thanks. It's a long story – maybe I'll explain it another time.'

He nods. 'Of course. Anytime you want to offload, though, I'm here.'

Her phone vibrates again, this time with a text message.

Been to police. Given all details. Up to them now. Will keep you updated. Kim x

Jess had been hoping for a call, to get more details, but it's doubtful there's much more Kim can say. She slides her phone into her bag and turns her attention back to Gabriel.

For over three hours, Jess focuses on the people whose company she's in. She's still waiting for her phone to ring, but in between that she loses herself in the conversation, and feels a flutter in her stomach when Gabriel brushes against her arm.

'I'd better get going,' she says, finishing her glass of wine. It's past eleven o'clock, and she's lost count now but she's had at least four drinks. 'I'll get an Uber.' *Again. I need to stop wasting money.*

'Let me order it,' Gabriel says. They can drop you off first then go on to my place. That way I'll know you're home safe.'

Jess laughs. 'I don't need protecting.'

'Oh, I can see that you're perfectly capable of looking after yourself,' Gabriel says, 'but just humour me, okay?'

Zara chimes in. 'I think I'm speaking for my sister when I say, yes, she would love to share an Uber with you.' Then she lowers her voice and taps him on the arm. 'Now hurry up and book it before she changes her mind.'

In the cab, Gabriel turns to her. 'So, what do you think? That was a total setup by your sister, wasn't it?'

Jess chuckles. 'I'd bet my life on it. She's determined to get us together, isn't she?'

'Yep. We might fall out over this. I mean, does she think I've got no taste at all?'

She lightly punches Gabriel's arm. 'Thanks!'

'You do know I'm just kidding, don't you? The truth is, I feel lucky that she thinks I'm good enough for you.'

'Maybe she's the one who's got no taste, then?' Jess smiles, and with it she realises how relaxed she is with Gabriel. That barrier remains up, though – the one that won't let her open up about her history to anyone new in her life. Will it always be like this? She's exhausted by it. She shouldn't have to hide who she is, what was forced upon her.

She takes hold of Gabriel's hand as the car pulls up outside her place. She's not going to hold back any longer. She is who she is, and he can choose to walk away if he can't deal with it. It's better to know sooner rather than later.

'Come in,' she whispers.

'Are you sure?'

'Yes. Come on.'

Once they're inside, Jess realises there's nothing she can offer him to drink other than black coffee.

'That's fine with me. And probably a good idea after all that wine at Zara and Ryan's. I don't want to make a fool of myself.'

'Well, I do make coffee that can rival Starbucks,' Jess laughs. 'You'll be flocking back here for more. Although, there's no milk. Sorry.'

'I'll take it however it comes. And that's not the reason I'd want to keep coming back here,' he says.

Jess understands what he means but she asks him anyway, just to hear him say it, because after the last few days she needs to lose herself in something else.

'Okay. I like you, Jess. I know we've only just met, but it's the feeling you get from people that matters, and I trust my instinct. I feel good being around you, like I can already be myself.'

Jess's cheeks burn. She wants to tell him that she knows exactly what he means, that she feels it too, but she stays silent. She knows what she wants, what feels right, and undoubtedly the alcohol is helping, but in this moment, all she wants is Gabriel. To wake up in the morning and for him to still be there. What happens after that doesn't matter. She's living in this moment, before it's gone. Before she wants it to go. 'Come here,' she says, gesturing for him to come closer. One thing is for sure – she is going to be the one who controls what happens here.

Afterwards, they lie together in her bed, and Jess watches Gabriel as he sleeps. She likes him, even more now, and she'd like nothing more than to give this a go, see what happens. But how can she when everything she thought she knew about her mother has been turned upside down? And she can feel herself clutching at what remains of her own life. Nathaniel's disappearance is concerning. There's no way Jess can forget about these things, and she doesn't want to. She owes it to herself, and to her mother, to know the truth. It doesn't matter what Lori might have done; all that matters is finding out who killed her, and silently Jess vows that she will do that, whatever it takes.

She reaches her arm across Gabriel's chest, taken aback by how familiar he feels, how comfortable she is lying beside a virtual stranger. Closing her eyes, she longs to sleep, just as he is, but it won't come easily for her tonight.

How can it when there could be someone out there who wants to silence Nathaniel French? Someone who might know that Jess has been in contact with him. Someone who might want to silence her too.

SEVENTEEN
JANUARY 1993

Lori

For over a week she's been coming to the café each day, sometimes with Jess, mostly by herself. The hope of seeing Nathaniel draws her here; she wants him to be here when she has Jess with her, just so that he knows, so that there's no awkward conversation. Then Lori will know whether he's really worth thinking about. And she definitely has been thinking about him. It's the first time since Danny that she's let her guard down, made herself vulnerable, and, rather than being scared, it feels good to know that she's still capable of feeling something. Her fear since she left him is that Danny has permanently killed off her ability to want someone. Men like Shane don't count. They are just something she needs to do.

Now she sits cradling a cappuccino, one of her law books on the table in front of her as usual, the words on the page swimming before her, refusing to sink in. She's too distracted. Every time the door opens, letting in a gush of fresh winter air, she looks up expectantly, but it's never Nathaniel. And now she's beginning to wonder if she'll see him again.

It doesn't matter, Lori tries to convince herself. He probably wasn't interested in her anyway. He was just being polite, killing time during his lunch break. She was foolish to get carried away. Yet when they'd spoken, hadn't she sensed something between them?

Finishing her coffee, Lori packs away her book; she is ready to leave, and to stop making a fool of herself by coming here every day in the hopes of seeing Nathaniel.

It's when she's standing, throwing her bag over her shoulder, that she sees him strolling towards her, that beautiful smile on his face.

'Ah, you're leaving,' he says. 'I was hoping I could buy you a coffee. Never mind, maybe next time.'

She's already had three cups. 'Actually, I can stay for one more. I'm not doing much.' She hopes she doesn't sound desperate. She's far from that; after Danny she really doesn't care if she ever meets anyone again. Still, she likes this guy.

Raising his eyebrows, Nathaniel slowly nods. 'Great.' He hangs his coat over the back of the chair opposite Lori's. 'Back in a sec.'

As she watches him head to the counter, she wonders how she will bring up Jess. She will just throw it out there, she decides. She's not, and never will be, ashamed of her daughter, or of being a single mother. And if Nathaniel has a problem with it, then she doesn't want him in her life.

'So, how are things with your sister?' Nathaniel asks when he comes back. He places two cappuccinos on the table and slides into his chair.

'Well, she's still not talking to me, but as long as she loves my daughter then that's all that matters.' There, she's done it now. He can like it or take a hike.

Nathaniel's eyes widen, but he's still smiling. 'You have a daughter? That's great. How old is she?'

'Two. Her name's Jessica. I'm not with her father.'

'You don't have to explain anything to me,' Nathaniel waves his hand. 'We're just two people having a coffee, getting to know each other. No pressure or expectation, okay?'

Lori nods, and exhales a deep breath. All the tension she hadn't realised she was bottling up drains from her body. 'So, how about you? Married? Any kids?'

'Nope. There was someone, a while ago, but after it ended I've just kept to myself.'

'Sorry to hear that. Sounds like it was difficult.'

'Relationships breaking up always are, aren't they? Even if it's what you both want.'

Something they have in common, Lori thinks. 'Yep, that's definitely true.' She thinks of Shane. Of the others. Of what she has done. The legacy of Danny Moore.

'Hey,' Nathaniel says, tapping the table. 'Let's not talk about the past, let's only focus on the future. How about going for a drink on Friday? Not just coffee, I mean a night out.'

'I'd like that,' Lori says. Nathaniel grabs a napkin and pulls a pen from his pocket. 'Here's my number and address. Sorry – I've got no paper.'

Lori smiles, reaches for a napkin. She writes down her details and slides it over to him.

Nathaniel looks at it and slips it into his pocket. 'Now, Lori Gray, tell me more about this course you're starting in September.'

Later, at home, she cooks dinner while Jess organises a tea party for her cuddly toys. Lori hasn't felt this way since the night she followed Danny and her whole life came crashing down around her. Nathaniel has given her hope; yet still she is wary. She'd thought she knew Danny. He was the father of her child, yet he harboured ugly secrets. She will never again make the mistake of trusting someone. No, she's already planning on finding out everything she can about Nathaniel.

EIGHTEEN

NOW

Jess

Jess sleeps fitfully, while beside her Gabriel barely stirs, lost to peaceful slumber. The alcohol should have helped anaesthetise her, yet the opposite is true. When her phone vibrates on the bedside table, she's ready to answer it, her senses heightened because it's nearly two a.m. This call won't be good news.

It's Harrison, and Jess is about to decline the call until she remembers that he's been kind enough to help her with Nathaniel. Still, it feels wrong to answer his call while she's lying next to Gabriel, both of them barely clothed. Pulling on her dressing gown, she rushes from the bedroom and answers as she heads downstairs.

'Jess, hi. Sorry it's so late. I just wanted to check in with you. I've been outside that man's building all day and night and there's been no sign of him. A few people have come and gone but none of them fit his description.'

'Oh.' Jess is disappointed, even though she already knows that Nathaniel is missing.

'Does he have a car?' Harrison asks. 'All the ones outside the flats have been driven away at some point today so I don't think any of them are his.'

Jess hadn't thought to ask Kim what car Nathaniel drives, if indeed he even owns one. It's not that unusual for people in London to forgo cars and depend on public transport, or bikes instead. 'I don't know,' she says, keeping her voice low. In the kitchen, she keeps the light off and pulls the door shut.

'It doesn't feel right, Jess. 'Why would he ask to meet you then not show up?'

'This is what I've been asking myself. I have no idea.' Jess explains about meeting Nathaniel's neighbour, and how Kim will have reported him missing by now.

'He didn't turn up for work? That's definitely not right, is it? Look, I'm worried about you, Jess. I don't want to scare you but all of this seems too coincidental. Right when he's about to tell you who did that to your mum, he disappears. Something really messed up is going on.'

Harrison echoing her own thoughts, validating what to most people might seem irrational, is a tremendous relief to Jess. There have been moments when she's wondered if she's losing her mind. 'What can I do?' she says. 'If I never hear from him again, then the truth disappears with him. I can't bear the thought of that.'

'I know. So many questions and so much uncertainty. It would be better if he is actually guilty. I mean, he still could be.'

Jess hasn't shared with Harrison what she's found out about her family. The secrets and lies. Her mother's whole life reconstructed.

'I'm worried about you, Jess,' Harrison says again. 'I don't think you should be on your own. I can come over now and we can try to work out what's going on?'

'I appreciate the offer but it's late and I'm really tired. I think—'

'I can't let you be there on your own. It's bad enough you

having to deal with it all but... I'm sure you've thought about the possibility that whoever did that to your mum is still out there? And you were the only witness. I'm coming now—'

'No, just stop!' Jess speaks too loudly, too defensively. 'Look, I'm fine. The truth is—'

'You're not on your own tonight.'

'How did you know?'

The silence that follows is loaded with pain and tension. She can feel it as if it's passed through the phone line.

'Because I know *you*,' Harrison says, eventually. 'Is this the guy you mentioned a few days ago?'

Jess feels her cheeks flush. 'Yeah.'

'That was quick. You must like him a lot if he's staying the night. I know you don't just fall into bed with someone easily.'

'I don't know. It's early days. And I've got a lot of other stuff going on, haven't I? Please be okay about this? I would if it was the other way around.' At least she hopes she would. That would be her intention, but who knows what hearing Harrison had found love again would do to her heart.

'But it isn't the other way around, is it? And I'm not the one who left you. Just what exactly d'you think will be different with this guy? Years down the line d'you think he won't want all the things I want? Or will he be just the next idiot whose heart and soul you destroy?'

Jess takes a deep breath. She can understand Harrison's anguish. 'That's not fair. Not everyone wants to get married and have kids. Gabriel might not want to. We're not even at the stage of discussing it. We may never be.'

'Just listen to yourself, Jess. Justifying your cruel actions. Good luck to you and that poor bastard, whoever he is.'

Harrison cuts off the call.

Sadness and anger amalgamate inside Jess as she stares at her phone, contemplating calling him back to tell him he has no right to behave this way. But the sound of footsteps upstairs forces her hand. Gabriel. Which means there is every possibility he's heard her conversation.

Rushing upstairs, still attempting to be quiet, Jess is surprised to find Gabriel still in bed asleep.

But she'd heard the unmistakable sound of footsteps. She knows she did. And there's nobody else in the house other than the two of them.

Jess wakes before Gabriel, and even though her body is weighed down with fatigue, she climbs out of bed and trudges downstairs.

While she's making coffee, she determines that she will go to the police today. At least telling them everything she knows will ease her burden. She's not a detective; how would she even know where to start with this? First, though, she needs to speak to her grandmother. No doubt she will spin the same story as Mionie, but at least then that will be one more person Jess knows she can't trust.

'Morning.'

Gabriel is standing in the kitchen doorway, smiling. 'You should have woken me,' he says, yawning.

She explains that she's only just got up herself, and offers him coffee.

'It'll have to be a quick one. I'm meant to be in Kent in half an hour to check how a build is going. It'll be a beautiful house when it's finished. I'm even thinking of living there myself.'

'You'll have to show me it,' Jess suggests, but she's distracted, only half focused on what he's saying.

'Yeah, let's do that. Maybe in a few weeks when it's got a bit more to it. It literally is just an empty shell at the moment. I can show you the plans, though.'

She nods and hands him his coffee. 'I'm sorry if I woke you

last night,' she says, looking away so that he doesn't see how loaded her words are.

'When? You didn't wake me. I slept like a baby,' he says.

'Oh. I came down for some water and could have sworn I heard you get out of bed'

'Nope, I definitely didn't. But I wouldn't have minded if you'd woken me up.' He smiles, and reaches for her hand, pulling her closer. When he kisses her, Jess makes up her mind that she must have been mistaken. It's easy in the dead of night to imagine sounds that aren't there.

Three hours later Jess is in Farnham, hesitating outside her aunt's door. She's always found her grandmother aloof, as if she's not that interested in her. She'd put that down to it being too painful, that perhaps Jess is a constant reminder of the daughter she lost. And now, she wonders if she could have made more effort herself. But Jess hadn't been aware that she'd been distancing herself from her mother's side of the family. Instead, it had happened organically, without thought or intention. Was it the same for them? Lori's death should have brought them all closer together, but now Jess is sure there were other reasons for this chasm between them.

Meredith isn't expecting her and it's better this way. Jess doesn't want to give her time to concoct a story, although there's every possibility that Mionie has already warned her that Jess has been poking around, asking questions about Lori.

She looks frail and thin as she answers the door, but even though she's well into her eighties, she's still a tall woman. 'Jessica! What are you doing here? Is everything okay? Did we plan this? I'm sorry, I don't remember...'

'Hi, Grandma. No, I was just passing and thought of you. Are you busy?'

Meredith looks back at the house and shrugs. 'Not particularly. Although I do have a a friend coming at one. Come in if you like. I... I don't know if I've got any coffee, though.'

'Don't worry, I can't stay long.'

Inside, Jess notices straight away how different her aunt's house appears. It used to be filled with ornaments and plants, yet now it feels as if Meredith is getting ready to pack up and leave. There are no photos anywhere, and now that she thinks about it, Jess can't recall ever seeing one of her mother in this house.

'I think I expected to hear from you,' her grandmother says, gesturing for Jess to take a seat on the sofa.

'Aunt Mionie told you I was asking about Mum.'

'Yes, she did. I do understand, Jess. It's only natural you want to know more about her. And Mionie and I are the ones who knew her the most. Yes, your dad loved her, but he only knew her as an adult.'

'And he also doesn't seem to want to talk about her much. I know it's hard for him.'

'Sometimes it's best to let sleeping dogs lie,' Meredith says. 'There's something *you* need to understand too, Jess. We're a private family – we always have been. And... your questions are stirring up some... old resentments and issues.'

Meredith must be talking about Uncle Neil, and the feelings he had for Jess's mother. She asks if this is what her grandmother means.

'Yes, that's some of it. But—'

'Neil said Mionie didn't treat her well.'

Meredith falls silent, frown lines adding to the wrinkles already present on her forehead. 'Oh, Jessica. I'm so sorry, but it's probably true. I've had many years to think about it and maybe I did sometimes sit on the sidelines and try not to get involved in their issues. I should have at least defended Lori when Mionie was overreacting. Accusing Lori of all sorts.'

'Why? Why would any mother sit back and let her daughter feel so isolated?'

The walls feel as though they will close in on her as she waits for her grandmother to answer.

'It's complicated,' Meredith begins. They were so young when it first started happening and I think they just fell into a pattern. We all did. You see, in their father's eyes, Lori was always the golden child. The perfect little angel who could do no wrong. That was hard on Mionie. Especially when she worked so hard to be successful. To get his attention. But it didn't matter what she did, Lori always came first.'

Anger swells inside Jess. 'So, Mionie was jealous of her?'

Meredith holds up a trembling hand, reminding Jess to handle this gently. 'When they were kids, Lori could do anything and she'd never get into trouble, at least not as far as their dad was concerned. I tried to balance it out, I suppose, by coming down harder on her, but Mionie just wanted their dad to... *see* her. So, as I said, she worked extra hard in school, and went to university and excelled in her career, while Lori just cruised along never really committing to anything.' Meredith sighs and stares at the beige carpet. 'It didn't change anything, though. Nope. Your grandfather was still besotted with Lori.'

Jess is incensed by what she's hearing. 'That doesn't excuse how she was pushed out. It wasn't *her* fault.'

'I know that. And I'm ashamed of how I let it happen with my... inaction. Lori was just... very different to us. Maybe we just didn't understand her. And she didn't understand us. She and Mionie would never have been friends if they hadn't been siblings.' She reaches over to the coffee table and pulls a tissue from its box, wiping her nose. 'But there was all that stuff with Neil. I'm sorry to say this, Jess, but we really believe Lori and Neil had something going on.'

Jess shakes her head. 'I don't believe that. Aside from

anything else, she loved my dad. And Uncle Neil didn't tell me anything had actually happened.'

Meredith folds the tissue and slips it inside her cardigan sleeve. 'Jess, your mother wasn't perfect. I don't think she was as committed to your dad as he thought.'

'And what does *that* mean?'

Meredith stares at Jess. 'I think you already know the answer to that. And Neil wouldn't say anything against Lori. He probably still loves your mother to this day, so it stands to reason that he'd say whatever he could to protect her memory.' She sighs. 'Even at the expense of my other daughter. Look, Jessica, just what is it that you want to know?'

'The truth.'

'The truth is that nobody's perfect. Not me, not you, and not your mother. Her life was a mess, but I like to believe she would have sorted herself out, if she'd had the chance. Wait here. There's something I want to show you.' Slowly, Meredith rises and shuffles into the hall.

It's almost five minutes before she returns, carrying a white shoe box. She sits down, clutching it to her chest before handing it to Jess. 'It's full of family photos of all of us, and there are loads of your mum. Your grandfather loved photography and he was always capturing shots of us all.' She smiles for the first time since Jess arrived. 'I wonder if that's where you get it from?'

'Possibly,' Jess says, although she's never heard that a love of photography was genetic. Anything is possible, though, Jess is beginning to realise. She opens the box and pulls out the photos, studying each one. What strikes her is that in every photo they all look happy, despite the animosity Mionie harboured. Jess turns to her grandmother and questions her about it.

'They say the camera never lies,' Meredith says. 'But that's where they're wrong. It does. We're told to smile for the camera, no matter what emotions we're feeling, or what's going on in our lives. Forget it all and just smile for a second, while snap, snap,

snap – to capture that one perfect moment in time, but it's not reality, is it?'

Jess has never looked at it this way, preferring to believe in the integrity of photographs, but Meredith has a valid point. 'There aren't any of my dad,' she says. 'How come?'

'Are you sure?' Meredith frowns and leans forwards. 'He must be in there somewhere. Although, if I remember right, Danny was rarely around. It was always work, work, work with him. He never seemed to make it to family get-togethers. How is he, by the way?'

'Same old Dad. Still a workaholic.'

Meredith smiles. 'Some things never change. Send him my love, won't you, dear?'

Jess nods, but she has no intention of revealing to her father that she's come here today. She places the photos back in the box and slips the lid back on. 'Can I ask you something else? When my mum was killed, who did you believe had done it?'

The colour drains from Meredith's face. 'Why are you asking that? Everyone knows who it was. It was that... that... Nathaniel French. I still can't believe he got away with it.'

'But what if it wasn't him?' Jess asks. 'The police couldn't find evidence to prove his guilt, could they?'

'No, but does that mean he's innocent? Or that he's just clever or lucky?'

'So, no doubts ever crossed your mind that it might have been someone who knew her?'

Meredith leans back against her chair; it's clear that this conversation is taking its toll on her. 'Well, of course we all speculated. We wondered whether Lori and... but no, that was ridiculous.'

'What?' It's got to be Neil that she's referring to, Jess is convinced of that.

'Um, well, we did wonder if... Danny could have—'

'My dad? There's no way!'

'I know. And anyway, the police very quickly ruled him out.'

Jess's heart races. She's never even entertained this possibility before. Her father. 'Did they... it definitely couldn't have been him, could it?'

'Oh, no, dear. He had a solid alibi.'

'Do you remember what it was?'

'Yes. He was in hospital, with plenty of witnesses to prove he wasn't well enough to leave his bed.'

Jess exhales, silently admonishing herself for even considering her father could be involved. 'Can you remember what he was in for?'

'Oh, Jessica, it was such a long time ago.' Her forehead creases. 'Um, I think it was a hernia operation or something like that. Now, please, Jessica, this is too much to talk about. I'm sorry, dear, but I'm just too old for raking up the past.'

Jess leaves not long after this. At least it appears that her grandmother has been honest, and she's confirmed Neil's story about Mionie's treatment of Lori. Maybe this quest for answers is futile, and Jess might never know why Nathaniel French turned up in her life, and disappeared just as quickly.

Before making the drive back to London, she sits in the car outside her grandmother's house and pulls out her phone to message Kim. But Nathaniel's neighbour has beaten her to it and there are three missed calls from her. With a lump in her throat, Jess calls her back.

'Kim, hi. I'm so sorry I missed your calls. I was—'

'Never mind that – they've found him. They've found Nathaniel.'

'Oh, thank goodness, where—'

'No, you don't understand. They've found his body. He's dead!'

NINETEEN

FEBRUARY 1993

Lori

He's not like Danny. Or any of the others. She could detach herself from them, but Nathaniel is different. It's as if his soul is trying to pull her in. But she's resisting. For weeks now he's slept on the sofa whenever she's stayed over at his place, and not once has he tried to work his way into bed with her. As much as this pleases her, this man is an enigma she can't work out.

Lori still won't let him come to her flat, and she doesn't know how much longer she'll be able to hold him off. It's especially difficult when he knows Jess is staying with her mother or sister.

Tonight, she's cooking for him at his place, and as she prepares a roast dinner, she watches him as he attempts to fix the video recorder. His heart is set on them watching a film together, yet he seems calm as he grapples with it. She admires this – Danny would have lost his temper and given up long before now.

By the time Lori's serving up dinner, Nathaniel has got it

working. He doesn't make a big deal of it, though – like Danny would have.

They sit down and eat, but there's something different about Nathaniel this evening. He's a fairly quiet man, but tonight he seems withdrawn, as though there's something bothering him.

'Is everything all right?' she asks, clearing away the plates. 'I hope dinner was okay?' He's eaten it all, but perhaps that was just out of politeness. Maybe she overcooked the beef. And the potatoes might have been a bit hard.

'It was perfect,' Nathaniel says. He starts washing up, but he's not concentrating, and there are remnants of food on the plates he's stacking on the draining board.

'Is everything all right at work? You can talk to me about it, you know.'

He smiles and sighs. 'I know. I feel like I can talk to you about anything. Except...'

'What? What is it?' Lori's heart seems to sink into her stomach. Her equilibrium is about to be disturbed, she knows it. This is all going to end up a mess like it did with Danny. The instinct to run – before she can hear what he's about to say – is powerful.

'Come over here,' he says, taking her hand and leading her to the sofa. 'I need to ask you something.'

Lori nods, but she's finding it hard to keep looking at him.

'Do you like me?'

'Of course I do.' She frowns. 'I wouldn't be here otherwise, would I?'

Nathaniel stares at the floor, nodding. 'I feel like you do. But then... physically, you know, you don't seem to... want me.' He fixes his eyes on her now and she feels like he's trying to read her mind.

'I *do* want to. I'm just... taking things slowly. After... I told you I had an awful break-up, didn't I?'

'Yeah, and I understand that, but—'

'Can you just give me a bit of time?' She moves across to him and nestles into his chest. It would be so easy to give in and lose herself in him, let their bodies find each other. But there are things she needs to take care of first, and she won't make Nathaniel a part of that.

'Whatever you need,' he says, standing. 'How about we go to Blockbuster and choose a video?'

After the film, he asks if she wants to stay the night, his eyes wide with hope.

'I'm sorry. I need to be at home for Jess when my mum brings her back tomorrow morning. She has an early appointment to get to.'

'No problem. Next time, then. Or I could even come to you?'

So, they're back here again. Just how long does Lori think she can avoid introducing him to Jess. 'Yeah, soon, I promise.'

Nathaniel nods. 'Whenever you're ready. Come on then, I'll drop you home.'

In the car, chat flows easily, making Lori believe that maybe he will be okay for a while longer. He's an easy-going person; surely as long as they keep spending time together then he'll realise she does like him.

Outside her block of flats, she kisses him quickly then runs inside to wave to him from her front window. It's what they do, so that Nathaniel knows she's safely inside.

But this time, when she gets upstairs and heads to the window, he's already gone, his car disappearing around the corner.

Lori's phone rings a few minutes later, when she's getting into bed. She's still getting the silent calls, but they've stopped bothering her. Instead, she just stays on the line, telling the person how pathetic they are, and that they can't scare her.

'Hello?' she says, preparing for her attack.

'Hey. It's me.'

It takes her a second, then she recognises the deep husky voice.

'Hi. What are you up to?'

A few minutes later, Lori is pulling off her pyjamas and slipping on a black dress. She checks herself in the mirror. It's perfect. Sexy but still classy.

Now she is ready.

TWENTY

NOW

Jess

Jess is so consumed by her whirlwind of thoughts that she doesn't notice someone is right behind her as she unlocks her front door. She leaps back the second she hears a breath, and pulls out her alarm, ready to fight with every inch of her being.

'Jess, it's me.'

'Harrison, what are you doing? You scared the hell out of me!'

'Sorry,' he says. 'I needed to see you. There's something I have to tell you.'

She shakes her head. 'It will have to wait. I've just found out that Nathaniel French is dead. His body was found. Shoved into a recycling bin.'

Harrison stares at her, his mouth hanging open. 'My God, that's awful. I'm sorry. But Jess, this is even more reason why I should come in.'

Jess shouldn't let him – every time she's around him the wall she's built up begins to crumble. And after the way he reacted when he learnt about Gabriel last night, she's convinced any kind of friendship between them is impossible. 'I just need to be alone.'

'Come on, Jess. We can talk it all through. Something worrying is going on. How do we know you're safe? What if someone knows you were talking to him?'

She's clearly not going to get rid of Harrison easily, and there is little fight left in her tonight. 'Only for a few minutes,' she insists.

Inside, Harrison hunts for some glasses while Jess marvels at how easily he can make himself at home in her place. This wasn't the property they'd rented together; she'd let him keep that flat – it was the least she could do after shattering his heart.

'Here, you need this,' he says, handing her a glass of wine.

Jess pushes it away as she fills him in on everything she's learnt from Kim. She's numb as she describes how they found him, with knife wounds so deep that there was no chance he could have survived, even if he'd been able to get help.

'So, the police don't know yet what happened?'

'They told Kim they think it was a mugging. His wallet, mobile and watch were all missing.'

Harrison shakes his head. 'That's just too coincidental, isn't it? And this happened on the night he was coming to meet you.'

'Yes. Not too far from his house. He must have been on his way when it happened.'

'Oh, Jess, what the hell is going on?'

'I wish I knew.' She eyes her wine glass, tempted just to have one sip. 'What are you doing here, anyway?' she asks, ignoring her urge.

'I came here to tell you something. After our phone call, I couldn't sleep so I went straight back to Nathaniel's. I didn't see him, but I noticed someone hanging around the block of flats. A youngish guy. Similar age to me, I reckon.'

'That could have been anyone. Other people do live in that building.'

'I know. But I watched him, and after a while he pressed Nathaniel's buzzer.'

'It could have been someone he knows?' But hadn't Kim told Jess that Nathaniel was a loner and she'd never known him to have visitors.

'True,' Harrison agrees. 'Did he have any family?'

'No – there was only a woman he used to be with, but that ended years ago, before he moved to London.' Elsbeth, Jess recalls. She needs to find her somehow. 'That's probably why the police are talking to Kim – she's the closest person to him.'

'This isn't right,' Jess says, 'I need to go to the police myself, and tell them that he approached me last week.'

'I agree. Jess, look...' He hesitates, just stares at her.

'What is it?'

'I'm just worried about you.'

'Don't be. I can take care of myself. I always have done.'

'I know, I just—'

Jess stands. 'I think you should go now. You could have called to tell me what you saw. You didn't need to come all the way here.'

Harrison doesn't move. 'Bethnal Green isn't that far away. Besides, I wanted to apologise. In person. For my behaviour on the phone. I had no right...'

'No, you didn't. We're not together any more, are we? That means we're both free to see whoever we want.' Jess picks up her glass and takes it to the sink, pouring the contents out.

Harrison watches her. 'I know that. I said I'm sorry.'

'Apology accepted. Now, please, I just need to be on my own.' She places the glass down too forcefully and it shatters on the worktop.

'Let me get that,' Harrison says, rushing over.

'No, please, can you just go now?'

The minute he leaves, Jess locks the door behind him and checks the windows are closed. Across the garden she can tell that her studio is locked up as is always the case. She's fiercely protective over everything in it.

She's glad she decided not to drink the wine Harrison poured – now she can drive to the police station in Sydenham. This is long overdue.

Her father is waiting for her when she gets home. She called him when she'd finished at the police station, telling him it was urgent that she sees him immediately.

'What's going on, Jess? I have to say, this is a bit out of character for you. Are you all right?'

'No, Dad. Let's just go inside.'

The thin smile that was on his face as she approached quickly disappears. 'I hope this isn't about that man. I told you—'

'*That man* is dead!'

There's a pause while her father processes what she's saying. 'What? How?'

She pulls him inside and closes the door, locking it behind them. 'Just sit down and I'll tell you everything.'

Whatever Jess expected her father to say, it comes as a shock when he leans back on the sofa and utters the words 'Good riddance.'

'Dad!'

'He was a piece of scum. Have you forgotten what he did?'

'That's just it, Dad, I don't think it was him. And remember, the police never charged him.'

'They were useless! It *was* him. He was always hanging about in that park, and he was seen that morning. I don't believe in coincidences. The police officer I was in contact with told me in confidence that they had no doubt it was him. And nothing's changed now, Jess.'

'Everything's changed!'

In response to her father's frown, Jess admits that she's been in touch with Nathaniel since that first meeting. To his credit, her father listens without interrupting, no emotion registering on his face. When she's finished, he sighs and buries his head in his hands.

'I've even been to the police, to tell them that his death might have something to do with what happened to my mum.'

Danny looks up. 'What exactly are you trying to do, here?'

'I just want some answers, Dad. How am I supposed to just carry on with my life when all this has happened? I can't.'

'Jess, just calm down.'

'I'm sick of trying to work things out and never getting anywhere. All I've uncovered so far is that I've been lied to by my family for years.'

Her father leans forwards, frowning. 'What are you talking about?'

'Did you know that Mum's whole family hated her? Apart from her dad, that is. But he wasn't around, was he? How did you not see all this?'

Seconds tick by while he digests this information. 'I might have had an inkling,' he admits. 'But Lori never talked about it and, to be honest, I didn't see her side of the family much.'

'I know. You were always too busy with work.'

He sighs. 'Yes, I was. I regret that heavily now. I didn't deserve your mother. Look, Jess, I can understand why you're confused. But I still stand by what I believe. Nathaniel French murdered your mother, right in front of you, and whatever he was doing by tracking you down, well that's got nothing to do with innocence.' He pauses. 'Maybe he wanted to just make sure you hadn't had some sort of memory recall, and could identify him. I'm sure that happens. We can look it up and see—'

'How do you explain the photo of him with my mum, then?'

Danny hesitates before he answers. 'Even more reason it was him. If they were having some sort of relationship, then maybe he got jealous or something. Yes, that must be what happened.'

'But she was with *you*, Dad.'

He falls silent, watching her closely, and Jess immediately knows that something is wrong. 'What is it? What aren't you telling me?'

His eyes gloss over, just as they always have done whenever she talks about her mother. 'Jess... I'm sorry I never told you this, but... I don't know who it was with, but your mother *was* having an affair.'

TWENTY-ONE

MARCH 1993

Lori

It's raining today, but Lori needed to get out of the house. The walls are closing in on her, and her new flat, which she's slowly grown used to – become fond of, even – now feels like a prison. Yesterday, when she came home from her walk with Jess, she was convinced someone had been following her. It wasn't that she'd seen anyone, but she'd *felt* it.

What if Danny has tracked her down? It hadn't been easy to make the move to a new flat in Clapham, but she'd done it to keep him away. It's possible he could have followed her back from her mother's house once he realised she no longer lived on Lessar Avenue. She's still got the same car; it wouldn't be too difficult to find her. It's not as though she's moved to the other side of London. Still, she has one thing she can hold over him. He won't want anyone finding out what he's done.

Lori walks along Upper Richmond Road, striding towards Putney High Street. Her coat is meant to be waterproof, yet she can feel the rain soaking through to her clothes. It's futile to fight it; she accepts that before long she'll be drenched, as though she'd dived into a lake. Lori already has too many battles she's fighting, so she slows down – she will let nature win this time.

She's in the bookshop in the shopping mall, browsing the psychology section, when she sees him. He stands across from her, staring directly at her. She jumps, and it makes him laugh.

'Hello, Lori. Where's my daughter?'

She looks around – the shop is fairly full, surely Danny won't cause a scene in here. Still, she needs to get away from him. She turns away too late; he is already grabbing her arm. 'This isn't a game, Lori. I want to see Jess. You can't keep her away from me.' He spits his words, and it frightens her. Another new side of Danny.

Lori wrenches her arm from his grip. 'I really didn't know you, did I?'

'What's that got to do with me seeing my daughter? Where is she? At your mum's? With Mionie? I'll go to both of them if I have to, Lori, so why don't you just tell me where she is?'

Lori hopes he can't tell her body is shaking. 'You won't do that, though, will you, Danny? You'll never risk everyone knowing what you've done.' Her words may be assertive but she's crumbling under the force of his character. That's how he's been able to lie to everyone.

He pushes a stray strand of hair from Lori's face. 'I just want to see Jess. That's all. You can do what you like – it's my daughter I need in my life.'

Hearing these words fuels Lori with strength. She stares at him for a moment until the words are ready to come out. 'Do you know what sickens me the most? You asked me to marry you. I never suggested it. *You* did that. And all the time you knew what life you were living. What you were doing.' She backs away. 'Over my dead body will you ever see your daughter again.'

And then she walks away, ignoring his demands for her to

come back. Only when she's outside, where now the rain falls even harder, does Lori pull up the hood of her coat and run.

She spots the bus that will take her to her street and increases her pace to jump on it, checking behind first to make sure Danny isn't following her. Only when there's no sign of him does she exhale. What if she'd had Jess with her? What if Danny had snatched her? These are the thoughts invading her mind as she takes a seat next to an elderly man, who moves over to give Lori more space than she needs. His kindness is too much, and she feels the sting of her tears as they pool in her eyes.

It's only when she gets inside her unfamiliar building and pulls shut the main door that Lori allows herself to relax. Although she'd planned for Jess to stay the whole day with her mum, so that she could lose herself in reading for the day and clean the flat, she needs her daughter with her. But first she needs the bathroom – she's been needing to go since she was in the bookshop.

At her front door, Lori stands frozen, staring at the words scrawled across her door in blood-red paint: BITCH. An ugly, cruel word, screaming its hatred at her.

If it didn't terrify her so much, she would laugh. She didn't think people actually did things like that other than in films or on television. But there it is, loud and clear. A message for Lori, an escalation of the silent phone calls.

She hurries inside and grabs a scrubbing brush and washing-up liquid from the kitchen, wiping the words away before any of her neighbours walk past.

'I wasn't expecting you this early,' Lori's mother says, standing aside to let her in. 'Jess and I were just about to do some painting. I've promised her.'

'It's okay,' Lori assures her. 'I'm not here to take her home yet. I just wanted to be with her. With both of you. Is it okay if I stay?'

Meredith closes the door. 'Oh, Lori, you are a strange one. I thought you desperately needed today to get things done. What's happened?'

Lori wishes she could talk to her mum, that she could share everything that's been going on. The good and the bad. But she worries her mother might not be open to hearing about Lori troubles. It would shatter the illusion of their perfect family. 'Nothing's happened,' she says instead. 'I just finished early, that's all.'

Her mother rolls her eyes and heads back to Jess, who's sitting in her highchair in the kitchen. 'I hope you haven't got fed up of studying already. You haven't even started your course yet.'

'Mama!' Jess screams when she sees Lori. And for just a moment, a sense of serenity washes over Lori. Her daughter makes everything okay.

'I'll make tea,' Lori says, ignoring her mother's comment, watching as she hunts for paper and paints for Jess.

'Not for me, thanks. I've just had one.'

Later, when Lori says she needs to get Jess home for a nap, her mother insists on letting Jess sleep there. 'She'll just fall asleep in the car, and that's not a proper nap, is it? She needs to be comfortable and lying flat.'

'Okay, Mum. We'll stay so she can nap.'

'I'll take her up. How about you tidy away the paint things?'

When her mum comes back down, she tells Lori they need to talk.

Overcome with uneasiness, Lori sits down. Her mother has never said anything like this before; most times she avoids any conversation with Lori that goes beyond asking how Jess is.

'Okay.'

'You know, Lori,' her mother begins. 'I've tried to stay out of the issues between you and your sister. At least since you've been adults. But... well, now I feel that I have to say something. Your behaviour is—'

'My *behaviour*? What are you talking about?'

'All this trouble with Mionie and Neil. What's going on, Lori?'

She should leave right now, go upstairs and get Jess, even if it means waking her. She's not sure she has the energy to defend herself right now. There is no point pleading her innocence – her mother's already made it clear she doesn't want to be stuck in the middle. Yet stubbornness keeps Lori rooted to her seat.

'I didn't do anything.'

'I'm just finding this all a bit strange. Neil has always seemed like a good man. What on earth would make him think about you in that way if he didn't have a reason to think you... oh, I don't know, Lori. It's all a mess. I think for the moment you should just stay away from them both. Mionie says you're always flirting with him. Is that true?'

'Mum! I have never done that.'

'And what does poor Danny think of all this?'

The mention of Danny's name renders her silent. She could tell her mum the truth now, to make sure nobody in the family mentions his name again, but it would just give them something else to blame Lori for. They will say it's no surprise that she chose the wrong man.

'He works so hard for you and Jess, and this is how you repay him. What would your father think?'

Without replying, Lori walks away, leaving her mother in the kitchen.

And as she's fixing Jess into the car seat, she acknowledges that her life is unravelling. Slowly but consistently. But Lori will do all she can to protect her daughter.

TWENTY-TWO

NOW

Jess

Her dad's words are the first thing she thinks of when she wakes up. *'Your mother was having an affair.'* And now, so much makes sense. When Jess had asked her father why he didn't tell the police, his reply was that he hadn't needed to, that the man had died in a car accident the day before Lori had died.

Jess needs to put this behind her now, and find a way to live with this new picture of her mother. It doesn't have to matter, and her father was quick to assure Jess that it had nothing to do with the love Lori had for her. Jess can be at peace with that, even though she will never know the truth about who killed her mother.

Nathaniel has gone, and she can only assume it was either a strong coincidence, or because someone has carried out their own form of justice. Hadn't he told her that he'd feared for his life all these years? Either way, Jess may never have an answer. It's been a week since he confronted her, and she won't put her life on hold any longer. Knowing her sister will already be up and getting ready for work, she reaches for her phone and calls Zara.

'Hey, sis, what's happened? Are you okay?' Zara sounds out of breath, and Jess imagines she's on her exercise bike, snatching some time before work.

'I'm fine,' Jess assures her. 'I just wondered what you're up to later? I could do with a night out.'

'Funny you should say that. Ryan was just organising drinks somewhere with Gabriel. Why don't we all get together?'

'I was thinking more of just us sisters. Would you mind?'

'Oh, hang on,' Zara says. In the background Jess can hear Ryan's voice. 'Sorry, Jess, Ryan's just saying that it's organised now. Please come with us, though.'

After some hesitation, Jess agrees.

'You don't seem keen to see Gabriel,' Zara points out.

'I am. I was just hoping you and I could talk.'

'Of course, sis, we will – they can chat about football or whatever, and we can talk in private. Okay, see you at Hemingways in Wimbledon. Eight o'clock.'

As soon as she's ended the call, Jess wonders if she's doing the right thing. Can she really just ignore everything that's happened, deny to herself that Nathaniel French ever came into her life? Yes, she decides. That's exactly what she needs to do. And work will be her saviour.

Around lunchtime, Gabriel messages Jess, telling her that he's looking forward to seeing her tonight.

Me too, she writes back, but she feels like a fraud as she presses send. She's not being honest with him, keeping such a big part of her life hidden. But the voice of reason in her screams out that it's nobody's business but her own.

For once, Jess is happy to stop working in the evening. She stands in front of her mirror, trying on clothes, forcing away all images of her mother doing the same thing, getting ready for a date with Nathaniel. The man who ended up killing her out of jealousy. Why would her mum do that to Jess's father? Jess hates making judgements about people, and she's far from perfect herself, but she needs to know why her mother needed to do it. She takes off the black skater dress she was planning to wear and searches for her jeans.

When she's ready she heads outside and locks up the house. She'll get the train to Wimbledon so she can have a drink tonight. She's never been one for excess, but this struggle to erase Nathaniel French from her mind is a challenge.

'Hi, Jess.'

She turns around and Harrison is walking towards her.

'You've got to stop doing this,' she says, shaking her head.

'I was on my way home from work and wanted to check you were okay.'

'I've told you before you could just call!'

'I wasn't planning on knocking. I just wanted to check no one was hanging around. Anyway, a phone call won't keep you safe, will it?'

Jess checks her phone. If there's any point making the trek to Wimbledon, then she needs to go now. 'I'm on my way out.'

'I can see that. Anywhere nice?'

'A drink with Zara. In Wimbledon.' Jess won't mention Gabriel – not after how Harrison reacted last time she'd spoken of him. 'I need to walk now, so...'

'Let me give you a lift. It'll be quicker.'

Jess checks her phone again. Does a quick calculation. 'Okay,' she agrees.

'Come on then,' Harrison says, jingling his keys.

In the car, he turns down the radio, much to Jess's annoyance. She could do with getting lost in some random music, instead of having to make small talk, or humungous talk, with her ex.

'I was thinking about Nathaniel,' Harrison says. He clearly has other ideas about this car journey.

'Well, I'm trying not to,' she warns.

'Did you go to the police?'

She tells him she did, and that now it's in their hands, and she's moving on. Putting it all behind her.

There's a brief pause as Harrison reflects on what she's saying. He knows her well enough to see that once she's made her mind up about something, nothing will shift her. 'Jess,' he begins. 'I know how difficult this must be for you, but the person who killed your mum is still out there, and most likely had something to do with Nathaniel's death too. What if they—'

'Don't say it! I'm not going to live my life in fear. Someone took my mum's life but I'm not going to let them ruin mine. Besides, I've found out some new information from my dad.'

Harrison glances at her before focusing back on the road. 'Oh?'

Jess shouldn't tell him – they're no longer meant to be in each other's lives and she's already let him in far too much. 'Forget it. It doesn't matter.'

'Of course it matters. Haven't I always been there for you?'

She has to admit that he has.

'Then let me be there for you now, even if it's just getting it off your chest so you can let go of it.'

But is it something Jess will ever be able to let go of? The picture of her mother is forever changed in her mind. She stares out of the passenger window, the London road a blur of static car lights. She should have got the train. 'My mum was having an affair,' she says. 'Dad knew about it. Well, he knew she was seeing someone, he just didn't know it was Nathaniel.'

Harrison glances at her. 'Oh, Jess, I'm sorry. How do you feel about it?'

'That I no longer know what kind of woman she was. But it's fine. I won't let it define me.'

'Course you won't. That's what I lo—'

'Stop! Don't say it. Can you just let me out?' She reaches for the car door.

'We're nowhere near Wimbledon.'

Jess doesn't care. She'll jump on the Tube, anything to get out of this car. 'Just let me out, Harrison.'

He pulls over into a bus stop. 'Just wait. Jess, if your mum was having an affair and your dad knew about it, do you think... what if he got angry with your mum or something?'

Cold dread fills Jess's body. Of course this thought has flitted through her mind before, but she's never allowed it to implant itself. 'No,' she says. 'It means Nathaniel probably did do it and he got angry because she wouldn't leave my dad.'

'Jess, I don't think—'

'Just stop!' She unbuckles her seatbelt and jumps out of the car, slamming the door behind her. 'It wasn't my dad,' she shouts into the car. 'He was in hospital at the time!'

And as she walks away, she prays that Harrison will leave her alone. Her mum's death is not the only thing she needs to leave in the past, for the sake of her sanity.

By the time she's reached Hemingways, the last thing Jess wants is a night out drinking. Or even talking. Not even to her sister. She hesitates outside the door, seconds away from turning around and heading home. Then someone opens the door to come out, and Zara sees her, beckoning her inside.

'And what time d'you call this?' her sister says when Jess gets to their table. She's over an hour late, and can only imagine the state she must look. Water drips off her hair and her damp jeans stick to her skin. 'Oh dear, what happened to you?'

'I'm taking a wild guess here, but could it be Jess got caught in the rain?' Gabriel stands up to help her peel off her coat. 'Are you okay?' he whispers.

'Yeah, I'll be fine. Let me just go and dry off a bit.'

When Gabriel offers to get her a drink, she gratefully accepts before rushing to the toilets.

She dries herself as best she can with the limited flow of hot air from the hand dryer, but doesn't feel much better when she gets back to the bar. But she's here now and she's determined to make the best of this evening. She's with people who care about her – whatever was, or is, going on with the rest of her family doesn't matter; she has Zara and Ryan. And maybe Gabriel too. It's early days, though, she warns herself. She can't let herself get carried away.

Later, when Ryan and Gabriel are deep in conversation about hybrid cars, Zara moves over to sit closer to Jess. 'You're not okay, are you?'

'I'm fine.'

'Jess. I know you. On the phone you said you wanted to talk. Has something happened? I could tell the second you walked in that you weren't right.'

It's inevitable that Zara will find out from their dad soon enough. 'Nathaniel French was found stabbed to death yesterday.'

Zara claps her hand to her mouth. 'Oh my God! What happened?'

'The police don't know yet, but it looks like a mugging.'

'Well, I hate to say this, but what goes around comes around, doesn't it?' And after what he did to your mum—'

'Zara! We don't even know if he was the one who...'

'But it must have been. They've never arrested anyone else for it, have they? Look, I'm so sorry this has happened, but at least he'll leave you alone now.'

But will the person who killed Nathaniel? Jess shudders, despite the warmth in the bar.

Zara taps Jess's arm. 'Hey, maybe it was done out of

revenge? I bet he had a lot of enemies. It might have all caught up with him.'

Before Jess can reply, the men turn their attention back to Jess and Zara.

'Another round, ladies?' Gabriel offers, pointing to their empty glasses.

'Not for me, thanks. I think I'll head home.' Jess pulls her coat from her chair. Her head is pounding, and it's nothing to do with alcohol. What Zara has said about someone killing Nathaniel out of revenge has planted a seed in her head, one she doesn't want to grow. The only people who would want revenge for Lori's death are Jess's family.

'But you've only just got here,' Zara moans, trying to grab Jess's coat. 'Come on, at least stay for one more.'

Jess shakes her head. She's aware of Gabriel watching her and she avoids his stare. 'I can't. I've got an early shoot tomorrow so I need to get some sleep.'

'I'll see you home,' Gabriel says, already standing and pulling on his coat.

'Looks like it's just us, then,' Zara says to Ryan.

'I'll make it up to you,' Jess whispers, giving her sister a hug.

Outside, the rain has eased up, falling only in soft spatters now. 'I don't think Zara was happy,' Gabriel says.

'I'll make it up to her,' Jess says. 'Maybe I'll do dinner for the four of us. Soon.'

Gabriel smiles. 'Sounds good. As long as you let me help with the cooking.'

'Deal.' Jess pulls out her phone. As much as she enjoys Gabriel's company, and spending another night with him would help her lose herself, she needs to be alone tonight.

'Look, you don't have to see me home, I'll just order an Uber. I've been doing that a lot lately. I should take out shares.' She smiles.

'No, I'm coming. I'll just get the driver to take me to my place after dropping you.'

Less than ten minutes later they're in the car, moving steadily through Wimbledon, the rush-hour traffic having petered out hours ago. She loves driving through the city at night. Safe inside a car.

Jess listens as Gabriel tells her about the project he's working on. It is a safe subject, and it delays the moment he'll ask more about her family. It is inevitable – like the sun rising each morning. She just needs to be prepared when it comes.

Outside Jess's house, the Uber driver parks across the road to let her out. Jess unbuckles her seatbelt and leans in to kiss Gabriel on the cheek.

'Do you want some company tonight?' he asks, smiling hopefully.

'Any other time, yes. But not tonight. Is that okay?'

'Course. No pressure at all. I've got an early start too.'

She kisses him again, this time on his mouth. 'Speak tomorrow, then.'

The rain pounds down harder now, splattering onto Jess as she rushes around the car to cross the road. She pulls her hood up and it blocks her vision. And by the time she's heard an engine revving, it's too late, and a black car hurtles towards her. She jumps back, smashing against the side of the Uber, the black car narrowly missing her as it screeches off and disappears around the corner.

TWENTY-THREE
MARCH 1993

Lori

'As much as I love being outdoors, it's a bit cold for a picnic,' Lori says, as she watches Nathaniel spread out the blanket and unpack all the food he's brought. She doesn't mention it, but there is far too much of it – sandwiches, cakes, crisps, sausage rolls – enough to feed a whole family, Lori thinks.

The sun shines down through the branches of the tree they've chosen to sit under, but it does nothing to ease the bitter chill in the air. 'Luckily, we're wrapped up. Well, I am at least.' Nathaniel laughs. 'I told you to wear your hat and scarf, didn't I?' He pulls his own woolly hat from his head and holds it out. 'Here, take mine. I promise it's clean.'

Lori shakes her head. 'I'll look ridiculous!'

'You could never look ridiculous, Lori Gray,' Nathaniel says, taking her hand. 'Even if you were wearing a dustbin liner.' He scratches his chin. 'Well, okay, maybe just a tiny bit ridiculous in a dustbin liner. But still cute.'

She rolls her eyes, and they both laugh. Yet despite his corny words, Lori loves the way he makes her feel, the way his words emit warmth around her like a comfortable blanket. She never felt this good about herself with Danny. Not surprising, given what he was doing. Nathaniel is different – she sensed it the moment she met him, and even though she's still on guard, with each passing day she feels her barrier dissolve.

Not enough to introduce him to Jess, though. No, she's not in that place yet.

While they eat, and Lori listens to Nathaniel talk, she thinks how easy it would be to lose herself in a life with him. She could forget everything that she's been doing, and all that took her there in the first place. Nathaniel would be a good father to Jess, Lori knows it.

But she can't stop now. She's only got a few months left before university starts; she will put it behind her then. Change her life. *There is no end, though, is there, Lori. Can't you see that?*

'You never talk about Jess's dad,' Nathaniel says.

Taken aback by his comment, Lori stares at him, her hand frozen with the sandwich she was about to take a bite of.

'Sorry, you don't have to talk about it. It's none of my business.'

She puts the sandwich back on her plate. 'He's not in her life. That's all there is to say, really. He will never be in her life.'

Nathaniel frowns. He must be deciphering her comment, attempting to work out the context. Perhaps he will come to the conclusion that Danny was abusive. As guilty as she feels for not explaining, Lori can't let herself get into that conversation.

'I'm sorry,' Nathaniel says. 'But I know you've got more than enough love for your little girl. She'll be fine without him.'

A tear forms in Lori's eye. 'Thank you for saying that.'

Nathaniel takes a bite of his sandwich, chewing it slowly. 'I'd love to meet her,' he says, when he's swallowed his bread. 'Maybe we could take her out somewhere? Bring her here to the park or something.'

A lump forms in Jess's throat. This is happening too quickly and she's not ready. Nathaniel has mentioned it before, but there is something different, something more earnest in his words this time. *How long can I keep fobbing him off?*

'I'm not ready for that,' she says quietly.

A moment of silence passes between them. Nathaniel wipes his hands on a napkin. 'You know what, Lori? I'm beginning to think that you'll never be ready. We've been seeing each other for months now and... it feels like we're not moving forwards at all.'

'This is about sex, isn't it?' If she has to make a choice, then Lori hopes this is the case. 'I told you it will take time for me to be ready. And it's not as if we don't do *anything*.' Lori loves every moment that their bodies are connected physically – she just refuses to taint him, and that's what would happen at the moment if they went any further.

Nathaniel brushes crumbs from the blanket. 'It's about *everything*, Lori. Our relationship isn't just about sex. It's about us being together. Properly. And Jess is your daughter. The biggest part of your life. Think about what you're doing – you're shutting me out.' He's raising his voice now, and it's the first time she's heard him angry.

A woman walks past pushing a pram. She smiles at them both, and Lori wonders if the woman's life is less complicated than her own. She hopes so. She wouldn't wish this on anyone. 'I know you're upset,' she says, turning back to Nathaniel. 'But maybe if you're not happy, if I'm not making you happy, then you should just walk away.'

From the way his face falls, Lori immediately sees how much her words have hurt him, how easily she appears to be letting go of what they have. She wishes she could show him that this is causing her pain too.

Silence hangs over them, and minutes pass before either of

them speaks again. 'Maybe you're right,' Nathaniel says. 'This isn't working, is it?'

Lori freezes. She knows what's coming now. She has pushed him too far and now there's no going back.

'I love you, but I can't do this any more,' Nathaniel continues.

Lori watches as he packs away the remaining food and tugs the blanket from beneath her. She should stand up and help him at least, but she's too numb. This isn't what she wants, but she can't find the words to try and stop it.

'I don't know what it is you're looking for,' Nathaniel says. 'But good luck finding it.'

And then Lori is standing alone under the tree, watching as the man she's only just realised she's in love with walks away from her.

TWENTY-FOUR

NOW

Jess

Gabriel and the Uber driver rush out of the car, both of them grabbing hold of her arms. She doesn't need help standing, though – it's her head that smashed against the Uber, and the explosive pain is like nothing she's experienced before.

'Are you okay, Jess? Talk to me!' Gabriel's eyes are wide with panic.

'I think I'm okay.'

The driver runs down the road in the direction of the car, but it's far too late – too many seconds have passed. 'He was going too fast,' he pants, when he makes his way back, crouching forwards to catch his breath.

'Did either of you get the number plate?' Jess asks, clutching her head. 'Or see what make of car it was?'

The two men glance at each other.

'Sorry... it all just happened so fast,' the driver says. 'It could have been a Golf or something? I didn't see properly. But if you need me to make a statement to the police...'

But what could any of them report? That a black car of

unknown make and model nearly ploughed into her? Whoever it was, they'll never be found.

'Is there CCTV here?' Gabriel asks, scanning the road for cameras.

'No,' Jess says.

'But there might be on the main road? Bus lane cameras or something? The police can track anyone by car nowadays.'

'It was some idiot driving too fast – I'm not going to waste their time.' Jess hopes that saying this out loud will help her believe it. 'I just want to go inside.'

The Uber driver straightens up and reaches into his pocket, pulling out a business card. He hands it to Jess. 'If you need me as a witness, then please call.'

She thanks him and starts crossing the road, scanning it carefully this time. She's normally so alert – how did that car manage to escape her attention? The only conclusion she can reach is that her senses have been dulled by the alcohol she's consumed this evening.

'Jess, wait.' Gabriel catches up with her. 'I'll come in with you and get another Uber in a bit.'

'You really don't have to.'

'I want to.'

Jess doesn't have it in her to argue, and she lets Gabriel take her hand.

Inside the house, Gabriel heads to the kitchen to get them both water. While he can't see her, Jess locks the front door. If he notices, she will just tell him that it's force of habit, something she always does when she's alone.

She's curled up on the sofa when he brings her a glass of water. 'How are you feeling?'

'Like I've been hit by a car.' She laughs, despite the seriousness of this situation. It wasn't just a random accident. The person in that car had been waiting for her, she's sure of it.

Gabriel sits beside her. 'Jess, you could have been... I can't even say it. The speed that car was going...'

She nods. 'I know, but if you don't laugh you'll cry, right?'

Gabriel frowns. 'It was weird. I didn't even hear it before it was right there in front of you. It doesn't make sense.'

'We just weren't paying attention. Alcohol has that effect on people, doesn't it?'

'I know, but... it's just strange.'

Jess needs Gabriel to stop looking too deeply into this. He is the one part of her life where she doesn't have to hold the heavy baggage of her past, or her present.

'I think we should call the police, Jess. Just to get that reckless idiot off the road. What if they do it to someone else? It could be a lot worse next time, just—'

'I'm fine. I just want to forget it happened.' She finishes her water and stands. 'I'm really tired.'

'Okay, I'll call—'

'Come on.' She holds out her hand. 'There's no point you traipsing all the way home now. You can go to work tomorrow wearing that, can't you?'

Her eyes snap open, and Jess is immediately alert. Something has roused her, yet the bedroom is silent. Her Echo Dot shows her it's three fifteen, too early to be so awake. She closes her eyes again and then remembers that Gabriel is here. That must be what woke her. She turns over and reaches out but the space next to her is empty.

Jess wonders if he decided to go home after all, if he couldn't bear the thought of turning up for work in yesterday's clothes. She understands; it's not something she'd be happy to do either.

She checks her phone but there's no message from him telling her of his plans. Jess throws off the duvet and shivers as she pulls on her dressing gown. Maybe he's left a note downstairs, although that's highly unlikely when he could have just texted.

The bathroom is bathed in darkness as she passes it, so he's not there. And when she checks downstairs, there's no sign of him in the living room. Just as she's about to check the kitchen, she hears a noise. The tap running. A glass being filled.

'There you are,' she says, opening the kitchen door. 'I thought you'd gone home.'

Gabriel smiles. 'Now why would I want to do that?' He lifts up his glass. 'Just needed water. Do you want some?'

'No, thanks. Let's go back to bed.'

'Ah, an invitation I can't refuse.'

Jess rolls her eyes. 'I mean to *sleep*!'

'Oh, that's a shame.' Gabriel laughs.

'Just a sec,' Jess says. 'I think the tap's still running. It's a funny one, you have to turn it really tight otherwise it leaks.'

Gabriel nods. 'I'll remember that. See you up there, I just need the bathroom.'

Jess heads back into the kitchen and sees immediately that the light in her studio is on. Her breath catches in her throat. She never leaves the light on – it's something she checks religiously when she's locking up. There's no way she left it on.

The key is still in its box in the corner cupboard, and Jess scoops it up before pulling a knife from the block on her worktop. Barely breathing, she unlocks the back door, closing it quietly behind her. Guided by the light from her studio, she makes her way down the garden and peers in to her studio. Nothing appears disturbed, and there's no sign of anyone in there.

She checks the door and it's still locked. Jess opens it and steps inside, relieved to see everything as it should be. Then she notices that the cardigan she always leaves hanging over the back of her chair is missing. She searches the studio but there's no sign of it. Strange. She never takes it out of there; it's always there for when she gets cold in the evenings.

Turning off the light, she locks up and makes her way back to the house. She must have been distracted and forgotten to turn the light off. There's no other explanation. And she must have absentmindedly taken her cardigan inside. She's been distracted lately. It will turn up.

But as she tries to get back to sleep, Gabriel already sleeping beside her, Jess is certain that she didn't make a mistake. In fact, she specifically remembers turning off the light this evening and wondering how the bulb has managed to last for so long.

Which means that someone was in her studio.

TWENTY-FIVE
MARCH 1993

Lori

Five days have passed since Nathaniel ended their relationship. The pain cut deeply at first; Lori had really begun to feel something for him, but she's come to realise that it's better this way. Danny is still in her head, consuming her, casting his heavy dark shadow across everything she does. She wants rid of him – physically and mentally.

Now, as she sits on the floor helping Jess stack blocks, she knows that she was right not to introduce her little girl to Nathaniel. Their relationship – or whatever it could be called – was as fragile as a butterfly's wings.

Lori is surprised he hasn't called, though, and that he could so coldly cut her out of his life. Men. They're all the same, even when they appear to be different. She won't let anyone fool her again.

'Maybe it's time to move again,' she tells Jess. Her daughter looks up at her and smiles, even though she won't really comprehend Lori's words. 'Far from here. I can try and transfer to a different uni. I don't have to study in London. We could go anywhere, Jess. Where would you like to go?'

'Ice cream,' Jess replies, giggling.

Lori strokes her cheek. 'Somewhere with loads of ice cream.' Maybe Brighton? Or Bournemouth? A seaside town would be nice, and far enough away from her family that she can write them out of her life for good.

But is that fair on Jess? Lori has already made sure Danny is out of the picture; it wouldn't be right to take Jess from her grandmother and aunt too. Still, Brighton isn't too far, and it will do Lori's family good to get out of London for a change. 'The world doesn't revolve around London, does it, Jessie?' Yet even as she says this she wonders how she'll manage out of the city that runs through her veins.

Jess giggles again and swipes the tower she's built, the blocks tumbling around her feet. 'Just like my life,' Lori says.

She's just finished making sandwiches for their lunch when the phone rings, startling her. Since she moved flat, she's had no silent calls, and nobody else has bothered to call her.

'Hello?' She forces her voice to be upbeat, to show whoever it is that she's not scared of them.

A few seconds of silence pass before anyone answers. 'Hello, is that Lizzi?'

Hearing the name she'd chosen at random the night she met Shane in the bar, Lori glances quickly at Jess then walks into the living room. She can still see Jess, but at least she's not right next to her. 'Yes, who is this?'

'My name's Alice Hewitt. Please don't hang up.'

'How did you get my number? Why are you calling me?'

'Can we talk?'

'No. My daughter's here. I can't.'

The line goes silent and Lori assumes the woman has hung up until she finally speaks again. 'Not on the phone. Can we meet somewhere?'

'I've got nothing to say,' Lori says, wincing because she knows that none of this is Alice's fault. And doesn't she owe this woman something? Women have to stand together, Lori thinks. There are too many people trying to make the opposite happen.

'Please, Lizzi.'

'Okay,' Lori agrees.

'I finish work in half an hour. Can you meet me in town? Oxford Street?'

'No. By the time I got a babysitter it would be hours before I could get there.'

'I'll come to you, then. You name the place.'

'Do you know Clapham Common?' This is the first place Lori can think of, and it's only after she's said it that she wonders why on earth she's suggested the place where Nathaniel ended their relationship. Lori explains exactly where they can meet.

'I'll find it,' Alice says.

For the entire drive to her mother's, Lori wants to turn the car around and go back home with Jess. They could curl up together on the sofa and watch TV, and she could pretend she's just a normal person, just like anyone else. Nothing else needs to exist, does it? But then she thinks of Danny and it fuels her to keep going. To finish what she has started.

Alice Hewitt. Lori bets the woman thought she was just like everyone else too, until this happened.

As expected, Lori's mother greets her with frostiness. Until just now, they hadn't spoken since Lori woke Jess up from her nap to get her out of the house, and there's been no clearing of the air. Even though it's unlikely that could ever happen between them.

'So, what's the big emergency this time?' her mother asks.

'I'm surprised you're even asking me after how you behaved last time I looked after Jess for you.'

It's always Lori's fault. But this time she's not just going to smile and accept it. 'Are you going to babysit or not? Please just tell me, because if you can't, I need to find someone else quickly.'

Her mother tuts and reaches out her hand for Jess. 'Hello, my darling. Come on, let's go and play with some toys, shall we?'

Before Lori drives away, she stares back at the house, and she's filled with sadness. She should need her mum, but she doesn't. Not emotionally. Lori should want to tell her what's going on in her life, to seek her advice, and at the very least need a hug from her. That's part of what a mother and daughter relationship should be. She will give that to Jess, no matter what. And that's why she's going through with meeting Alice Hewitt now. Lori will face the consequences of her actions.

The woman is nothing like Lori has imagined. In her head, Alice Hewitt was a dowdy woman, older. She sounded it on the phone, at least. But seeing her now, Lori realises how mistaken she was to make these assumptions. Assumptions which were based on a voice on the other end of the phone, and a husband's biased remarks.

Alice Hewitt stands by the park entrance, anxiously scanning faces. She is beautiful, despite the pain she wears on her face like make-up. She's dressed in a long denim skirt and a leather jacket; sunglasses sit on top of her head, nestled into her dark curly hair, despite the lack of sun today.

Lori considers walking right past her. Alice won't know what she looks like, so it would be easy to do. Then she remembers the urgent plea on the phone; lying behind it must be a desperate need for answers, and only Lori can provide them.

Yes, after what she's done, it's her job to try and heal this woman.

'Alice,' she says softly, walking towards her.

Alice looks straight at her, unsmiling, looking her up and down. 'You're Lizzi.'

Lori nods. 'Shall we walk?'

'Is there a bench we can sit on? I had surgery on my ankle not long ago and it still hurts if I walk too far.'

A maelstrom of guilt swirls inside Lori. This woman just can't catch a break. 'Of course. I'm sorry to hear that,' she says, leading the way into the park. 'There are a couple of benches a bit further down.' Lori points into the distance. 'Can you make it that far?'

'Yes,' Alice snaps. 'I got here, didn't I?' She gestures to her leg. 'You're probably wondering what happened, but it's none of your business.'

Lori looks away, focuses on the path ahead. 'I wasn't going to ask. You don't have to tell me anything. You're the one who wanted to meet.'

Alice turns and stares at her. 'Yes, I did. And I have to say – you aren't what I expected. You seem so... oh, forget it. Look, where's this bench? I really need to sit down now.'

'It's not far,' Lori says.

Both women are silent until they reach the bench. As soon as she sits, Alice leans down and rubs her ankle, wincing as she does so.

Lori averts her eyes, scanning the park instead. Dark grey clouds threaten to erupt above them, and Lori didn't think to bring an umbrella. There aren't many people around, and suddenly she is nervous. What if it's Alice who has been making those phone calls? She could be the person who painted that obscenity across Lori's door. 'Why did you want to meet?' Lori demands.

'How funny that your tone is full of animosity, when *I'm*

the one who's been wronged. First of all, I want to know why you told me. I mean, the real reason. See, I've been thinking about it a lot, and the only thing that makes sense is that Shane ended it with you and you were on some kind of revenge kick.'

Lori shakes her head. 'That's not it at all. Please believe me, Alice. It wasn't my intention to hurt you.'

A loud cackle erupts from Alice's mouth, attracting the attention of an elderly man passing by with a walking stick. He turns and stares at them for a moment before shuffling on.

'Well, that's exactly what you've done,' Alice says. 'You slept with my husband, knowing he was married. What kind of messed up bitch are you?' That word. The same one that someone scrawled across her door.

'Everything I said to you on the phone is true. He was coming on to me in a bar one night and told me he was separated. Then I found out he wasn't and... I always intended on telling you. Right from the first second. Men like Shane—'

'Oh, spare me! You're just trying to make yourself feel better. That's it, isn't it? So, you felt guilty and told me to ease your conscience.'

'No, that's not it at all. Please believe me, Alice.'

'Did you know I was pregnant, Lizzi?'

Lori's eyes dart to Alice's stomach. There's no way to tell how far along she is under her leather jacket.

'Oh, don't bother looking,' Alice snarls. 'I said *was*. I had a miscarriage when all this happened.'

Instantly Lori feels sick. 'My God, I'm so sorry!'

'Actions have consequences, don't they? And now, because of what you did with my husband, I've lost my baby.' She turns away from Lori, rubs her eyes with her hand. 'I was going to call her Jennifer if it was a girl. I hadn't thought of a boy's name yet. Maybe Eli. Something a bit different. But I was sure she'd be a girl.' Alice turns back to Lori. 'I'll never know now, will I? Just think about that, won't you. I want you to always remember those names. Jennifer. Eli. They're going to haunt you, Lizzi.' She stands up, wincing. 'You shouldn't have told me. You've wrecked our lives – mine, Shane's. Probably your own too, from the look of you. I hope it was worth it.'

It's Lori who is crying now. 'But you deserved to know the truth, Alice.' She remembers her hands shaking as she made the anonymous call to Alice, to tell her what her husband had been doing. 'Shane wasn't worthy of you, was he? Leaving him is the best thing you could have done.'

'You're not GOD! Alice shouts. 'Or some kind of puppet master. You can't control what people do.' She leans forwards and grabs Lori's wrist. 'Just one more thing before I go. Watch your back, Lizzi.'

TWENTY-SIX

NOW

Jess

Gabriel has gone by the time Jess wakes. It's past ten o'clock, and she can't remember the last time she slept so late. She's frustrated that she's missed a good couple of hours of work time, but it's Saturday – she shouldn't be so hard on herself.

He's left Jess a message on her phone.

Didn't want to wake you. Hope you're feeling okay this morning. Will call you in a bit to see how you are x

It's only now that Jess recalls the events of yesterday. The black car narrowly missing her as it sped down the road. The light left on in her studio. And although she has no evidence, she's convinced that everything is tied to Nathaniel French. But the dead don't speak, and whatever knowledge he had has gone with him.

What if she's just being paranoid? There's the possibility that Gabriel is right, and the driver of the car was simply being reckless, paying scant attention to the road. She'd been in such a rush to get inside – maybe she just hadn't paid enough attention? And the studio light? People do things like that all the time, and Jess can't just think of herself as an exception. Yes, she notices things, details, but lately her attention does seem to be slipping.

After her shower, Jess attempts to do some editing. But the legacy of last night – a crushing headache – forces her to give up after only an hour.

Zara calls, her words a rush of shock and concern. 'Gabriel told us what happened. I can't believe it. Are you all right? You could have been...' The missing word taunts Jess. *Dead*. Like Nathaniel French.

'I'm doing okay. Just a bad headache from where I smacked it against the Uber.'

'Oh, Jess. I can't believe all this stuff keeps happening to you. If you'd only stayed a little longer at Hemingways. Look, I'm heading over to Mum's for lunch soon – please come, I'll pick you up on the way.'

Jess is about to protest – on top of everything else, she doesn't want to put Carolina out – but the thought of staying here alone all afternoon is a grim prospect. 'Okay,' she agrees. 'I'll come with you.'

'Great, I'll let Mum know.'

Carolina lives in a top floor flat in a prestigious block near Wimbledon tennis courts. She rejected the idea of buying another house after divorcing Jess's father, and is more than content to live in this low-maintenance property. As bright and spacious as it is, Jess would feel claustrophobic living here. She needs outdoor space. The tree-lined communal grounds are pleasant enough, but afford little privacy.

'Something smells nice,' Zara says, as they step inside and give Carolina a hug.

Carolina beams. 'That's your lunch. I'm trying a new risotto recipe I found online.'

'Oh, Mum, a sandwich would have been fine,' Zara says.

'Well, it's not often my two girls come for a visit together, is it? Let's make the most of it.'

Jess gives her a hug. 'At least let us help you.'

It's nice to lose herself in preparing lunch, and Jess lets their chatter fill her head. She's fully aware this is only temporary respite, but she'll cling on to every second while she can.

On the way over there, she'd asked Zara not to mention the incident with the black car to Carolina, but it's slipped her mind that her stepmum will know about Nathaniel's death.

'I heard about that man dying,' Carolina says, when they've finished eating. 'Your dad told me.'

'Mum!' Zara chimes in. 'Jess might not want to—'

'It's fine.'

'Oh no. Sorry, love. You don't have to talk about it,' Carolina says. 'To be honest, none of us should waste our time even uttering his name. What goes around comes around, doesn't it?'

'He was never charged, though, was he?' Jess says. 'So, we don't know.'

Carolina takes Jess's hand. 'I know, love. You're right. And it's not really fair for me to comment on any of it. I didn't even know your dad then. I only know this: Danny is still convinced to this day that it was Nathaniel French. Anyway, I'm sorry. I'm not one for rumours or hearsay. I'm just concerned that this is affecting you. How are you feeling about it all?'

'It's very bizarre,' Jess begins. 'I have no memories of my mum at all, and when I look at pictures of me as a baby with her, it's like looking at someone else's life. And then I feel guilty that I'm betraying her by not remembering, or not feeling the right kind of pain.'

Carolina strokes her cheek, just like she used to when Jess was a child. 'Oh, Jess. There *is* no right kind of pain. What happened to you is not a common experience – thank goodness – but that probably makes you feel even more alone. I hope you know that you can talk to me and Zara about anything? We're your family and we're here for you.'

In the absence of any words, Jess squeezes Carolina's hand. 'I know,' she says eventually. 'Can I ask you something?'

'Of course.'

'Did Dad ever tell you that my mum was having an affair?'

Carolina's eyes widen. 'No, he didn't. Why do you think that? From everything I've heard about your mum, it doesn't sound like something she'd do. She loved your dad tremendously.'

'Dad told me.'

'Oh.' Carolina pauses. 'Well, he never said anything to me. And I'd definitely remember something like that.' She pauses, pushing her knife and fork closer together. 'I will say this, though: it doesn't matter. People's lives can be complicated, and we don't know what she was going through. She was still your mother and she loved you, that's all that matters. Don't let her memory be tainted.' She sighs. 'I wish that bloody man had never showed his face. That's what's started all this, Jess. You haven't been yourself since he appeared, have you?'

Jess glances at her sister, who offers a thin smile.

She wonders if she's ever been herself. How could Jess possibly be the person she was meant to be when her mother was taken from her so early in her life? She doesn't say this to Carolina, though, not when she did her best to try and give Jess a normal life. 'I'll be fine,' Jess says instead.

'Of course you will. You always are.'

Zara gets up to give Jess a hug. 'We're here for you, sis. Always.'

. . .

Jess is not good at letting things go, blocking them out until they erupt. She prefers to deal with whatever comes her way, face it head-on and set it free. She didn't do this with her mum's death, not to start with at least, and it took a toll on her.

She's sitting in her studio with the door locked, staring at her computer. She's entered the name Elsbeth into Google, but without a surname any type of search is futile, and as expected Jess has come up with nothing.

Picking up her phone, she calls Kim. She doesn't want to involve her in this, but she's got to explore every avenue. Especially if she is in danger.

'Hello, Jessica. How are you doing?' Kim's voice is warm, fuelling Jess with confidence. 'I was just thinking 'bout you, wondering how you're doing.'

Jess tells her she's okay, and explains what she needs from Kim. She holds her breath until she gets a response.

'I'm home now if you want to come over?'

Kim is almost unrecognisable. Her tanned skin is paler, and there's no hint of make-up on her face. 'I've been in complete shock since it happened,' she tells Jess. 'I keep expecting him to knock on the door. And hear this: yesterday I actually went to call him on my mobile until I remembered. Crazy, eh? And what awful luck. He was in the wrong place at the wrong time. I don't know if that makes me feel better or worse.'

'It's terrible. Is that what the police still think, then? That it was just random?'

'Seems so. They don't tell me a lot, but that's what I can gather from the little they do pass on.' A loud sob erupts from Kim.

Jess feels sorry for this woman. Judging from all the photos displayed in her flat, she clearly has a big family, people around who love her, yet Nathaniel's death has clearly affected her. 'He meant a lot to you, didn't he?'

Kim nods. 'More than I even realised.' Tears glisten under her eyes. 'I curse myself for... for not letting him know how important he was to me. And for not paying more attention to him when he'd been so out of sorts.'

Jess reaches into her bag for a tissue and hands it to Kim. 'Please don't blame yourself. I'm sure he knew how you felt. And I bet the feeling was mutual.'

Kim nods, dabbing at her eyes, and it takes her a minute to regain her composure. 'So, you said he was a friend of your mum's? And you wanted to let him know that she'd... passed away?'

Jess nods. After what happened to Nathaniel, she hates lying to Kim, but it's too late now to take back what she initially claimed when she first came looking for Nathaniel. Lies give birth to more lies, she thinks now. 'Yes, he was very close to my mum years ago. He and his partner, Elsbeth. Did Nathaniel ever mention her?'

Kim's eyes narrow. 'Yeah, he did talk about her sometimes. I think the relationship ending really scarred him. At least that's the feeling I got.'

'Is there any chance you know where I can find her? It's just important that I let her know about my mum. And she should know about Nathaniel too, of course.'

Kim studies her for a moment. What if she can see through Jess's lies? 'I suppose you're right, although I doubt she'd care. Apparently she just left him one day with no explanation. Packed her stuff and left while he was at work. Not a word. Ghosting they'd call it today. She doesn't sound like a good person.'

So, Nathaniel has lied to Kim. It's understandable, though, that he'd want to keep hidden the reason Elsbeth left him. 'That's cruel,' Jess says.

'Anyway, I don't know where she is now.' Kim shrugs. 'Could be anywhere.'

'Do you know her surname at least?'

'Ah, as a matter of fact I do. Only because it's my mother's maiden name too. Shaw.'

Thank goodness for coincidences. And Elsbeth isn't the most common name, so Jess should be able to track her down if the woman has any social media presence. 'Thank you, Kim. That's really helpful.' Jess stands and heads towards the hall.

'You could have asked me this on the phone,' Kim says, following behind. 'Why did you come all the way to Sydenham just for this?'

To get out of the house. To feel like she's doing something to get her life back in order. Because she's afraid. 'You've been so kind to me, I just wanted to pay you a visit. To say thank you properly.'

'Well, visitors are much appreciated,' Kim says. ''Specially now.'

At the front door, Jess thanks her again. 'Actually, there was one other thing I wanted to ask. Have you ever seen anyone hanging around the flats? Male, around thirty? Black hooded top. Jeans. Dark hair. Does that sound like anyone who lives here or visits anyone here?'

'Well, aside from that description being able to fit most young people, nobody comes to mind.'

'Nathaniel never had a visitor like that?'

'Nobody ever came here to see him. Like I said before, he kept himself to himself. I think I was the only friend he had.' Once again, Kim's eyes well with tears.

'I'm sorry, Kim. Can I make you a cup of tea before I go?'

Kim laughs. 'Oh, you are a sweetheart. No, thank you. I'm heading out in a minute to meet a friend. She'll take my mind off it all.'

Jess passes Nathaniel's door as she leaves, and for a moment she stops outside it, staring, as if it will provide her with answers.

In her pocket, her phone rings, snapping her back to reality. Gabriel. A voice she needs to hear right now.

'I'm taking you out for dinner,' he says. 'No arguments. Unless you're not feeling well?'

'No, I'm fine. And dinner would be nice. Thank you.'

Right after she's found Elsbeth Shaw.

TWENTY-SEVEN
MARCH 1993

Lori

It's nearly nine o'clock by the time Lori parks up outside her flat with Jess. Seeing Alice Hewitt, Shane's wife, has left her shaken. Alice's parting words are still haunting her, refusing to leave her alone. '*Watch your back.*' A clear threat.

She hadn't felt ready to pick up Jess straight away – there was no way she wanted her daughter to sense her fear. It could damage her, couldn't it? Lori had read about that in a book when she was pregnant. She needed to keep her baggage away from Jess, to make sure that she always felt safe around Lori. She also didn't want her mother asking questions.

So, for a couple of hours she'd sat in different coffee shops in the high street, avoiding the one near the park where there was every chance she'd bump into Nathaniel.

Jess has been asleep in the car seat but she wakes up as Lori unclicks her belt and carries her in. 'Come on, little one. Let's get you into the bath, it's almost bedtime.' At least her mother has fed Jess, leaving Lori one less thing to worry about.

She puts Jess down while she grabs her bag from the car and

Jess runs across the road. 'Stop! Come back!' Lori rushes after her, scooping her up. 'Mummy's told you not to run off, haven't I? It's not safe.'

Jess smiles up at her. 'Want to go in,' she says.

Once they're safely inside the building, Lori puts Jess down to walk. They're only on the first floor, and Jess can manage the stairs with Lori holding her hand.

She notices it the minute they reach the top stair. Her flat door is open. Just a crack. Lori freezes. She knows she didn't leave it open; she specifically remembers dropping her keys on the floor as she'd locked the door. 'Stop, Jess, come here,' she whispers.

She cradles Jess in her arms while she tries to work out what to do. They haven't lived here long so Lori only knows one of the neighbours, an elderly woman called Janice. She's been friendly enough whenever Lori's passed her in the corridor but they've never said more than a few words. She needs to keep Jess safe, though, so right now there is no other option.

Light spills out from the gap under Janice's door, so there's every chance she's still up. Without hesitation, Lori knocks on her door, still holding Jess, who rests her head on Lori's shoulder. 'Want to go home, Mama,' Jess says.

'We will, sweetheart, I just need to do something quickly, so I need you to stay with Janice just for a few minutes, okay?'

Jess doesn't say anything but nestles further into Lori's shoulder.

It's a few moments before Janice calls out from inside her flat. 'Hello? Who is it?'

'Hi, Janice, it's Lori from next door. I think I've been burgled and I was wondering if you could just watch my daughter for me for a second while I check the flat. I don't want to take her in there yet.'

The door opens, and a head pokes out. 'Oh dear, how awful! I didn't hear anything.'

'I can't be sure, but my door's open and I know I didn't leave it like that.'

'You should call the police, dear. You can come in and use my phone.' Janice opens her door.

'I will, but I just want to check the flat first. Just in case I've got it wrong. But I don't want Jess to come in there. Would you mind just watching her for a few minutes? I'll be as quick as I can.'

'Of course, leave her with me.' Janice beckons her in. 'Ah, bless her, it looks like she's fallen asleep.'

Jess peers down and sure enough, Jess is asleep again. This will make things easier for Lori, now at least she doesn't have to worry about Jess crying for her. 'I'll just put her on the sofa if you don't mind keeping an eye on her?'

'Not at all. I'll watch her like a hawk. I'm used to it, dear – I have four young grandchildren, you know. Let me just get a blanket.'

Lori thanks her and settles Jess on the sofa. 'Mummy will be right back,' she whispers, stroking Jess's forehead.

'Be careful,' Janice calls out. 'What if they're still in there?'

But Lori doesn't answer – she's too busy mustering all her courage to step inside the place that's meant to feel safe, that's meant to keep her daughter safe. She pushes the door open and it slams back against the wall. Turning on the light, Lori sees straight away that the narrow hallway doesn't look disturbed, and it doesn't feel as though there's anyone in there. Perhaps she did leave the door open after all? Her head had been all over the place so she can't rule out a lapse in concentration. *But I know I dropped the keys. I was carrying too much. I even cursed when they slipped from my hand.*

The living room is just as she left it – there's not much in it other than a sofa and dining table and the TV still sits on its stand, the video recorder right beneath it. Definitely not a burglary then.

But when she steps foot in the bedroom and takes in the scene, Lori is paralysed, a tidal wave of nausea rising up inside her. The cupboard doors have been flung open, the contents stripped bare. Every item of clothing and footwear she owns is cut to shreds, discarded in a pile on the bed. Her underwear too. All the books she owns have been massacred, their covers and pages ripped and scattered on the carpet like fallen confetti. She rushes to her bedside table, the place where she keeps her important documents, and there they are – her passport and driving licence – shredded beyond repair like everything else she owns.

The horror of it is too much, and Lori's body and brain must have shut down because she's not crying. No, she's staring at the destruction as if it's happened to someone else. A scene from a movie. Not her life.

Finally, it hits her when she checks the kitchen and sees the crockery set she saved up for months to buy shattered into pieces. The mugs too. Even Jess's plastic toddler plates and cups have been thrown to the floor.

Lori rushes to the bathroom and throws up in the sink. She knows with just a glance that she has no towels left, and even the shower curtain hangs in shreds.

Everything Lori owns has been destroyed. There's nothing left but the clothes and shoes she's wearing.

Now the tears come hard and fast. *What have I done? And how am I ever going to keep Jess safe?*

For five minutes she sits on the bathroom floor, unable to steel herself to move. But she needs to get Jess. Janice will tell her to go to the police, but there's no way Lori can do that. This was not a burglary – this was a personal vendetta. Revenge. Whoever did it touched nothing of the landlord's – it is only Lori's possessions which have been damaged beyond repair.

When her body allows her, she pulls herself off the floor and makes her way next door.

'I was worried about you,' Janice says as she lets Lori in. 'Is everything okay? Please tell me you just left the door open by mistake?'

Lori doesn't need time to work out that she can never tell the police, or anyone else. She can't have them prying into her life and finding out what she's done. No, she will deal with this alone. 'Everything's fine,' she tells Janice. 'I was stupid and forgot to close the door in my rush to get Jess out.'

'Oh, what a relief!' Janice says. 'And it's easily done. It's hard trying to get a toddler ready to go out, isn't it? Even if she is a little angel like your Jess.'

Lori nods, heading for the living room where Jess lies sleeping on the sofa. 'It's really hard. Anyway, I'm so sorry to have taken up your time.' She carefully lifts Jess. 'I've just realised we've left Jess's favourite cuddly lamb at my mum's house so I'll have to rush back there and get it. I think we'll stay the night there so that Jess's bedtime doesn't get any later.'

'You can leave her with me,' Janice offers. 'It's no problem. No point taking the chance of waking her by getting her into the car. And it's so late, isn't it?'

'Thanks, but we'll be fine. My mum will love to have Jess stay the night. You know, special grandma time.' Lori heads towards the front door.

'Of course, dear. Well, let me know if you need anything. And thank goodness it wasn't a burglary. I shudder to think of someone coming in here and doing that while I'm right next door.' Janice says goodbye and shuts the door.

Lori holds Jess tightly and kisses her forehead. She needs to get her away from their flat and then come back to sort out the mess. Remove every trace of her damaged possessions.

She drives until she finds a phone box, then she parks right next to it. Leaving Jess sleeping in the car, she rushes inside to call her mum, her eyes fixed on Jess inside the car the whole time. When her mum answers, Lori explains that there's been a flood at her place, and she's relieved when her mother is warm towards her.

'Oh, that's awful. Poor little Jess. She must stay here, of course. Both of you.'

'Actually, Mum, I need to get back to wait for the plumber.' Is that who people call when something like this happens? Lori has no idea. 'And the landlord's on his way. He hasn't got his key so I'll need to let him in.'

There is silence, and Lori imagines her mother's eyes rolling. 'You drop Jess then and get back,' Meredith says, finally. 'I'll take care of her.'

Sneaking into her own flat alone, attempting not to be seen by Janice, would be laughable if the situation wasn't so menacing. Lori makes it inside, and quietly closes the door, locking it behind her. She doesn't turn on any lights, but finds the torch that she keeps in a kitchen drawer.

For two hours she fills bin bags with her damaged clothing and scrubs every inch of the flat. She can't bear the thought of there being traces of some stranger left behind, even ones that can't be detected by the naked eye.

In the hallway, Lori stops. In the darkness she can see something white by the door. Moving closer, it becomes clear that an envelope has been slipped under the door. It definitely wasn't there when she checked the flat while Jess was with Janice, and she's quite sure it wasn't there when she came back alone. Which means someone must have left it there while she's been clearing up the mess.

It's probably Janice, leaving her telephone number or something. In case of an emergency. This conviction reassures Lori as she rips open the envelope. Then she reads the words, each one of them like a bullet piercing her skin.

Now you know how it feels to lose everything you have. But it's not quite everything, is it? Which means I'm not finished.

Struggling for breath, Lori rips the paper into shreds and pushes it into one of the bin bags. She needs to get out of here, to leave London, even, and get Jess away. Neither of them will be safe if they stay. Moving flat has made no difference.

She gathers the bin bags and checks outside her door before dragging them out. Thankfully, no light shines under Janice's door, so she must be asleep. Lori will buy her some flowers to say thank you, as soon as she feels safe.

It takes several trips to the bins outside the building to dispose of all the bags, but eventually she throws the last one in. It's Thursday so they'll be collected tomorrow, all evidence of the break-in eradicated.

Back in her car, Lori stares up at the building which was supposed to symbolise a fresh start after Danny. Now, though, it will never feel like home. Lori needs to move quickly. To get her and Jess out of there, somewhere far away. At least she has her Peugeot. It's old but reliable, and will certainly get them across the country. And she has her savings from the video shop. That will last them long enough to get settled somewhere and then she can try to transfer her university place.

Tomorrow she will go to the charity shop and pick up some clothes for her and Jess. Thankfully there are spare clothes for Jess at her mother's and some in the boot of the car. Lori has it all figured out.

And tonight there's someone she needs to say goodbye to.

TWENTY-EIGHT

NOW

Jess

Jess has often cursed social media, despite needing an online presence for her business. But right now she is grateful for Facebook; without it she wouldn't be staring at image of the woman she believes could be Nathaniel French's ex-partner. Elsbeth Shaw.

Jess doesn't know whether they were married or not – all she learnt from Nathaniel was that he met her ten years after the murder, and that Elsbeth left him around a year ago. Which means that they were in a relationship for almost twenty years.

She's an attractive woman, with thick light hair and blue eyes, and Jess is surprised how different she is to her mother. 'You didn't have a type, then, did you?' she whispers to no one.

Elsbeth's profile is private, but Jess uses her business account to send her a message. She only hopes that Elsbeth checks her junk folder.

Hi Elsbeth,

My name is Jessica Moore and I wondered if we could talk?
My mother, Lori, is the woman who was killed in that park in
1993.

Jess clicks 'send', and now it's a waiting game.

'You seem distracted,' Gabriel says. He studies her, and she realises she isn't doing a good job of focusing on their evening. 'Is everything okay? Is it your head?'

'I've taken a lot of paracetamol so I'm fine now.' This isn't exactly true, but Jess refuses to make a big deal of it.

'You do like Greek food, don't you?'

Jess smiles. 'The food's lovely. Sorry, it's... been a long day.' She reaches across the table and strokes his arm. 'I'm just tired.'

Although Gabriel returns her smile, it's quickly replaced with a frown. 'You can talk to me, Jess. About anything. I know we've only just met, but... it's strange isn't it? Because I know your sister and Ryan, I feel like I've known you for years.'

Yet there is so much Gabriel doesn't know about Jess, none of which she's willing to reveal to him now.

'How about I stay at yours tonight?' he suggests. 'I try not work on Sundays if I can help it so we could have a lie in then go somewhere for a late breakfast.'

'You mean brunch?'

'Yeah, but I hate that word!'

Jess laughs, and even though it sets off the dull ache in her head that's become a constant companion since the incident with the black car, it enables the rest of her to feel good. And Gabriel's suggestion is just what she needs. 'How about we stay at yours this time, though? I'd love to see your place.'

The smile vanishes from Gabriel's face. 'Oh, I thought I'd told you – I'm having some work done on the kitchen so it's a bit of a mess at the moment. It'll be finished soon, though, and then

I'll invite you over and cook dinner for you in the revamped kitchen. Show off my skills.'

'That sounds great,' Jess says, masking her disappointment. It would have been nice to have a night away from the house, and to see what kind of place Gabriel calls home. It's hard to get to know someone when you have no idea how they live. And Jess doesn't just want to fall for the image she holds of him; she wants her feelings to be based on the reality of Gabriel.

When he heads to the bathroom, Jess checks her phone. There's no reply from Elsbeth.

Back at her house, Jess notices immediately how cold it is. 'I'll put the heating on,' she tells Gabriel. Jess doesn't feel the cold as much as most people, so it's strange that she's noticing the absence of any warmth now, especially wearing the thick roll-neck jumper she has on. She heads straight for the kitchen and opens the boiler cupboard, pressing the switch for the heating. Nothing happens. There's no sound of the ignition kicking in and when she checks, the flame hasn't appeared. 'That's odd,' she tells Gabriel, who appears right behind her. 'It's a fairly new boiler. I only had it installed about a year ago. It's definitely broken.'

'Let me have a look.'

Jess moves aside so that Gabriel can check it, but she knows any attempt he makes will be futile. If she can't do it, then it's unlikely he'll be successful. Her dad always taught her how to fix things around the house, and her ability to do most small jobs is something she's proud of.

'You're right – this thing's not kicking in. I'm guessing it's still under warranty?'

She nods. 'But that doesn't help at this time of night. Nobody will come out now unless I pay an extortionate amount for an emergency plumber.'

'Hmm, you're right. But listen, I'm happy to pay for it. We

can't freeze all night, can we? And I'm guessing the hot water won't work, either.'

'No. But I'm not letting you pay. I'll just call them in the morning and wait until they can get someone out.' She pauses. 'But we do have another option. We could go to yours after all? I know it's a mess but at least it will be warm. We can have showers in the morning.'

'I guess, but we're here now, aren't we? It would take ages to get back to mine, and I'm exhausted. We'll be fine with a couple of blankets, won't we?' He pulls her towards him. 'And there are other ways we can keep warm.'

Lying in bed next to Gabriel, Jess concedes that he was right to stay here and make the most of the night. And under the duvet, nestled into the crook of his arm, it's easy to forget that there's no heat in the house.

'I want to know more about you,' he says, kissing her forehead. 'Who is Jessica Moore? You don't talk about yourself much.'

She turns her head and looks up at him. 'That's because I'm not a narcissist,' she chuckles. 'It's not good to talk about yourself all the time.'

'All the time, yeah, but never?'

This is it, then. This moment has come too soon. 'What is it you want to know?' Jess asks.

He shrugs. 'I don't know. How about... where do you see yourself in ten years?'

She sits up in bed. This question she can deal with. 'Hopefully my business will have expanded. I'd like to employ staff eventually. It's already getting to a point where I have to turn down jobs because I can't fit them in.'

'I love your ambition,' Gabriel says, kissing her arm. 'What about having kids? Can you see that in your future?'

Her answer comes with no hesitation. She won't make the same mistake she made with Harrison. 'No. That's not something I want to do.' Jess studies Gabriel's face, but it's hard to read his reaction. 'You're shocked, aren't you?'

'No.' He pulls himself up and leans against the headboard. 'I actually think it's good that you know what you want. Or don't want. Can I ask why? Not that I think everyone should want kids. I really don't think that at all.'

There is no way Jess can explain the reason to Gabriel. How could she possibly reveal that she's terrified of ever being a mum because of what happened to her own mother? Having a toddler would be too painful for Jess. 'I've never felt maternal,' she lies. 'And I feel fulfilled without needing to be a mum. Don't get me wrong, if Zara and Ryan have children, then I will be the best aunt they could possibly have, but that's it for me.' She stares at him, again trying to read his thoughts. Again failing. 'How about you? Be honest.'

'This might surprise you, but I feel the same,' he says. 'Having kids is not something I've ever wanted. I love my nieces and nephew but... and this might sound selfish... I love my life as it is. Can't see myself changing my mind, either. I've got too much I want to do. Travel the world, experience things I've never done or seen. Let's just say I've got a serious amount of living to do.'

Every word Gabriel says fills Jess with relief. His response is vastly different to Harrison's. *'Let's just see how you feel further down the line. Things change. People change. None of us can truly know what we'll want in ten years' time.'* She'd tried to tell him that she wouldn't change her mind, that she is fixed on this and nothing will move her, but he'd refused to believe it. Even when she told him the reasons for not wanting to be a mother, Harrison still tried to convince her to keep her options open, even suggesting more counselling. Eventually, when that failed, he started on the idea of marriage, but Jess knew that sooner or later the topic of children would come up again. Harrison comes from a large family – it stands to reason that he'll want that for himself one day.

With Gabriel it feels different. But she still needs to tread carefully; they've only just come into each other's lives, and the timing of it still bothers Jess.

'Well, it looks like we're on the same page, then,' she says, kissing his cheek, then his lips.

'Wait,' Gabriel says, holding her arms. 'There are some things I do need to tell you. I want you to know me properly, so there are no surprises later on.'

Time freezes, and with it her heart seems to pause. She'd thought this was too good to be true. But she's grateful that he's telling her whatever it is now, before she invests any further into this relationship. 'What?' she asks, holding her breath.

'I've... God, this is difficult to talk about. I've, um, suffered from depression on and off throughout my life. And it's because something happened when I was sixteen and it changed me.' He looks away from Jess, unable to meet her gaze.

She takes his hand, to let him know that whatever it is she will still be there. *But how can I promise this when I don't know what he's about to say?* 'What happened?' she asks.

He takes a deep breath. 'It's hard to talk about... but we got burgled when I was sixteen. Two men broke into our house one night when we were all home. My parents and me and my brother. I didn't hear anything, didn't even wake up. But... my dad confronted them and they... attacked him. With one of our own kitchen knives. He died in hospital the same night.'

Jess leans in and wraps her arms around him. 'Oh, Gabriel, I'm so sorry. That's just... I have no words.' She pulls him closer. 'That must have been... your poor mum.'

'Luckily, she didn't wake up so she didn't see anything. Actually, I don't know if that makes it better or worse. She found him in the kitchen the next morning.'

'Did they catch who did it?'

He nods. 'Only because the bastards had stolen a car. The neighbour had heard a commotion and wrote down the number plate just in case. The next day, when they realised what had happened, they told the police what they'd seen. It was an open and shut case – the police tracked them down and found our stuff in a flat they were staying in.'

'I'm so sorry, Gabriel. Zara never said anything—'

'Ryan and Zara don't know. In fact, I don't tell many people. But you're... well, I really like you. And I want to be in your life to see where we can go. And to me that means full disclosure.'

Jess snuggles into him and they lie like this, each of them alone with their thoughts. She should tell him about what happened to her mother; Gabriel's past is not too dissimilar to her own, and there will never be a better time to share it with him. But the words remain hidden. Tonight is about Gabriel's story, not her own. When, and if, she is ready to tell him, her disclosure will be for another time.

Jess doesn't remember either of them falling asleep. She wakes to her phone vibrating on her bedside table, the glaring digits on her Echo Dot showing her it's nearly two a.m.

She hasn't had a chance to greet the caller when the person begins to speak.

'You're not safe,' are the words Jess hears.

TWENTY-NINE

MARCH 1993

Lori

It's raining again, icy sharp pellets that shoot down and pierce her skin, making her shiver. The coat she's wearing isn't waterproof, but now it's the only one she owns. Water drips from her hair and she can barely see in front of her as she crosses the road to Nathaniel's flat.

He won't let her in, she's sure of that, but what's she got to lose by trying? She's sure he is a kind man, that no matter what happened between them he would never turn away someone in need of help. Lori turns around and glances at the car. It's her plan B, and she's prepared to spend the night in it if she has to. She'll just listen to the radio, let it soothe her to sleep until dawn.

When he answers the door he stares at her, taking in her bedraggled appearance. Everything seems to happen in slow motion, as though she's watching a film of herself rather than being a participant in her life. Then Nathaniel is talking and at first she doesn't hear his voice – she only knows that his lips are moving.

'Lori? Lori, what's happened? Quick, come in. You're soaked!' He holds out his arm and she lets him lead her in.

'I'm sorry,' she says once they're in his flat, rain dripping into a puddle on his carpet. 'It's been an awful day.'

'I'm guessing this is about more than just the rain?' he says. 'Wait here while I get you a towel. Do you have any clothes you can change into?'

Lori shakes her head.

'Then I'll find something you can wear. Sit down, I'll be right back.'

'But I'll get your sofa wet. The carpet's already soaking.'

'Don't worry about any of that. Just sit.'

Lori sits on the floor and draws her knees up to her chest, resting her chin on them. Shrinking herself, and curled up like a foetus, she is the epitome of someone in distress.

Nathaniel returns, handing her a towel. 'Here's a hooded top and some joggers. They're too big but at least they're dry.'

Lori thanks him and pulls herself up. 'I'll go and sort myself out in the bathroom. Is it okay if I have a shower?'

'Knock yourself out. Have you eaten? I know it's late but I can rustle up something quick. Then we can talk.'

'You don't have to do that.'

'It'll only be cheese on toast or something. Maybe beans? Not sure I've got anything else in.'

'That sounds lovely. Thank you.' Lori can't remember the last time she ate.

She makes her way to the bathroom but turns back when she reaches the door. 'Nathaniel? Why are you being so kind to me?'

He shakes his head, lets out a melancholic sigh. 'I think you must already know the answer to that. But if you don't, it's enough for you to know that I'm kind to everyone.'

Lori feels better when she's washed and changed her clothes, and running Nathaniel's brush through her hair is comforting. She counts the brush strokes to distract her mind. Fifty. More than enough. And now she has to leave this bathroom and explain herself to the most decent man she's ever known.

He's in the kitchen, two plates of cheese on toast laid out on the table. 'Come and sit. Let's eat before it gets cold.' He pulls out a chair for her. 'I didn't know what you'd want to drink so I've just got water. It felt weird to get wine out. But if you want some...'

'Water's fine. Thank you.'

Nathaniel cuts into his toast. 'Well, this is strange, Lori, isn't it? I didn't think I'd ever see you in my flat again.'

'I owe you an explanation.'

He points to her plate, at the untouched food. 'Eat first. We'll talk after. Not much worse than cold cheese on toast.'

Lori smiles, and takes a bite. She hadn't realised how hungry she was until she tasted Nathaniel's food. They're both quiet while they eat, yet it's not an uncomfortable silence.

Afterwards she helps him clear up, and then he suggests they talk in the living room. They sit at opposite ends of the sofa and he doesn't push her, but waits patiently for Lori to speak.

'I'm sorry for turning up like this. And for being in such a state. Someone broke into my flat tonight... and I can't go back there. Jess and I weren't home at the time, but it just feels like I've been... violated.'

Nathaniel leans forwards. 'That's awful. I'm sorry. Thank God you weren't home. Did they take much?'

She's at a crossroads now – she can keep up a pretence, present the manufactured version of herself to Nathaniel, or she can finally allow herself to be honest.

And then he will despise her forever. And maybe even himself for falling for a woman who could do the things she's done.

It's all in the past, though. I'm starting over and never looking back. I am no longer that person.

All it takes is a fraction of a second for Lori to decide. And once the words are out, she can never take them back.

'No, they didn't take much. I think they must have got disturbed.' These words will surely choke her, drenched as they are in deceit.

'Well, that's a small mercy. Still, I can see why you're shaken up.'

'Can you just... hold me?' Lori hasn't planned to ask this, but now that she has it's what she wants more than anything.

'Is that a good idea?'

'The best one I've ever had,' Lori says, moving closer to him, wrapping her arms around him and pulling him into her. Her mouth finds his and it feels better than it ever has. She can tell he's resisting her, even though he responds. But nothing has ever felt more right to Lori. She peels off the oversized hooded top Nathaniel has given her, and pulls him onto the floor.

'Oh, Lori, are you sure about this?' he whispers.

She doesn't speak, instead showing him how sure she is.

Afterwards, they lie on the floor, their bodies entwined as if their limbs belong only to one person.

'Now *that* I definitely didn't see coming,' Nathaniel says, smiling and kissing her forehead.

Neither did Lori, but she doesn't say this. Talking about anything will spoil this moment, and she wants to freeze it, live in it for as long as she can. She clings to Nathaniel, breathes in his scent.

'You're welcome to stay here as long as you like,' he says, stroking her back. 'Jess too, of course. I can soon make the place child-friendly.'

And now she must speak, because what she's doing isn't fair.

'Jess and I are leaving London,' she says, pulling away. The words come more easily than she's imagined because putting this life behind her is what she must do above all else, for Jess's sake, despite what's just happened with Nathaniel.

He sits up, pulling on his T-shirt. 'What? For a holiday?'

'No, we're starting a new life far away from here. I'm sorry, Nathaniel. It's what I came here to tell you. I didn't mean for... anything to happen.'

For too long he remains silent, fumbling around to pull on the rest of his clothes. Embarrassed by her nakedness, Lori rushes out to the bathroom and grabs her clothes. They're still damp, but she throws them on.

'So, let me get this right,' Nathaniel says, when she comes back. 'You came here to sleep with me for the first and last time. To get my hopes up that we could finally have a proper relationship. You didn't give me a choice in the matter, you just went ahead and made it happen.' His voice is calm and measured, yet somehow this worries Lori more than if he'd shouted.

'I'm so sorry – I didn't plan for this to happen, it just felt right. To both of us, I think?'

'That's probably exactly what a rapist would say.'

His words render her silent for a moment. 'I didn't force you to sleep with me,' she manages to say.

'No, but you mislead me. You could have told me before that you were leaving. It would have been a different story then.' He shakes his head. 'When did you decide this? Is this about the burglary?'

'No. It's something I've realised we need to do. I don't know where we'll go but I'll transfer my university place when we get settled somewhere.'

'Well, haven't you got it all figured out?' His voice is louder now. 'It must be nice to have everything all planned out. You know, I thought *I* did. I thought you and I were going somewhere.' He shakes his head. 'What a fucking idiot I've been.'

The swear word takes her by surprise – she's never heard

Nathaniel curse like this before. Danny often did, she would have expected it from him, but not the man standing before her.

The next thing Lori's aware of is that he's lunging towards her, grabbing her arm. 'Do you know what you are? You're an evil bitch.' And then he pushes her away. She stumbles and falls to the floor, landing on the discarded pile of Nathaniel's clothes.

She's not hurt, but the humiliation burns her cheeks, and the pain and anger on Nathaniel's face is more than she can bear. Without a word she stands up and leaves, slamming the front door behind her.

Outside his door, she stands for a moment, leaning against it for support. She doesn't blame Nathaniel for his reaction; what she's done is cruel and thoughtless, and she should have stopped to consider his feelings instead of selfishly acting on her own impulses.

And then she hears him crying.

Her hand instinctively moves to knock on the door, and she envisages herself throwing her arms around him and telling him she won't leave, that they can be together and make this work.

But she can't. She is no good for Nathaniel, just like Danny was no good for her, and she needs to walk away and never look back.

THIRTY

NOW

Jess

'I said you're not safe.'

Jess sighs. 'What are you talking about, Harrison?' His middle of the night calls are becoming a regular occurrence, and it doesn't sit easily with her.

'I bumped into Zara yesterday. She told me what happened to you with that car. Is everyone blind? Am I the only person who can see what's going on here?'

With a glance at Gabriel, still sleeping undisturbed, Jess slides out of bed. 'You can't keep calling like this,' she hisses, once she's on the stairs.

'Jess, listen to me. This isn't about me trying to get back together with you. I know it's over. This is about me actually giving a damn what happens to you.'

She shakes her head, even though Harrison can't see her. 'I don't want to talk about this.'

'Even your stepmum's worried.'

'You saw Carolina?' Jess sits on the bottom stair.

'Yeah. She was with Zara. I bumped into them in Oxford Street yesterday.'

Jess saw them both yesterday and neither of them mentioned they were going out. Or maybe they had and she hadn't been listening; her head has been all over the place.

'I'm fine,' Jess protests. 'And what exactly did Carolina say?' Zara had sworn she wouldn't tell her about the incident with the black car.

'Don't worry, she doesn't know about that car running into you. Zara told me when Carolina had a phone call she needed to take.'

'Just how long did you spend with my family?' Jess shouldn't be outraged. She and Harrison had been together for years and he'd become a big part of the family. Everyone was fond of him, even her dad. He'd been the first boyfriend she'd had that Danny had approved of.

'We just went for coffee. It's no big deal. I haven't seen them for ages. It was Carolina who suggested it.'

This sounds about right. Carolina had been heartbroken when Jess had announced that she and Harrison were no longer together. And her stepmother had tried everything to convince Jess to change her mind, that she and Harrison could work out their issues.

'Why are you calling me now?' Jess snaps. 'Couldn't this have waited? It's three a.m.'

'Jess, I never thought I'd hear myself saying this, but I'm actually hoping that guy you're seeing is there with you. I don't want you to be on your own.'

'His name's Gabriel and yes, he *is* here. Sleeping. Like *I* should be.'

'Okay,' Harrison says. 'I get it. But we really need to talk. There's a lot of stuff I've been thinking about, and I think you should be considering it too.'

'I don't need you involved in this. I can handle it on my

own.' But hasn't she already dragged Harrison into her mess? 'Anyway, tomorrow's not good for me. I actually have a day off for once and I'm spending the morning with Gabriel.' She's flooded with guilt as she says this.

'Then I'll come in the evening. Please, Jess.'

It would be easy to agree, to renege on her determination to do this by herself – perhaps it is the fondness she will always feel for Harrison, even though she can't be with him. But it's also the fact that she knows he is right. She won't be safe until everything is out in the open and she knows what Nathaniel was about to tell her. The search for the truth will be like hunting for a grain of rice in the Atlantic Ocean, but she won't give up until she knows who wanted to silence Nathaniel.

'Let me think about it,' she tells Harrison. 'I'll message you. Look, I have to go now.'

Jess hangs up and immediately checks Facebook to see if there's any reply from Elsbeth. Still nothing, and it's looking increasingly unlikely that she'll hear from her at all. Trying not to be disheartened – it hasn't been that long since she sent the message – she heads back to bed, reaching out to hold Gabriel, who is still asleep.

She should have known she wouldn't be able to lie in. Her eyes snap open at six forty-five and she reaches for her phone again. This time there's a message, and even though she's staring at Elsbeth's name, Jess struggles to believe the woman has actually replied.

I'm sorry about your mum. I almost didn't reply but there was no way I couldn't. I can meet you today (Sunday) before I leave for Spain on Monday. You'll have to come to me, though, and I live in Oxford. I notice you're in London, so not too far.

*Meet me at The Grand Café on the high street. I'll be there at
11 a.m.*

Jess wastes no time replying, thanking Elsbeth and assuring
her that she'll be there. Then she heads to the shower. It's still
early, but she wants to be ready to leave. Gabriel will be disappointed, but she can't dwell on that. This is important. As soon
as this is over, she'll be free to focus on their relationship.

She's is getting dressed, throwing on jeans and a jumper,
when he wakes up. 'You should have waited for me,' he says. 'I
could have joined you in there.'

Jess sits on the bed and kisses him. 'I'm really sorry but
something's come up. A photoshoot I can't turn down.'

He sits up. 'Oh. Well, how about I come with you? I'd love
to see you at work. I'm in awe of anyone creative.'

'Maybe next time? This client is someone who wouldn't
appreciate me bringing anyone along. Some people don't feel
comfortable in front of the camera, so having an audience
would just make it more difficult.'

'Hmm. I hadn't thought of that,' Gabriel says. 'Next time,
then.'

Jess slips her feet into her trainers, laces them up. 'What
will you do today?'

'A few friends are playing football – just a friendly game.
Might tag along.'

'I didn't know you were into football.'

'Well, there's probably quite a bit you don't know about me.'
He looks away. 'And some stuff you do.'

'I'm so sorry about your dad,' Jess says, hugging him.

'It's okay, we don't have to keep talking about it. I just
wanted to share it with you. It's actually made me feel closer to
you.'

'Me too,' she says. 'Anyway, I know we can't have that
brunch, but how about a quick fry-up?'

'Have you got sausages? Bacon? Tomatoes?'

'No. Scrambled eggs, then?'

Gabriel laughs. 'Sounds perfect.'

Jess has never set foot in Oxford, and moments after arriving she regrets that her first visit here won't allow her time to explore the beautiful, historic city. She's too anxious to take much of it in, but she's not oblivious to the city's rich architecture and grand buildings. This city has a completely different feel to London, not as claustrophobic, but Jess is fully aware that she needs to be more alert than ever in these strange new surroundings.

It's not hard to find The Grand Café, and Jess is early, so it's likely that Elsbeth won't be here yet. There's nobody in there who matches Elsbeth's profile picture, so Jess sends her a message to let her know she's arrived, before making her way to an empty table.

It's almost half past eleven before Elsbeth arrives, striding in and scanning faces, much like Jess had done over half an hour ago. Jess had worried that Nathaniel's ex might not look like her picture, but she is unmistakable.

'Thanks for coming,' Jess says, standing as Elsbeth approaches. 'Sorry, I had to order a coffee. Let me get you something. What would you like?'

Elsbeth slides into the chair opposite, and places her large handbag on the chair beside her. 'I'll wait until they come over. Anyway, I'm the one who should apologise. I told you eleven o'clock, and here I am half an hour late. Sorry. I was on the phone having to sort something out with the airline. I fly out tomorrow so it couldn't wait. I don't have too long, I'm afraid.'

'Is it a holiday?' Jess asks.

'No. I'm moving abroad. I own a house in Spain and felt like now was the time to leave all of this behind.'

'I lived in Portugal as a kid,' Jess says. 'After my mum died. It was where my dad took me to escape what happened.'

'I'm so sorry. I can't imagine how that must have felt.' She pauses. 'You're here to ask me about Nathaniel, aren't you? That's the only possible link I have to your mother's story.'

Jess nods. 'I'm sorry. I realise this must be difficult to talk about.'

'Much harder for you. Anyway, how is it you know about me?' She holds up her hand. 'Wait. Before you answer, I need to make one thing perfectly clear. I don't want to know anything about what Nathaniel is doing now. I've left that part of my life well and truly behind. But I'll answer anything you need to know.'

Jess hesitates. She came here prepared to break the news to Elsbeth that Nathaniel is dead, but after this declaration, she no longer feels able to. It's not her place. And it's conceivable that Jess might not have found out about him being murdered. If she hadn't met his neighbour, she'd be none the wiser. 'I'll only tell you what's relevant to me finding out more about my mother's death,' she promises. But this is murky ground, ethically.

Elsbeth nods.

'Nathaniel tracked me down just over a week ago. I don't know how he found me. He told me that he didn't kill my mum, and said it was important that I know that.'

'I see. It must have been very difficult being face-to-face with him.'

'It was,' Jess agrees. 'But even more than that, I couldn't understand why he would spend so long searching for me to tell me that if it wasn't true.' Jess pauses, waiting for Elsbeth to say something, but a response doesn't come. 'He also told me about you, and how he'd let you down by lying to you. I got the feeling he wished he could take it all back.'

'That's the trouble with life,' Elsbeth says. 'We don't have the power to retract our actions. What's done is done. I've moved on and I'm happy now.'

A young woman comes over to take Elsbeth's order.

'Flat white, please.' She looks at Jess. 'Another for you?'

'Still got mine,' Jess says. When the waitress walks away she turns to Elsbeth. 'What kind of man was he – when you were together?'

Elsbeth sits back in her chair. 'Nathaniel was always kind. He never raised his voice, even when we were arguing. I have to admit it was infuriating. Sometimes I wanted him to shout, just to make myself feel better for losing control.' She smiles. 'We met at work. Feels like a lifetime ago. He didn't seem interested in me for a long time, not romantically. But we became friends, and that's when I realised he was in love with someone else. Lori.'

Jess will never get used to hearing her mother's name coming from the mouths of strangers. It will always feel like a violation.

'He didn't try to hide it,' Elsbeth continues, 'and I understood. I wasn't going to let myself feel threatened by a poor woman who was no longer here. I just used to listen to him, and let him talk about her as much as he wanted.'

Jess admires this. It must be hard to know that the person you love still belongs to someone else, even if that person is no longer here. 'What kind of things do you remember him saying about her?'

'Oh, I don't know. It's been such a long time. After being friends for a while we got together and then he stopped mentioning her as much. He never made me *feel* second place, and eventually I no longer felt it. Life continues, doesn't it? I'm sorry, that must be hard to hear. But I just want you to understand that Nathaniel and I eventually had what I thought was a healthy relationship, where it was just about the two of us. I wouldn't have stayed with him otherwise.' She frowns. 'I haven't answered your question. He'd just say things like he didn't think he would ever love someone in that way again.'

'It must have been awful when you found out what he'd done,' Jess says. 'How did you find out?'

'Now that, I remember clearly. It was only a year ago. We were moving house and he'd had to pop into work for something, so I was finishing up the packing on my own. I found a newspaper cutting in the cutlery drawer, hidden underneath the drawer lining. I don't even think Nathaniel had remembered putting it there. You see, he lived alone in that place, and when I eventually moved in, he must have forgotten all about it.' She rolls her eyes. 'It says a lot for my cleaning, doesn't it, that I never even pulled up the lining of that drawer? I just used to wipe it down. I curse myself every day for not finding it sooner. Over twenty years of my life I wasted.'

Jess nods. 'What did you do when you found it?'

'I was devastated. And terrified. The first thing that went through my mind was that I'd been living with a murderer for all those years. I started to load my things in the car. Luckily, they were already packed. I just wanted to get out of there before he came back. My sister had said I could stay with her until I found somewhere else. But as I was getting in the car, Nathaniel came back and found me. So, I had no choice but to confront him.'

It occurs to Jess that Elsbeth is just another victim of her mother's murderer. Whether that was Nathaniel or someone else, Elsbeth's life was torn apart by the aftermath.

'I've never seen anyone look so shocked in my life. He just stared at me for ages, and then the tears came and he begged me to come inside and hear him out. He told me he hadn't done anything, that he'd never been charged. But I couldn't listen to him. Because even if he was innocent, he'd kept such a huge part of his life a secret and destroyed all my trust in him. Where can you go from there? Absolutely nowhere with that person.'

Jess nods. 'Did he tell you he knew who had done it?'

'No, but he did say there were a lot of issues with her family, and that she also had an ex in the picture. Nathaniel vowed that he was going to make it his life's mission to find out who was responsible.'

And that seems to be exactly what he had done.

The waitress appears with Elsbeth's coffee. She takes it and stirs in some sugar.

'He told me he'd been in trouble with the police before,' Jess says. 'And that's why they were so intent on suspecting him. Do you know anything about that?'

'Yes. But that incident was my fault, not Nathaniel's.'

'What do you mean?'

'I've always been very outspoken,' Elsbeth begins. 'And... we were at the supermarket one time when this man barged in front of me to get to the till quicker. It was really busy that day and we'd already been queuing for a while. It was before they had smart tills. Anyway, I couldn't keep quiet and I told him how rude he was, that he should wait his turn. The next thing I know, he's in my face shouting and screaming at me, looking like he wants to do me some serious harm. Nathaniel quickly stepped in and tried to get him away but the man wasn't leaving me alone. Next thing I know, Nathaniel's pummelled him in the face. The man fell backwards and split his head on the floor.' She sighs. 'I'm not proud of what happened, but it wasn't Nathaniel's fault. Not really. He was just defending me. I know it sounds strange, but it was his kindness that drove him to do that. It got on his record, of course.'

Jess contemplates the significance of this. 'So, he could be violent.'

'I suppose it's hard to argue with that,' Elsbeth agrees, 'but I can tell you this: I'd never seen him violent in any way either before or after that.'

'Do you think he killed my mum?' Jess asks. It's not that she believes Elsbeth has all the answers, she just needs to grasp hold of anything she can.

'The truth is, I don't know. I would say no, definitely not, but you hear all the time about people who commit crimes being the nicest neighbours, or husbands or wives. Pillars of the community. What does that mean? People present the image they want us to believe in. So, I'm sorry but I don't know either way. And if the police couldn't find out, then I doubt you'll ever get the answer you're looking for.'

This is exactly what has tormented Jess, even though she's come to believe that Nathaniel couldn't have done it. That there's someone else out there who doesn't want the truth to emerge. 'Nathaniel was wrong about something,' she says. 'My mum was having an affair with him – she was with my dad when they were together.'

Elsbeth stares at her. 'I had no idea. He never said.' Her eyes narrow.

'I'm not sure if he knew.'

'Well, that's interesting,' Elsbeth replies. 'It's made me remember something that didn't seem important at the time. It wasn't long before the day I found out. I'd come home from work and I could hear Nathaniel arguing with someone. I couldn't hear exactly what it was about but I was sure I heard someone mention Lori's name.'

Jess leans forwards. She needs to cling to every word Elsbeth speaks, because she has a feeling that this is the last time the woman will be willing to say anything.

'They stopped talking when I came in, but the atmosphere was filled with tension,' Elsbeth continues. 'Have you ever had that feeling? When you just *know* you've walked in on something you weren't supposed to hear?'

Though Jess can't recall an incident like this, she gets the point.

'The man he was with left after that, and when I questioned

Nathaniel about it, he said it was just someone from work. I asked him what they were arguing about and he said they hadn't been. He said they'd been talking about an incident at work – something someone could be in trouble for. And when I said I'd heard him say Lori's name he said I must have been mistaken.' She rolls her eyes. 'I trusted him so thought nothing more of it. And when I found the newspaper years later I didn't give any thought to this incident because it had happened such a long time before.'

Jess's heart rate is increasing, she feels it without having to check. 'What did this man look like? Would you recognise him if you saw him again?'

'I don't know. Dark hair. Good looking. Similar age to Nathaniel. Maybe a bit older.'

She doesn't know what makes everything suddenly come into sharp focus. Perhaps it's the adrenalin coursing through her body. An instinct. Jess pulls out her phone and flicks through her photos, holding it out to Elsbeth when she finds the one she's looking for.

'Is this the man Nathaniel was arguing with?'

Elsbeth stares at the photo, frowning.

Seconds tick by before she finally answers. 'Yeah, that looks like him. An older version, at least. Who is he?'

Jess takes a deep breath. 'That... is my dad.'

THIRTY-ONE

APRIL 1993

Lori

Everything is set. She just has to get through four more days, and then she and Jess can leave this place. Ninety-six hours, that's all. She can do this. Lori would leave today if she could, but she didn't want to let Nigel down at the video shop. He's been kind to her when she's needed to change shifts at short notice because of something or other with Jess. So, she's working her notice.

Lori loves London, it's the only place she's ever known, but the fear of staying is far greater than the fear of leaving.

Meredith calls from the kitchen. 'I thought you were working today?'

'I am. But not until four.' Lori's had no choice but to stay at her mum's for these last few days, but she hasn't whispered a word about her plan to leave with Jess. She knows what would happen if she did. Her mother would try and stop her. Convince Lori that there's no way she'd manage somewhere else on her own, that she needs her and Mionie. Lori doesn't want to hear it. She's leaving before it all catches up with her.

'I'm just popping out for a bit, then,' her mother shouts. 'I'll be back in time for you to go.'

Lori's in the living room, writing a letter to Nathaniel. She feels dreadful about the way things went the other night; it's important that she makes peace with him. He's a good man, and she wants him to know she'll always care for him.

'What are you doing there?' Her mother stands in the doorway, arms folded, watching Lori.

'Just making some notes for uni.'

'Hmm. Oh, Lori, I hope this is it for you. I hope you don't drop out. It's so important to see things through in life.'

'I know, Mum.' Lori turns to Jess, who sits on the floor watching television.

'And don't let Jess watch that thing all day, will you? Too much TV isn't good for toddlers.'

'I know,' Lori repeats.

'And how long did you say you'd need to stay here? Surely sorting out your flat won't take the landlord that long?'

'Four more days and then we'll be out of your hair.'

Her mother sighs. 'Oh, having little Jessica here is no trouble at all. Anyway, I'm off. See you later, then.'

Once she hears the front door close, Lori glances at the television. She shouldn't feel guilty; Jess doesn't watch that much, and besides, Lori doesn't know when she'll get a chance after they leave London. She doesn't own a TV and she needs to be careful with money. She's booked a hotel in Exeter where they can stay while she looks for somewhere to live. Lori's never been there – she chose the place at random by looking at a map of the UK, closing her eyes and pointing at the page. Her decision was confirmed when she did some research in the library and found out all about the University of Exeter.

Thinking of it now makes Lori smile. She and Jess will have a good future, they just have to get through these four days. She turns back to her letter, for a moment considering asking Nathaniel to come and visit her once she's settled. It would mean introducing him to Jess, but that will be fine once they're away from here, and this toxic life is far behind her.

The doorbell rings, startling Lori. She's been lost in her letter writing. She won't answer it – nobody knows she's here so it will be someone for her mother. 'It's okay, sweetheart,' she says to Jess, who's turned to look at her. 'We don't need to get that.'

Lori begins writing again, but whoever is out there presses the doorbell again. Twice. Three times. She'd better see who it is. It must be important, and she doesn't want to give her mum another excuse to admonish her.

The second she opens the door she knows she's made a mistake.

'Hello, Lori.' Danny flashes a menacing smile. There is only one reason he's here. 'You're a hard girl to find,' he says. 'Aren't you going to let me in?'

'No,' she hisses. 'You need to leave. Now.'

'Is my girl in there?' He peers into the hallway, and must hear the sound of *Tots TV* because suddenly he is smiling. 'I know you and my Jess are here alone. I saw Meredith drive away.'

'Leave us alone, Danny. I'll call the police!'

He laughs. 'And say what? That your ex wants to see his daughter and you won't let him. That's the only thing I'm guilty of.'

'That's not true, though, is it Danny?' It feels good to stand up to him, to say what she should have said when she found out what kind of man he was.

'I just want to see my daughter.' Without warning, he barges past her and heads straight for the living room.

'No!' Lori shouts. But it's too late. By the time she catches up with him he is already scooping Jess into his arms. Lori falls silent as she witnesses the joy on Jess's face, her tiny arms wrapped around Danny's neck. 'Dada!' she shrieks.

Lori's chest tightens. 'You need to go now,' she urges, as calmly as she can manage.

Jess snuggles further into him, and it's as if Lori's heart is being wrenched from her body. She's spent too many months shielding Jess from the pain Danny has caused; she has dealt with her toddler questions about his whereabouts, and has done her best to make sure Jess never feels the gaping hole he has left in her life. And now, without warning, all the hard work she's put in has crumbled away. This is exactly what Lori wanted to avoid.

'Jess,' Danny says, 'why don't you play for a minute while I talk to Mummy in the kitchen – is that okay?'

Jess nods and lets him put her down. 'TV,' she says, pointing at the screen.

'If that's what your mum lets you do, then fine,' Danny says.

He shuts the door when they get to the kitchen. 'I'm not letting you keep her from me,' Danny says. 'She needs me in her life.'

'Wrong. You're exactly what she doesn't need in her life.'

Danny shakes his head. 'I never had you down as vindictive, Lori.'

'I'm doing whatever I can to protect my daughter from—'

'Protect her from me? I'm not the one she needs protecting from. It's you! What kind of mother keeps her child from her dad?'

'The kind who knows what kind of person you are. You're a sick person, Danny, and I can't let you be around Jess.'

Danny falls silent, then nods slowly. 'Have it your way, then. Just so you know, though – I'll do whatever it takes to have Jess in my life. You're insane if you think I'll just walk away and leave her.'

'Do what you have to do, Danny. I'm not scared.' Because in

ninety-five hours she and Jess will be heading away from this place. Lori heads to the worktop and picks up the phone. 'Now, if you don't get the hell out of here, I'm calling the police.'

Danny throws his head back and laughs, walking towards her and shoving his face so close to hers that she can smell the mint chewing gum he's rarely without. 'I never loved you,' he spits. 'Maybe I thought I did, but you were a big mistake. Jess, though, is the best thing that's ever happened to me, and there's no way I'll let you force me out of her life.'

'Get out.' Lori forces the words out, her whole body shaking.

To her surprise Danny backs away and heads out into the hall. It takes her a moment to compose herself, and in that time she hears him talking to Jess, explaining that he'll see her again soon.

Then it falls silent, and Lori visualises him leaving the house with Jess, getting her into the car and driving away. She rushes from the kitchen, stopping only when she takes in the sight before her.

Danny is standing by her bag, with Jess holding onto his leg. In his hand he holds the prospectus Lori was sent from the University of Exeter and the hotel booking letter she'd tucked safely inside it.

'Well, well, well,' he says. 'It looks like someone's been planning to run away and start a new life somewhere. You do know that's never going to happen?'

THIRTY-TWO

NOW

Jess

She's always been in awe of her father. A figure of huge strength in her life, Danny is a man who was able to carry on and raise her to be the best she could be, despite the pain he lived alongside. The resemblance between Jess and her mother is striking, so she knows her father will see Lori every time he looks at Jess.

Now, however, as she stands outside his front door, her image of him lies shattered. He's been lying to her and she needs to know why.

'Jess! I wasn't expecting to see you today. Come in!' He's in a good mood, and this will be to her advantage. 'I was about to make coffee. Want one?'

'No, thanks. I was just passing on my way home from a shoot and thought I'd stop in and say hi.'

Danny smiles and hugs her. 'Well, I'm always pleased to see my girl.'

Unless I'm talking about Nathaniel French.

In the kitchen, Jess watches him spoon coffee into a cup. He feels like a stranger now and it sickens her. First her mum, and now her dad. She wants to be wrong. 'Dad, I need to ask you something. It will really help me put all this stuff with Nathaniel French behind me. I need to move forwards and start living my life again.'

'Course you do. I just want you to be happy, love. I know it unsettled you, but he's gone now, hasn't he?' He shrugs. 'Sometimes we get what we deserve in life.'

'Did Mum get what she deserved?'

He turns away. 'No, course not.'

'Even though she had an affair?'

'I never held that against her when I found out. Sometimes things are complicated in relationships, aren't they?'

'And the man she was having an affair with – it wasn't Nathaniel French?'

'No. I only saw Lori with this man once, and it wasn't him. He was lying to you, Jess. I don't know how he got that photo of the two of them but it couldn't have been real.'

Jess nods. 'So, you've never met Nathaniel? Never even bumped into him in the street?'

'Jess, why does this feel like an interrogation? Again.'

'It's not. I just want to be clear on a few things.'

'No, I never set eyes on that man before he was arrested. The first I saw of him was in the papers.'

Something inside Jess's body withers and dies. She wants to believe that Elsbeth was mistaken, but there had been no doubt in the woman's mind, even all these years later. Jess had insisted that she look again, urged her to be sure. Her reply had been that she'd always been good with faces. Names she forgets, but faces stay forever ingrained in her memory.

Jess struggles to speak. 'Dad, I know you went to Nathaniel's home, years after Mum died. Nathaniel's ex-partner confirmed it. She said she came home and found you both arguing. He told her you were a work colleague.'

Her father has never been lost for words in Jess's presence.

With his face stripped of colour, he seems to diminish before her, and it crushes Jess; it can only mean one thing.

'Okay. I lied to you, Jess. I did go to Nathaniel's flat. Just once.'

Jess pulls out a kitchen chair and sinks into it, fearing her legs won't hold her up if she stays standing. 'Go on.'

Danny clears his throat. 'When the police couldn't make a case against him, I became a bit... well... obsessed. I wanted to keep track of him, and watch his movements carefully in case he ever tried to do anything to another woman.' He sighs. 'I did it for ages, until we moved to Portugal.'

'No, Dad, this was years after that. You're still lying!'

He frowns. 'I just can't remember the details, Jess. It was years ago.' He pauses. 'Yes, I did start following him again. I needed closure. Then one day I decided to confront him at his flat. I went there when I knew he'd be home. He didn't even recognise me when he opened the door. I was sure he would, but no, not even a flash of recognition. I forced my way in and accused him of murder. I said the police might not have been able to charge him but I knew he was guilty.'

'And what did he say?'

'He just repeated over and over that it wasn't him. And then his girlfriend came home and I didn't want to upset her so I stopped shouting. I didn't want to drag her into it. She hadn't done anything wrong. Well, apart from falling in love with a murderer.'

Jess is unsure how to respond. She wants to believe her dad, but he lied to her just minutes ago. And if he can lie once...

'I didn't want to tell you because this is exactly what I've tried to protect you from all these years. I hope you can see that, Jess?'

'Why go there? What did you want to achieve by confronting him? Or did you want to... hurt him?' *And if you wanted to hurt him then, maybe that feeling never left you.*

Before he can answer, her father's phone rings. It's on the table right in front of her and she sees Carolina's name on the screen. 'You'd better get that,' Jess says.

He hesitates but then picks up his phone. 'Carolina! Hi, love. I'm just with Jess at the moment, can I call you back?'

Jess stands up. She can't hear Carolina's words but she's willing to bet the call is to express her concern for Jess.

'I have to go,' she says, turning from her father.

'Wait, hang on!'

But Jess is already walking away.

'I need to see you. Can I come over?'

There's no hesitation in his answer, and when she gets to his house, he's standing at the door waiting to let her in.

'This is a surprise,' Harrison says. 'It's usually me turning up at your place. What's happened? Are you okay?'

'No,' she says. 'And I shouldn't be here, but there's no one else I can talk to about this.'

'You'd better come in then.'

He leads her into the living room. 'I've never seen you like this before, not even when Nathaniel came up to you on the street. Sit down and tell me everything.'

So Jess does, even speaking aloud the thought she hasn't allowed herself to consider since she left her dad's. Yet it feels good, and now she's convinced that Harrison will tell her how ridiculous she's being to even consider it.

'Your dad? I mean, that's... well, not beyond the realms of possibility. It's often the people closest to the victims, isn't it?'

'The police didn't suspect him, though. He had an alibi.'

Harrison frowns. 'But what was it?'

'He was in hospital having a hernia operation. And what stronger alibi is there than that?'

Harrison nods. 'True. But... what if he didn't actually do it himself? Maybe he got someone else to do it for him? If he knew he was going to be in hospital, then it could have been planned to coincide?'

Jess shakes her head. 'No... he wouldn't... I can't even believe I'm talking about this. It makes me sick to my stomach.'

'I know your dad, Jess, and he's definitely a man who wouldn't have liked his fiancée cheating on him.'

And that's exactly what worries Jess. 'He would have been a suspect, though, wouldn't he, to start with at least? Even if he was in hospital. Wouldn't they have checked him out. Phone records. Things like that?'

'Remember, mobiles weren't around then. Or emails. No internet. People must have used phone boxes to do dodgy stuff. So I'm not sure what they would have found. And they would have been satisfied with his hospital alibi, wouldn't they?'

'This is my dad we're talking about. You know him, Harrison. He's not a murderer. And the police would have known if he was lying to them, especially after they couldn't prove it was Nathaniel. Surely they would have kept on looking, even if the police did believe they'd already found the person responsible?'

'In an ideal world.' Harrison sighs. 'But we both know this isn't one. Cases get messed up all the time. Things go wrong and people get away with stuff.'

'This is awful,' Jess says. 'I feel like I can't trust anyone. I'm running around in circles trying to work out... what? What exactly am I hoping to achieve? All I'm trying to do is get my life back, put all of this to rest. Yet the only thing I seem to be doing is destroying my family.'

'But isn't it more important to know the truth?'

'Yes. How did you get so sensible all of a sudden?' She smiles, but the truth is that Harrison always has been sensible and rational. An adult opposed to the child she often felt like.

'I think you should come and stay here, Jess. Just for a while.

I don't like the idea of you being alone. Even though it sounds like you're not always on your own.'

Jess looks away. Everything is so new with Gabriel that she doesn't want to make a big thing of it, despite feeling that something is pulling her towards him. And further away from Harrison. Gabriel understands why she doesn't want to be a mother and isn't likely to try to change her mind.

'Does he know anything?' Harrison asks. 'This new guy in your life.'

'No. We haven't known each other long – I'm not just going to blurt it out.'

Even though Gabriel shared his own trauma, and I missed the perfect opening to be honest about mine.

'You told me right from the start,' Harrison reminds her.

Yes, she had. But she was a different person then. She had yet to learn that her past could wreck her relationships. She won't be burnt twice. 'That was different. We'd already known each other a while, hadn't we?' Harrison had worked for her dad, so she'd assumed he must already know. Workplace gossip was rife at her dad's company. Jess had realised that when she'd helped out for a couple of months one summer when he was short staffed.

When she doesn't reply to Harrison's comment, he changes the subject. 'Would it do any harm to dig a little deeper? Maybe question your dad again about the time he went to Nathaniel's flat. See if you can catch him out in another lie.'

'There's no way I can do that. He'll see what I'm doing and he'll know what I'm accusing him of. Once that's out there I can never take it back.'

'No, I guess not.'

'And doesn't it seem likely that whoever did it was the one who also killed Nathaniel?' Jess asks.

'It's plausible.'

'Then that could also be the same person who tried to

plough into me with that car. But my dad would never hurt me. Never.'

'That's true. If I've learnt anything from working with your dad, it's that you and Zara mean more to him than anything. Including his company.'

Jess believes this too, but the fact remains that her dad lied to her.

'Maybe the person in the car never intended to hurt you. What if it was just meant to scare you off? There were two witnesses, so whoever was driving would have to be insane to try and hurt you in that way. Doesn't that seem the most likely scenario?'

Jess has considered this, and the fact that it's probably the same person who somehow got into her office and left the lights on. And she still hasn't found her cardigan. Hearing this theory from Harrison, though, breathes life into it.

'He loved my mum. He was distraught when she was killed.'

Harrison walks over to her and takes her arm. 'I'm so sorry I don't have any answers for you, Jess.'

'I'm not a detective, am I? It's not like I can solve any of this and then live happily ever after. What am I supposed to do?'

'You need to go to the police,' Harrison says. 'Tell them everything. And you need to be vigilant.'

She will never again let her guard down. The car incident had caught her by surprise, probably because she'd been drinking, her senses dulled. 'But how can I tell them about my dad? I can't have them interrogating him when I don't know for sure he's done anything at all.'

'You know he went to Nathaniel's house, years after he was a suspect. Isn't that enough? And what if he's the one who... wanted to stop Nathaniel talking to you?'

Jess can't go to the police, not without knowing more. She needs something incontrovertible first.

'I can be there with you,' Harrison continues. 'You don't have to be alone in this.'

Jess can't listen to this. She won't be pulled back into him, regardless of what's going on in her life. Above all else, it's not fair to him. No matter how she feels about him, she won't get involved again, not when she caused him so much pain and would only end up hurting him more.

'I've got to go,' she says, grabbing her bag and rushing out.

'Jess, wait!'

But she doesn't.

Her phone rings as soon as she steps onto the street, pulling her hood over her head because it's raining now. It's got to be Harrison, who will plead with her to come back. Is he using her father as an excuse to get close to Jess again?

She reaches for her phone, ready to firmly tell him to give her some space, until she realises it's Zara calling.

'Hi, sis. Are you okay?'

'I'm the one who should be asking *you* that,' Zara says.

Jess continues walking towards the Tube station. 'I'm fine. You saw Harrison then. Had coffee with him.' She doesn't mean to sound resentful, although she's sure that's how it will come across. There is anger inside her, though – not with him, but with whoever did that to her mum. And Nathaniel. *And probably me too, if I'm not careful.*

'Oh, yeah. That was strange. Seeing him again after all these months. Mum was delighted, of course. She always loved Harrison. Anyway, I was calling to see if you wanted to come over. I've got wine and snacks and we can watch something on Netflix. I'll even let you choose what we binge.'

'Thanks. That does sound like just what I need, but I'm so tired, Zara. I could do with an early night. Another time?'

'Okay.'

'Where's Ryan? Is he out tonight?'

'I'm surprised you don't know. He's gone over to Gabriel's. They're having a football night with a whole bunch of them.'

Jess stops walking. 'At Gabriel's? Are you sure?'

'Definitely. Why?'

'He's having his kitchen refurbished and his whole place is a mess. It has been for weeks. He said it's not fit to have any guests.'

Silence follows, and Jess wonders if they've been cut off. 'Zara?'

'Yeah, um, that's weird. His flat definitely isn't being refurbished. I was there the other day picking up Ryan.'

'Oh. I must have misunderstood.' But Jess hadn't. She knows without doubt what Gabriel told her about his flat. His excuse for not inviting her there was impossible to misinterpret.

Zara laughs. 'You probably weren't listening. He probably could have told you he's a spy for MI5 and you wouldn't have taken it in. You've been so distracted lately. It's understandable, of course. All this stuff with Nathaniel French.'

'Don't tell Gabriel any of this, will you? I don't want him thinking I'm not interested in him.'

'It will be our secret,' Zara replies. 'Listen, are you sure you won't come round?'

'No, it's an early night for me. Soon, I promise.'

They say goodbye and Jess continues on her way to the station, anxious to get home. It's dark now and every passing stranger could be a hidden threat.

Not only has her father lied to her, but now Gabriel too.

And Jess needs to find out why.

THIRTY-THREE

APRIL 1993

Lori

There's a puce-coloured ring around her wrist, where Danny had gripped her so tightly she thought he'd snap her arm. Lori had fought back, punching him with such force that he reeled backwards against the wall. And this had bought her just enough time to grab Jess and charge upstairs.

Locked in the bathroom, she'd cradled and soothed Jess, wiping away her toddler's tears as fast as they'd fallen. She'd tried to ignore Danny pounding on the door, shouting and cursing, and covered Jess's ears and sung to her to drown out the noise. 'Daddy's just not well. He doesn't mean to shout at us,' she'd told Jess. It was the only thing she could think of.

Several minutes passed before the house fell silent. And ten more before Lori dared to open the door and venture out. She'd heard the front door slam, but it could easily have been a ploy to coax her out. Danny frightened her; a feeling he'd never evoked in her when they were together. Not even when she'd found out the truth about him.

'You're daydreaming again, Lori,' her mother says, snapping

her back to where she sits on the sofa, the book she's reading closed on her lap. 'You need to watch that, you know. Anything could happen to Jess while you're in one of your... trances.'

'It's not a trance,' Lori insists. 'I'm fully aware of what's going on. And Jess is napping upstairs.' Every admonishment her mother hurls her way is painful, but she has to keep focused. Only three more days and she will never have to listen to this cold and harsh tone again. Of course she'll bring Jess back to visit, but Lori will stay far out of the way, avoid the toxicity that's been present in her life since her dad died. Probably even before that.

'It's great that you're taking your studies seriously but do you think you could help me with dinner? Mionie and Neil are coming, and I don't have much time.'

Lori freezes. 'You never said anything.'

'Didn't I?' Her mother frowns. 'It was a last-minute thing, really. She called this morning.'

'Does she know I'm here?' Lori places her book down, turning over the corner of the page because she's lost her bookmark. Her mother hates that.

'Um, I don't think it came up. Why?'

'Because she hates me!'

'Lori! Nobody hates you. I wish you'd stop thinking that the world is against you. And Mionie's far too busy at work to waste time with sibling rivalry.'

'I didn't say anything about sibling rivalry.'

'Well, I just assumed that's what you meant.'

'Forget I said anything.' Lori refuses to argue or explain. She's already shaken up after the violent confrontation with Danny; the last thing she needs is more conflict.

The evening comes too quickly, but to Lori's surprise, dinner runs smoothly. Mionie seems overdressed in a lace evening dress, but she's in good spirits and, if anything, is warmer towards Lori than she's ever been. She clearly hasn't shared the details of what happened with Neil to their mum, and this will be for one reason only: Mionie doesn't want the illusion of their perfect relationship shattered.

'Neil and I have set a date,' her sister declares when they've finished the profiteroles her mum has made from scratch.

Meredith beams, clapping her hands together like an excited child. 'Well, it's about time. Fantastic news. Isn't it, Lori?'

Her cheeks heat up but she manages to nod, and raises her glass of wine. 'Congratulations to you both.'

'Well, this calls for champagne,' her mother declares. 'I'm sure I've got a bottle. Let me just go and check.'

Mionie holds up her hand. 'Not for me, Mum. I'm on call tonight. But the three of you go ahead. Neil and I can celebrate later.' She turns and smiles at Neil.

'I've got some elderflower you can have instead. I'll just go and fetch it.'

Icy silence falls upon them once Meredith has left the room.

'You look surprised, Lori,' Mionie says after a moment, with a twisted smile.

'I'm very happy for you,' Lori responds.

'Are you?' Mionie hisses.

Lori glances at Neil and sees he's staring at his empty plate. He should say something, stand up to Mionie like he should have done long before now. Do what's right.

'Yes, I am.' She says this firmly, keeping her focus on what's just around the corner: a new life with Jess.

Her mother comes back in, a bottle of champagne in her hand. 'Here we go. Found some.'

Never has Lori been more grateful to see her mother.

'And what are you all whispering about?' She gets some clean champagne flutes from the cabinet.

'Nothing,' Mionie says. 'I was just telling Lori how lovely it will be for her to have Neil as her brother-in-law. *Family*.' Her emphasis of this word leaves Lori in no doubt as to what Mionie's trying to do.

'Yes, how lovely for all of us.' Her mother pours their drinks and raises her glass. 'To Mionie and Neil – what a perfect union!'

Lori drinks hers far too quickly. Anything to help her get through what's left of this evening.

Someone's pager beeps.

'I'm being called in,' Mionie says, already standing. 'Sorry to cut the evening short, Mum.'

'Not at all, you go. Save some people. Neil can stay and finish his drink. I'll drop him home.'

Lori watches Mionie kiss Neil before rushing out. She can't recall a time when she's seen her sister so affectionate with him. It's all for Lori's benefit.

'I'll go and check on Jess,' Lori says, scraping her chair back.

'Let me,' her mother says, walking off before Lori can protest.

And now she is alone with Neil, silent tension wrapping itself around them.

'I'm sorry for everything, Lori,' he whispers after a moment. 'I was an idiot for telling Mionie how I felt. I've had a lot of time to reflect on it, and, well it was just stupid. I should have known you didn't have those same feelings for me, but if I'm honest, I hoped that maybe a tiny part of you did actually feel something.'

'I *did*, Neil. It's called friendship. Since when did being able to talk to someone and open up to them mean you want to be with them? That's utter crap!'

Neil hangs his head. He's not used to Lori being so assertive, shaming him. 'I know.'

'What are you doing, Neil?'

'What?'

'I mean, why are you marrying Mionie? You don't love her.'

He looks at his hands, scratching them until white marks appear. 'I'm marrying her because it's what I want to do.'

'For convenience? Because that's what important doctors do to keep up appearances?'

'Those are your words, not mine.'

'But they're the truth,' Lori insists. 'And you must know how messed up that is? You're stopping Mionie having the chance to find someone who really loves her. And d'you know what, Neil? I can't let you do that to her. Too many men destroy women's lives and I'm not going to stand by and watch you do that to my sister.'

'What exactly are you saying, Lori?'

'You need to leave her. You're not good enough for her. You're lying about your feelings and it's time to tell her the truth. Be honest. You owe her that.'

'I *was* honest, remember? And she wouldn't listen. She just wouldn't hear it.'

'Then you have to make her listen. And you have to do it now. Tonight.'

Neil shakes his head. 'I... I can't. We're getting married, Lori. Next summer. It's what I want. A wife. Children one day. All of it.'

'And it doesn't matter who it's with?'

Again, he avoids looking at her. Neil understands what she's saying, he's just too caught up in his lie of a life to acknowledge it. 'I'm not telling Mionie anything. We're getting married.'

Lori sits with this declaration for a moment, analysing it, weighing up her options. There is only one.

'If you don't tell her, then I will. And before you say it, no, she doesn't listen to me, but I'll make sure the rest of the family know too. Mionie would never let your relationship continue if everyone knew you'd declared you had feelings for me. You know that as well as I do. Mionie cares too much about what people think.'

Finally, Neil looks directly at her. 'I never had you down as a bitch, Lori.' He lowers his voice. 'I can't let you do this. Do you understand? I'm never going to let you ruin what I've got.'

Before she can respond, her mother flounces in, announcing that Jess is snoring softly. 'Oh, good, you've finished your drink,' she says to Neil. 'Shall we get going? There's a programme I want to watch and it starts in half an hour.'

Without a word to Lori, Neil stands up and walks out, not once glancing back.

THIRTY-FOUR

NOW

Jess

Rays of February sunlight seep through the blinds in her bedroom, forcing Jess awake. She barely slept, but she forces herself up, needing to get on with the day before the inevitable confrontation with Gabriel. One thing Jess won't stand for is being lied to.

It's eight o'clock when his text comes. Light-hearted and charming, he asks if she wants to grab lunch today.

Jess calls him – she might as well get this over with.

'It's nice to hear your voice so early,' he says. 'Even if it's only over the phone.'

'How's your kitchen renovation going?' she asks.

There's a brief hesitation before he answers. 'Good, yeah. Fine. So how about lunch today, then? There's a great place in Covent Garden we could go—'

'No, thanks. I don't like liars.'

Gabriel falls silent for a moment. 'What... what d'you mean?' he says eventually.

'I know you're not having your kitchen redone. In fact, it's in perfect condition, isn't it?'

'Jess, listen, I—'

'Save it. Don't bother explaining. We haven't known each other long enough for this to be a big thing. Let's just end this, whatever it is, now.'

'I know this is new between us, but please will you just hear me out?'

She stays silent, torn between ending the call and listening to whatever excuse Gabriel is about to deliver.

'The truth is,' he begins, 'I was embarrassed.'

'Of what?'

'I really like you, Jess, and I just wanted to give you a good impression of me. I'm a property developer, aren't I? And, well, my flat isn't the standard you'd expect from someone who builds luxury homes. I just didn't want you to see it yet, not until you got to know me better.'

'That's ridiculous! I couldn't care less what your flat's like.'

He sighs. 'It's small. And dull. I haven't really put much effort into it because I'm so busy doing up other properties.'

'You must have realised Zara would tell me she'd been there. We talk a lot. You know that.'

'I know. I wasn't expecting her to turn up that day to pick up Ryan.'

'Do you know how this all sounds?'

'I know, I know. I'm ashamed that I lied to you. And that I thought you'd be put off me if you saw my place. I know you're not that kind of person.'

Seconds tick by.

'Jess, are you still there?'

She doesn't reply.

'How about we have dinner tonight instead of lunch. You can come to my place afterwards. I'll let you see all of me, I promise.'

'Okay.' Jess sighs. 'Dinner tonight. But you come to mine.'

'Yeah, of course. Thank you for hearing me out. And for believing me.'

Jess ends the call and immediately dials another number. It's time to find out what Gabriel is up to.

'Did you bring everything?'

Harrison holds up a plastic bag. 'It's all in here. Everything we'll need.'

Jess moves to hug him, but then reconsiders. She wants to be fair to him – what they're doing now doesn't change anything.

'Thank you. I really appreciate this.' Jess closes the door behind her then leads him through to her studio.

'So, are you going to tell me why you want to spy on your boyfriend.'

'He's not my boyfriend. Not really.' *And he never will be.*

'But you're in a relationship and you don't trust him? This doesn't sound like you, Jess. Normally at the first sign of deceit you'd be telling him to take a hike.'

Yes, she would. But this is about something else. 'I can't explain what's going on, but I think he has something to do with Nathaniel appearing in my life. Something to do with my mother. It's all too much of a coincidence.'

Harrison sits on her desk chair. 'That doesn't make sense.'

'I know. But I'm trusting my instinct here. He can't be trusted. Think about it. He came into my life just before Nathaniel did,' she explains.

'Still doesn't mean much.'

'I told you on the phone I think he's been snooping around the house. Someone left my studio lights on the other night and he was here. I know I didn't do it.' She looks at Harrison, sees the disbelief etched on his face. 'When you called me that night,

I heard him moving around upstairs but he said he didn't get up at all. Then there's the car nearly ploughing me down. He was right there with me – who else would have known the exact moment I'd get back home?'

Harrison sighs. 'I suppose that could mean something. But still, it's not really evidence, is it?'

'You're right. And I didn't think anything of it until he lied to me about the flat. I told you what happened on the phone. And I know it's all circumstantial, which is why I need to find out, one way or the other.'

'But isn't it plausible that he *is* actually embarrassed about his place?'

Jess studies Harrison's face. 'You surprise me. I thought you'd jump at this chance to get him out of my life.'

'If he isn't who you think he is, then yes, I will help you. I'm just trying to keep an open mind, that's all. Don't let your mind get clouded.'

Harrison is right. Which is exactly why he's here now, holding a bag full of mini cameras and everything she'll need to set up surveillance in her office. 'Either it's him or it isn't.' She points to the bag. 'That will help me figure it out either way.'

She's surprised when Harrison walks over to her and takes her arms. 'Jess, I just don't want you to get paranoid about everyone in your life. This isn't a film. This is real life.'

'And look what happens in real life. My mum was murdered right in front of me and then the man accused of murdering her turns up in my life and is killed soon after. *That's* my real life.'

'Point taken. Look, I just don't see what Gabriel has to do with your mum or Nathaniel.'

'That's what I need to find out. Now are you going to help me or not? Because I can figure all that camera stuff out myself.'

'I know you can. But I said I wanted to help, and that's what

I'm here to do.' He peers into the bag. 'Just give me an hour in here and it will be done.'

Jess thanks him, while, for the second time, resisting the urge to hug him.

True to his word, Harrison is finished in less than an hour. He walks into the kitchen beaming at her, and for just a second Jess almost forgets they're no longer together. 'Come and look. He'll never notice them.'

In her studio, Harrison explains where he's hidden the cameras. 'I've even put one outside so you can keep an eye on anyone entering the garden. The whole of your studio's covered. And look, this is how you'll check the camera feeds.'

Jess listens while he explains how to access the cameras, the whole time hoping she'll never see Gabriel on them. There's no way back for them now, even if he has nothing to do with Nathaniel turning up, but she doesn't want to believe she's been fooled so easily. Not when she's spent her whole life being on high alert.

'You need to be careful,' Harrison warns, pulling on his coat. 'I really don't like this. Why don't you just go to the police?'

'Because they'll think I'm crazy. I need something concrete first.'

'Please make sure you keep me updated. I won't stop worrying otherwise.' He sighs. 'Don't ignore my calls or messages, Jess – it makes me worry. And then I do things like turning up here in the middle of the night.'

Jess promises she'll always answer.

Harrison offers a thin smile. 'I hope you know what you're doing.'

She doesn't. But she knows she has no choice.

. . .

Waiting for Gabriel to turn up, Jess feels numb, anaesthetised. Then comes the surge of anger that he has infiltrated her life in this way. *Don't jump to conclusions*. But that's exactly what she does because life has taught her to assume the worst.

What she's not prepared for is the pang of regret she feels when she lets him in. How quickly things have changed between them. Still, she pushes that aside and focuses on getting through the evening.

'Thanks for giving me a chance,' Gabriel says, hanging up his coat. 'I know you'll find it hard to trust me now, but I swear to you, I will never lie again. About small things or the bigger things that may come up. You have my word.'

'I believe you. What's in the bag?'

He holds it up. 'Ingredients for the dinner I'm cooking you tonight. To apologise.' He smiles, and Jess wonders if this charm works on other people. He's convincing, she'll give him that. 'Thai curry,' he adds. 'I've never done it before, but don't worry, I'm not a bad cook.'

'I'll take your word for that.' She forces a smile. 'Okay, what can I do to help?'

'Nothing. You go and relax.'

Jess nods. 'I think I will. Let me know if you can't find what you need.'

Sitting with a book in the living room, her stomach is tight, her hands clammy despite the warmth of the house. It's been so many weeks since she picked up this novel that she's lost track of what's happening, and no she has no interest in it. It doesn't help that her focus is elsewhere. She closes her eyes and listens to the clanging in the kitchen, and only when she's convinced he's lost himself in cooking does she abandon her book and sneak into the hall.

Gabriel's coat hangs on a hook by the door, and silently she heads towards it, plunging her hands into his pockets until she finds what she's looking for. She's lucky that he hates the feel of his jeans' pockets being weighed down.

'Are you okay?'

Jess freezes. Gabriel is watching her from the kitchen doorway. 'Yeah, your coat had fallen on the floor, I was just hanging it back up.'

'Ah, thanks. It's a crumpled mess anyway so probably isn't even worth hanging it up.'

'How's that dinner going? Need any help?'

'Nope. Everything's under control.'

Jess smiles. Yes, it is. Because now she's got what she needs.

She forces her food down, even though it's not bad for a first attempt at a Thai curry. She knows she's talking too much, acting out of character, that if Gabriel is guilty of anything, then this could easily make him suspicious, but being quiet is not an option. There can be no doubt in his mind that she's made peace with his lie. That all is forgiven.

The phone call comes when they're clearing away the plates. She'd wondered if Zara would go through with it, but she has, despite Jess not answering any of her questions. Now it's time for her to put on a performance.

'Uncle Neil? Yes. Oh... oh no... I'll be there right away.'

She hangs up and faces Gabriel's questioning stare. 'Is everything okay?'

'No... um, my aunt's been rushed to hospital. It doesn't look good. And my uncle is at a conference in Leeds so it will be hours before he can get there. He's asked if I'd go and be with her until he gets back.'

Gabriel stands. 'Come on, I'll drive you.'

'Thanks, but it might be better if I'm on my own. My aunt doesn't know you and it might make her uncomfortable. But stay here. I'll be back once my uncle gets there.There's no reason for you to go home, is there?' She strokes his arm.

'Okay, I'll stay. But let me know if you need me to come. And let me know when you get there safely.'

'Thanks. I will.'

Jess rushes out, fully aware of Gabriel's gaze resting heavily upon her.

THIRTY-FIVE
APRIL 1993

Lori

'So, you're really doing it? Leaving London? That's... brave.'

Lori turns to Belle and smiles. 'Not brave at all. It's just what I need to do. What I *want* to do.' Yet her words are laced with sadness because Lori is a London girl through and through; she doesn't know if she can fit in anywhere else. She can't and won't stay here, though, with the walls closing in on her. Everyone around her an enemy.

Working in the video shop tonight is putting her on edge. Since her flat was broken into she's managed to get away with day shifts, but Nigel was desperate so here she is until ten p.m. Thankfully Belle is working with her tonight; Lori might have just called in sick otherwise, despite her determination not to let Nigel down.

'I'll miss you,' Belle says, sorting through some videos a customer has just returned. 'And not just because your replacement sucks. Fergus. He looks about twelve and can barely work the till. And, get this, he knows nothing about films. Don't think he even watches any. He probably doesn't even have a TV.'

'Well, that's not required for the job, is it?' Lori says.

Belle chews her lip. 'I s'pose not. What I'm trying to say is, he's not you. He won't fill the gap you leave behind.'

Lori hugs her friend. 'Thanks for saying that.' She wonders if she'd be in this position now if Belle had turned up to the bar that night. Lori would probably never have talked to Shane otherwise. She would have had a girls' night with her friend and her life wouldn't have taken the turn it did.

She can't dwell on that now – what's done is done. Besides, she's more worried about the people she already had in her life. Danny. Neil. Her sister.

The shop door opens and Lori jumps. It's just a mother with her teenage kids. Lori needs to get a grip. There are cameras in here so surely nobody would do anything to her while she's at work.

'Are you okay?' Belle asks. 'You look weird. Are you sick?'

'No, I'm fine. Just need a quick break. Want a coffee?'

'Never say no to caffeine. Not too milky,' Belle says, as Lori heads towards the staffroom.

She's spooning coffee into their mugs when someone raps on the door. Lori freezes. It can't be Belle – she'd never leave the shop unattended. And she wouldn't knock, either. Spinning around, she's stunned to see Mionie standing there, folding her arms.

'Your colleague let me come up,' she says.

'Oh, okay.'

'You're probably shocked to see me here. But I wanted to have this conversation away from Mum. She's been through so much already after Dad dying so suddenly. The last thing she needs is to hear what I've got to say.'

'Would you like coffee?' She offers Mionie one of the mugs.

'No, I don't want coffee. Sit down please, Lori.'

Like an obedient child, Lori does as she's asked, hating herself for complying so easily. Despite how her sister is making it seem, Lori has done nothing wrong. At least not to her family. 'Look, if this is about Neil, then I've already explained myself. I did nothing, and—'

'This isn't about Neil. This is about *you*. And what you've done to Danny.'

Lori's chest tightens. 'What are you talking about?'

'Cut that innocent crap out, Lori. You know what you've done. It's... dreadful. I mean, you flirting with Neil was bad enough, but this... I can't even say it.'

Lori stares at her. 'No, say it. Because I have no idea what you're talking about.'

'I saw you a couple of weeks ago. In a bar. All over some guy. It was disgusting. Carrying on like that when you're with Danny. And you have a little girl. And there I was, thinking you were after Neil. Well, maybe you still were. Nothing would surprise me.'

Nausea shoots through Lori's body, the contents of her stomach desperate to escape.

Mionie shakes her head. 'Now you know what I'm talking about, don't you? And there's no point denying it because I was right there staring at you. You didn't see me. Too busy.'

Lori knows exactly what her sister's talking about. If it was two weeks ago, then it would have been Rohan. He'd been kind and sweet, and Lori had desperately wanted him to push her away, to realise he was making a huge mistake. To stop both of them.

'You disgust me,' her sister says. 'You've been with Danny for, what, eight years? It's despicable. How could you do that to him? He works such long hours for you and Jess, so you can have a good future together. And this is how you repay him while he's hard at work.'

Lori shakes her head. 'No... it's... you don't understand.' She should tell Mionie the truth. Let it all come out now because then maybe her family will take her side for once. They might even be united against Danny – she's never considered that possibility. Perhaps they will be able to understand her. But before she can give them life, the words die in her mouth. She only has one more day to get through. They will never need to know.

'I'm telling Danny what I saw,' Mionie says. 'I won't be complicit in your deceit. He has the right to know.'

Lori can't help but smile at the irony. This is exactly what she had said to Neil yesterday, the universe playing its cruel joke on her.

'Please, Mionie,' she begs. 'Can you just let me tell him myself. I'll do it tomorrow after work, I promise. If I haven't done it by then, you can tell him yourself. It will be better for him coming from me. How do you think he'd feel if you're the one telling him?'

Her sister ponders her request for a moment, the passing seconds fuelled with tension. 'You'd better do it,' she snaps. 'And then he can decide what to do about it. If I were him, I'd take Jess as far away from you as possible. Dad would be so ashamed. His golden child doing this kind of thing.'

And with those parting words, she turns away and strides out.

Lori can't move after that. The confrontation with Mionie has shaken her up, and she knows that, ultimately, it's because she still cares what her sister thinks of her. What her mum thinks. Somehow, despite everything, she loves them and she longs for their love in return. She couldn't bear it if they knew what she'd done.

She doesn't know how long she sits alone in the staffroom, her Blockbuster polo shirt stained wet from her tears, but eventually Belle appears and rushes over to her. 'Oh, Lori, I heard you arguing but couldn't leave the shop floor until there were no customers. I've locked up. I don't care if Nigel finds out. This is more important. What on earth's happened?'

Lori stares at her friend, feels her kindness wrapping itself around her body, drawing her in. 'Oh, Belle, I've done something terrible. And I can't take any of it back now. It's too late.' Tears stream down her cheeks.

'Tell me everything,' Belle says. 'Just get it all off your chest.'

So Lori does.

THIRTY-SIX

NOW

Jess

The first thing she notices when she steps inside Gabriel's flat in Battersea is how modern it is. Minimal. Neat and tidy. There's no colour in here. Greys and whites. No warmth. She sees this even though she hasn't turned on any lights, and is using only her phone torch to guide her way.

It's a fairly small flat, yes, but hardly a place anyone would be embarrassed about, property developer or not. Everyone's different, though, so she needs to keep an open mind. What strikes her the most is that it doesn't look lived in, but is more like a hotel room. As if he spends no time here at all.

The kitchen could do with some attention, but Jess wouldn't have noticed that if Gabriel had invited her here. She wouldn't have cared about his surroundings, would have made no judgements about his home. Her own is far from perfect, with a long list of improvements she needs to make. A work in progress, she likes to call it.

With no idea what she's looking for, Jess hunts through cupboards and drawers. It's a violation of his privacy, but hasn't he also done that to her? And he could be in her studio right now, with free rein to take his time with his search. Thinking of this, she pulls out her phone and accesses the cameras. They take a moment to load, but when they do she sees that all is still back at her house, her studio undisturbed.

A loud thud makes her freezes, her hand suspended in mid-air. Someone is in here. In the hallway. Her pulse is racing. She looks around for something to dive behind, but the kitchen is open-plan. There is nowhere to hide.

Thump, thump, thump. Turning off her phone torch, she grabs a kitchen knife and heads towards the hall. Jess doubts she'd ever be able to go through with stabbing someone, even in self-defence – just the thought of it sickens her – but having the knife in her hand might be enough.

There's nobody in the hall. She hears the heavy thud again and realises it's coming from the flat upstairs. Music pounds from above, and sweat squeezes from Jess's body as she makes her way to the last door off the hallway.

The bedroom is no more lived in than the rest of the flat, and so few clothes hang in the wardrobe that Jess begins to wonder if Gabriel lives here at all. She's never seen him wearing the same clothes twice, so it's odd that what she's looking at is the extent of his wardrobe.

The only other furniture in here is the bed and a bedside table, which on inspection contains nothing incriminating. No evidence of a link between him and Nathaniel or her mother. Jess's confidence begins to waver. She's got this wrong. All Gabriel did was lie. A stupid yet harmless one at that. If it had been anything more sinister, then why would he have let Ryan and Zara in here? He knows how close Jess is with her sister; it would have occurred to him that they'd talk.

Jess wonders if she's losing her mind. If PTSD has reared its head. She's read a lot about how victims of traumatic events can block things out, bury them so deeply that they forget they've even experienced them. She's often wondered if she's hiding the memory of her mother's death. Even if she thinks she can't remember that morning in the park with her mother, who knows what dormant memory might lay trapped in the recesses of her brain? This is a fear she's lived with her whole adult life, and it terrifies her more than the thought of never knowing who did that to her mother.

Sitting on Gabriel's bed, Jess checks her phone again. All is still undisturbed at her house. She owes Gabriel an apology for this. She needs to be honest about what she's done tonight, even if it means their relationship progresses no further.

Something catches her eye as she's standing up. The tip of a white trainer. Sticking out from under the bed. Panic sets her body alight until she realises it's not attached to anyone's leg. It never occurred to Jess to look under the bed.

Jess kneels down on the soft grey carpet and shines her phone torch underneath the bed frame. Other than the trainer, its matching one far against the wall, there's something else. And the minute her fingers clasp the cork noticeboard that lies on the floor, she knows that everything is about to change. Before she's fully slid it out, she can see her mother's smiling face. The newspaper headlines that scream of the horror in the park. All pinned neatly in place. Alongside them are recent photographs of Jess. Walking along what looks like Camden High Street. Others of her outside her house. Getting into her car. Out on photoshoots. The one thing they all have in common is that Jess remains oblivious to the glare of the camera.

'What is this?' she says aloud, while fear like she's never experienced sluices through her body, turning her cold. 'Who the hell are you, Gabriel?

Many thoughts compete for attention in her head as she drives home, taking a long route around the edge of London to buy herself more time. She should call Harrison and tell him what she's found – she'd promised him an update and so far he's messaged her four times. *I'm okay,* she'd finally replied just to stop his barrage. But she is anything other than okay as she heads towards her house, and closer to the man she knows nothing about.

On the passenger seat, hidden under her bag, is the kitchen knife from Gabriel's flat. She's ready to use it now if she has to. Even just a slash to his arm or leg should buy her enough time to run. But first she needs to know what link he has to her mother. As much as she's tried to work it out, she can't fathom any explanation.

The house is swamped in darkness as she pulls up and parks outside. Gabriel had WhatsApped her half an hour ago to check how her aunt was, and Jess had told him she was asleep. She'd let him think she was still waiting for her uncle to arrive. She wants Gabriel to be unprepared for her return home.

Jess lets herself in as quietly as she can manage, with the knife hidden up her sleeve. She is ready.

'What are you doing, Jess?'

She screams, her heart feeling as if it's trying to escape from her body. Gabriel stands in the living room doorway, no lights on behind him. 'You scared the life out of me!'

'Sorry.' He steps towards her. 'Why are you creeping around? I thought you were still at the hospital. You didn't tell me you were coming back.'

'I... my uncle arrived quicker than expected so I left. I'll go back again tomorrow to check on her.'

Gabriel nods. 'Okay. That's enough. How about you stop lying and tell the truth?'

THIRTY-SEVEN

APRIL 1993

Lori

As she begins to speak, Lori knows this is the beginning of the end. Everything will unravel now, the truth laid bare for everyone to make of it what they will.

'I'm not naive,' Lori tells Belle. 'I know men cheat. Women too. But this was another level of deception. I only found out because I followed Danny one night. We'd just had an argument and I wanted to apologise to him. I'd been putting all this pressure on him for us to live together. All I wanted was for us to be a proper family for Jess. I mean, we were engaged. He'd been the one to push for that, not me.'

Belle nods, and takes hold of Lori's hand. 'What happened when you followed him?'

'He didn't go to his place. He drove to a different house. In Chiswick. And then he got out of the car, walked up to the front door and pulled out his key to open the door. A woman was there at the door. It was as if she'd been waiting for him. They hugged and kissed, as if they hadn't seen each other for a long time.'

'Oh, Lori, I'm so sorry.'

But this is not the end of Lori's story, and now that she's started she needs to see it through. Right to the end.

'At first, I assumed he'd been cheating on me. That was bad enough and I was already prepared to cut him out of my life. But something about it felt weird. I can't explain. I think I just knew there was more to it.'

Belle frowns. 'What do you mean?'

'She was older, for one. A lot older than me. I know that doesn't really mean anything, but I did some digging around. I followed her and found out she worked in a primary school in the office. I walked in there one day and said I wanted to look around because my daughter was due to start school soon. I saw the name on her lanyard: Mrs M.C. Moore. Danny's surname. I later found out her name was Marion.'

'Oh my God, Lori, that's awful.'

'I didn't see him for a few weeks after that. We'd argued so I expected him to stay away for a while, and let things cool down. It gave me time to work out what to say. Anyway, he turned up one night as if nothing had happened, bleating on about how he missed me and Jess. I confronted him and told him I knew all about his wife. The double life he was leading. I screamed at him that bigamy was against the law. Do you know what the worst thing was? He tried to act like a victim because I'd been following them both.' As she recounts the events to Belle, Lori relives all the pain of the night she saw him with his wife.

Belle hugs her, tells her to take her time.

'But then he actually seemed relieved that I'd found out,' Lori continues. 'He said he was never planning to leave his wife, and that he'd thought of me as an escape from his life.'

'Oh, don't tell me.' Belle rolls her eyes. 'The bastard said his wife didn't understand him, right?'

Lori shakes her head. 'No. It wasn't like that. He said he and his wife couldn't have children. They'd tried for years and nothing happened. It put a lot of stress on their marriage, but he said he still loved her.'

Belle's eyes are wild with fury and she sits there shaking her head.

'He said when I got pregnant it blew his world apart, but there was no way he wasn't going to be a father to Jess.' Tears blur her vision, and all the pain Lori has felt because of Danny's actions is unleashed.

Belle finds her a tissue and sits close to her until she can speak again.

'His wife didn't know, either, so she was just as much a victim as I was. I told him he was never going to be part of Jess's life. And do you know what he did? He just laughed and said he'd take me to court and no judge in his right mind would keep him away from Jess.'

'That bastard. I would have throttled him! And then I would have told his wife all about it. Introduced myself as his fiancée of eight years,' Belle says.

'I did think about that,' Lori admits. 'But then it hit me that she might forgive him and that maybe the two of them would try to take Jess from me. They both had good jobs, a nice house. What did I have? I was about to be a full-time student so what court would think that Jess was better off with me?'

'Of course she is! You're her mother and you love her to pieces. It doesn't matter how much money you've got – you provide a loving, stable home for her. And he's a man who was about to commit a crime.'

'I don't think he had any intention of going through with it,' Lori says. 'I mean, look how he freaked out about us just living together. He would have fobbed me off until, what? His wife managed to get pregnant?'

'Evil bastard. Men like that...'

Belle's indignation spurs Lori to continue. 'I... I'm not proud of what I did next. But I was devastated, and didn't know how to deal with it. I just... got it in my head that I needed to make men pay for cheating on their wives. Not just Danny, but any man I came into contact with who was a cheater. It happened by accident, really. I didn't plan it, but once I started I couldn't stop.'

That's when she tells Belle about the night they'd arranged to meet in that bar. How, when Belle didn't show up, Lori got talking to Shane, quickly realising he was married. How she slept with him just so she could tell his wife she was better off without him. And how she didn't stop with Shane. 'I did it for months,' she admits. 'With lots of men. And I was proud of myself for revealing these despicable men to their wives. I... I didn't stop to consider what I was doing to the women. That only hit me when Shane's wife confronted me and told me she wished she'd never known. That's when I realised that I can't play God, even if I thought I was doing some good.'

'Oh, Lori. I don't know what to say.'

'It's okay. You probably hate me. But no more than I hate myself for what I did.'

'How many were there?' Belle asks.

'I don't know. I lost count. I was doing it for months.' She looks at her friend. 'I didn't always sleep with them. Please believe me. Many times I didn't have to. But I'd make sure enough happened to prove that they really were cheats.'

If Belle is shocked, she's hiding it well. 'And you always told their wives?'

'Or girlfriends, yes.'

'But how did you find them?'

'It wasn't that hard. I'd go through their address books, mostly.'

'Sounds like a full-time job. No wonder you never wanted extra shifts in this place.'

'I suppose in a way I was trying to rid the world of some evil, after what Danny did to me.'

Belle wraps her arms around Lori, pulls her close. 'I might not agree with it, but I do understand. And actually, in some ways it's a brave thing to do. So, it's over now? You're not doing it any more?'

'No, never again. That's why I'm taking Jess away from this place. Starting fresh. A clean page. It was getting... unsafe.'

'Good. But what was all that stuff with your sister? She didn't find out, did she?'

'Not quite. She saw me with someone in a bar and threatened to tell Danny. None of my family know what happened with him. They think we're still together.'

Belle's eyebrows rise. 'Why? Why wouldn't you tell them what he did?'

'Because they would find a way to blame me. They'd say I couldn't even pick a decent man. And he's Jess's father. I wanted to protect her from that.'

'You should tell them, Lori. What he did is not your fault. He misled you with years of lies. He's lied to them all too. They'll realise that, I'm sure. He fooled all of you.'

Maybe Belle is right. Besides, she's leaving the day after tomorrow, so it doesn't really matter what they think of her. She will tell them all about Danny, and make sure that if anything ever happens to her, he never gets custody of Jess. She won't tell them about what she's been doing, though. They aren't like Belle – they would never understand.

Lori turns to her friend. 'Will you promise me something? Please don't ever tell anyone what I've done. No one. No matter what. Will you promise? I can't have another person on this earth knowing what I did. I can't risk Jess ever finding out when she's older.'

'Of course. It's not my business to tell. You know you can trust me, don't you?'

Lori hugs her. 'Thank you.'

'We'd better get back out there before customers start complaining they can't get in. I don't need Nigel on my case.'

Lori follows Belle back to the shop floor, smiling for what feels like the first time in far too long. After tomorrow she will be out of here, far away from Danny, and she and Jess will never look back.

THIRTY-EIGHT

NOW

Jess

'I don't know what you mean,' Jess tells Gabriel. 'What am I supposed to have lied about?' And then it occurs to her that she is not the one who needs to explain herself.

'You see, a funny thing happened after you'd gone,' Gabriel says. 'I suddenly didn't remember locking my car. So, I went to my coat to find my keys and they weren't in the usual pocket. I'm a bit funny like that – I always keep them in my right pocket. Always. Most people probably wouldn't give that any thought, but it's something I'm very conscious of. Then I remembered that you'd picked my coat off the floor and hung it back up. Apparently. But you'd not mentioned anything about my keys falling out, so I checked them. And I'm sure I don't need to tell you the rest because you're probably holding them right now, ready to put them back before I realise they're missing?' He takes a step towards her.

In a fraction of a second Jess reaches into her sleeve and brandishes the knife, stepping away from Gabriel. 'Don't come any closer. Get back, right back!'

Gabriel frowns, holding up his hands. 'Jess? Wait! What are you doing? What's going on?'

'Who the hell are you?' she hisses.

'You know who I am. What are you doing with that knife? Look, I get—'

'Shut up and sit down in there.' She gestures to the living room. 'Just do it now or I'm calling the police.'

Gabriel edges into the living room. 'The police? What for? Jess, what is it you think I've done?'

'You must have realised that I've been to your flat. That I know all about you. But one thing I don't understand is what the hell you've got to do with my mother. So, start talking. Now!'

Gabriel perches on the sofa. 'What do you mean you know all about me?'

'I found your sick obsessive pictures and newspaper articles. Hidden under your bed. All about my mother. And those pictures of me. And I'm seconds away from calling the police.' In her other hand Jess holds up her mobile. 'I'm all ready to dial. So go on, explain yourself. What the hell have you got to do with my mother?'

He buries his head in his hands. 'Look, I'm sorry you had to find out like this. I... I wanted to tell you, but the more time I spent with you, the harder it became. I was having such—'

'Don't give me that crap about how much you like me, Gabriel. None of it was real. I want to know why and how you wormed your way into my life.'

'Look, I'll tell you everything, just please put that knife away. You're making me nervous. I'm not here to hurt you in any way, Jess, I promise.'

'And I should believe that because so far you've shown yourself to be highly trustworthy?' She waves the knife. 'I'm keeping hold of this.'

'The truth is... I'm an investigative journalist. And I've been drawn to your mum's case since I first heard about it years ago. I mean, I'd heard about it growing up – everyone did, didn't they? – but something about it haunted me. And then I got the idea that I wanted to write a book about it.'

Gabriel might as well be speaking another language. This is so far from what Jess has imagined that her brain struggles to make sense of it. 'You're lying,' she says.

'No, I'm not. Look.' He reaches into his pocket and pulls out an identity card. 'I work for *Metro* newspaper.'

Jess moves to the other side of the sofa, sits down on the arm. Still holding the knife, she faces Gabriel. 'So, you used me to get a story for your paper. Isn't that illegal or something?'

'No, not exactly. And it's not for the paper. It's a cut-throat industry, Jess. I really am sorry, but I've been desperate to write this book.'

'You could have just come to me and asked.'

'And what would your answer have been? No. I already approached your dad about a year ago and he slammed the door in my face. Literally.'

That sounds like her dad. 'We're a private family. There's no way we'd want my mum's story published. It nearly destroyed my dad having to read about it in the papers all those years ago. There's no way he'd want to go through all that again.' She forces away the image of her dad arguing with Nathaniel French. 'I can't believe you've done this,' she says. 'So your plan was to draw me into a relationship to get me talking?'

He hangs his head. 'Not to start with. I just... it was Ryan and your Zara I got close to. I was hoping I'd meet you through them, but my idea was to see what they would say about it all, being so close to you. But then Zara got it in her head that we would be good together and she arranged the date. I honestly didn't push that. Not at first. I'm sorry.'

What he's revealed does nothing to detract from his callous

actions. 'And that stuff about your dad. That was all lies, wasn't it?'

'He did die. But it was a heart attack, not at the hands of a burglar.'

'And Ryan and Zara? How did you get to know them?'

'I did meet Ryan through property development. But it's my brother who runs the family business, not me. I might have just manipulated things a bit so that the two of them would end up working together.'

The lengths Gabriel has been to are astonishing. Jess doesn't know how much longer she can bear to have this man in her house, but she has so many more questions. And Gabriel might know something useful. 'Do you know what happened to Nathaniel French, then?'

He nods. 'Yes. And I'd only just talked to him at his house.'

'You talked to him?' Jess asks, before remembering Harrison describing a young guy hanging around Nathaniel's building. 'When? What did he say?'

'It was the night he went missing. He said he was on his way to see you. He told me that he didn't do it, but he'd found out who did and he was on his way to tell you.'

Jess feels a wave of sadness. Perhaps it's because of the way her mother looked in that photo with him. Whatever had taken place between them, Nathaniel had clearly made her happy. 'Do you... did you believe him?'

'Yes, I did. In my job I've been trained to look for the signs of lying, and he didn't exhibit any of them. He was a terrified mess. Something had him spooked. And with good reason – look what happened to him.'

'And he didn't give you any hint?'

'Nope.'

'Did he tell you he knew my mum?'

Gabriel's eyes widen. 'No. I did not know that. How did I not know that?'

'Nobody did.'

'I wonder how the police didn't find out,' Gabriel says.

'Because it seems only two people in the world knew, and one of them died.'

'I'm sorry, Jess. I'm so sorry for all of this. I never meant for things to go as far as they did with us, and I should have stopped it when you invited me in that first time. I really did like you, though. I still do. Maybe—'

'Don't even think it!' She won't accept his apology, and doesn't want to hear any more about what they've done together. All she wants to do now is drill Gabriel for as much information he can offer. He's spent years researching her mother's case; he must know even more than she does. Possibly more than anyone in her family.

'Tell me something, then. In all your time researching, have you ever come across anything that might point to the person who killed my mum?'

'I'm not a police officer. But I do have my suspicions.'

'What suspicions?'

'Think about this. If it wasn't Nathaniel – and I'm not saying I believe he was innocent – but if it wasn't, then who was the closest person to your mum? That's who I'd start with.'

There is no hesitation in Jess's answer. 'My dad.'

'Exactly.'

'But he was in hospital when she was murdered. Having surgery.'

'Hmm. But there are other ways to – sorry to say this – do that to someone. Getting someone else to do it is one of them. And your father has a bit of money, doesn't he?'

This is precisely what Harrison had suggested. Still, on instinct she rushes to defend him. 'Now he does. He didn't have his business back then. He was doing okay, but wouldn't that kind of thing cost a load of money?'

Gabriel shrugs. 'You just asked me what I thought. And I've

said it, that's all. I'm not insisting that's what happened. And there was no reason for your dad to want her dead, was there?'

The affair. Was that enough of a reason? She knows her father likes to get his own way, needs control. It's part of the reason his business has been so successful. She doesn't mention this to Gabriel. She won't give him any information about her family.

She changes the subject. 'You've been snooping around my office, haven't you?'

Gabriel frowns. 'No, I swear to you I haven't. I realised early on that you don't hoard any information about the case, that you've tried to stay away from the details. The only thing I did that's... well, questionable, was to send someone in posing as a client. A friend of mine called Melinda. She was meant to book in for an appointment then see if she could find anything. But at the last moment she felt bad and changed her mind.'

Jess had forgotten about that woman. At least it's not as sinister as the alternative. 'Well, someone else has been in my house.' She tells Gabriel about the lights being on in her studio. 'And there's the incident with the car. Someone wants to scare me. Or worse.'

'I thought that was an accident?'

'It might look that way, but... forget it. I'm not saying another word to you about any of this.'

'Jess, I can help you,' Gabriel pleads. 'We want the same thing, don't we? Closure on your mum's murder. We could work on this book together. Maybe there's someone out there who knows something but has kept quiet all these years. A book – especially if it takes off – could open up this case again.'

She shakes her head. 'No way. I'm not helping you profit from the trauma my family experienced. And I'll put a stop to any book you try to publish.' She stands up and drags Gabriel from the sofa. 'Now get the hell out of my house.'

THIRTY-NINE

APRIL 1993

Lori

It's five thirty when Lori wakes, far earlier than she normally would. Today is their last full day in London and she wants to make the most of it. To soak up the memories the city holds, breathe the air into her lungs and say goodbye to some of the places that mean something to her. In the afternoon she plans for them to visit Oxford Street, Covent Garden and Piccadilly Circus, before her last shift at work.

Beside the bed, Jess stirs in her travel cot before settling down again. The one time Lori wants to be up early, Jess is showing no sign of being ready for the day.

She tiptoes downstairs to make coffee to bring back to the bedroom. Her mother is an early bird and Lori doesn't want to bump into her yet. She wants to eke out this peace, live in the serenity for as long as it can last.

Confiding in Belle last night has cleansed her, rid her body of the toxic life she was living in the false belief that she was doing some good. She trusts her friend, and knows that nobody will ever hear of it.

On her way back to her bedroom, she walks past Mionie's old room and a rush of sadness overwhelms her. Sisters are meant to be close, there for each other. As of last night, Neil still hadn't told Mionie anything. Lori had overheard their mother talking to her on the phone and all they'd spoken of was the wedding.

Jess hasn't woken by the time Lori finishes her coffee so she decides to have her shower, taking the baby monitor with her.

While she's washing her hair, it occurs to Lori that all her fear has evaporated. She knows she's made many enemies over the last few months, but just like the water from her shower, it's washing over her, unable to penetrate her skin. She's going to tell her mother all about Danny tonight, and about Neil. Everything will be out in the open – well, almost everything; nobody needs to hear about the methods she employed to help women who have been lied to and betrayed. Already she feels better, lighter, just knowing she will do it.

'Mama!' Jess calls out, wide awake the moment Lori gets back to the bedroom, wearing her mum's spare bath robe, her hair wrapped in a towel.

'Good morning, sweetie. Shall we get you up and have some breakfast?' She lifts Jess out of her cot, cuddles her against her chest.

Jess nods. 'Hungry.'

'And then how about we go to the park? It looks like a lovely morning.'

It's already warm, despite the early hour. It took Lori longer than she'd hoped to get Jess ready, but now they're finally out, and she smiles as she pushes Jess towards the Common in her buggy. She's counting the hours until tomorrow, but she will miss London, and she will miss her family. At least what they could have been. Maybe she could have tried harder with her sister. Lori has always been aware that their father was harder on Mionie. Was that her fault? She doesn't think so. She was just a child; she didn't do anything to garner favouritism. They were just alike. He saw himself in her, he told her once. It had made her float on air to hear that.

Lori sings 'Frère Jacques' as they head towards the park – one of Jess's favourite songs – her eyes squinting in the sunlight. She should have checked the weather forecast and brought her sunglasses, but she's not going to let anything spoil this moment. They'll be leaving early tomorrow morning, so this will be the last time she walks around the Common.

The park is deserted other than a man jogging in the distance. Lori feels a vague stab of recognition looking at him, but he's too far away for her to be sure. She shrugs. She won't let paranoia ruin this day.

Turning back to the path ahead, she tells Jess her plans for the future. 'Once I've finished uni, I'll get a good job at a law firm, Jess, I promise. And then we'll be able to do whatever we like. Travel the world. Have experiences. We can even go on holiday. Won't that be nice?' She's heard Lanzarote has an eternal summer.

'Toys!' Jess says, squealing.

Lori leans down and strokes her cheek. 'Yes, baby, and toys. But not too many. I want you to learn the value of money.' She knows Jess won't fully comprehend what she's saying but she's enjoying talking. Dreaming. Just the two of them in their own little world. 'I'll never let anyone hurt you, Jessie,' she whispers, her words merging into the spring air, drifting away.

Something smashes into her face. Lori's so shocked that she doesn't immediately register the searing pain, the blood trickling down her forehead. It's only when she sees the large rock lying near the wheel of the buggy that she is able to move. She looks around but sees no one. Maybe it fell from above? But there's nothing but clear blue sky. Clutching her head, she rushes round to check on Jess, whose eyes widen with fear as she takes in the sight of Lori. 'Mama!' she screams, and then bursts into tears. The blood is oozing now, a steady crimson waterfall. Lori needs to get out of here.

But as she stands up, the brick flies towards her, and there is nothing she can do to get out of the way. The shadow of someone behind it. Vague. Blurry. She's aware that something is happening – she's losing consciousness.

Seconds later she's lying on the ground, and through eyes blurred with a curtain of tears and blood, Lori sees a face she recognises standing above her. 'Please,' she manages to say. 'Jess...' Her voice is frail, drowned out by Jess's thunderous wails. 'Please... don't let her see me like this...'

Somehow Lori fixes on the familiar eyes – the wild panic, or perhaps it's just a mirror of her own.

'Jess will be fine.' The voice sounds alien, though she knows who it belongs to.

The last thing she hears is Jess calling out. 'Mama! Mama!'

Then there is only darkness.

FORTY

NOW

Jess

Alone in the house, Jess double locks the front door and checks all windows. Still clutching the kitchen knife, she peers into every room, making sure she really is alone. Gabriel's story appears to be true, but she still doesn't trust him; he could have been doing anything in her house since she left him alone. What he did to her sickens her, but she'll deal with that later. For now, she needs to focus on getting evidence to take to the police. Evidence that might destroy her father. She needs to know what he was doing the night Nathaniel was killed.

Ignoring Harrison's call, she waits for her phone to stop ringing then calls Zara. When it goes to voicemail, Jess leaves a message telling her everything she's found out about Gabriel. 'Don't trust him,' she says before ending the message. 'And tell Ryan to stay away from him too.'

For the next hour, Jess trawls through the camera footage, but there's no sign of anyone in the garden. The doorbell rings and her body freezes. It's after midnight. Fighting her fear, she rushes to the window and peers out, relieved to see it's Carolina.

She opens the door and rushes into Carolina's arms. 'Oh, Jess, I had to come straight here. I was asleep but Zara just called and told me about your message. She's babysitting for a friend who's on a night shift so she couldn't come herself.' She leads Jess in and closes the door behind them. 'I can't believe that man. How dare he? Let me get you something to drink.'

'No, I'm fine, thanks. Will you just keep me company for a bit?'

'Of course, love. You know you don't have to ask. I'll stay for as long as you need me. I can only imagine how shaken up you must feel. Zara said that you and Gabriel had really hit it off? How awful for you to have to go through all this.'

Carolina heads into the kitchen, flicking on the kettle.

'It was early days, but I'd started to like him,' Jess admits. 'I don't care about that, though – I care about being lied to. And what it all means.' She turns to her stepmother, reaches for her arm. 'Carolina, I need to ask you something, and it might be difficult to hear, but please just hear me out.'

'I'm not going to like this, am I? But I'm listening.'

Jess takes a deep breath. 'I'm worried about Dad. About what involvement he might have had... in my mum's death.'

Carolina's jaw drops. 'Oh, Jess! Where is this coming from? Is this what that Gabriel's said to you? How could your dad have possibly...'

Jess shakes her head. 'It's just something I need to rule out.' She stares at the floor, unable to look Carolina in the eyes. 'I don't *think* he did it, but I also need to *know* that he didn't, if that makes sense?'

Ignoring the boiled kettle, Carolina sits at the table, buries her head in her hands. 'Yes, I suppose it does. It just feels strange even talking about this. To be honest, it turns me cold. What exactly makes you think this?'

Jess sits beside her. 'I know you loved him. You still do.'

'Yes, we may have had our issues in the end but I care about him a great deal. And I'm telling you now, I can't comprehend for one second that he'd do anything to hurt anyone.' She pauses. 'I know he likes things done his own way. Everything has to fit into his neat little boxes, doesn't it?' She rolls her eyes. 'I think that's what drove me crazy in the end. But he has a good heart and, like I've said before, he adores his girls. Would have done anything for you.'

'That's what's scaring me. If he thought Mum was having an affair, what if in his head he thought I was better off without her in my life? What if he wanted to take me away from her? No court would have let him have me when she was such a good mum, would they?'

Carolina bites her lip. 'No. But I don't think he would have ever expected to get sole custody of you. He was so busy with work, I can't imagine that was his ideal situation. Looking after a toddler isn't easy. He knew you were better off with Lori so I think he would have been happy just to have you in his life. Anyway, they were still together, weren't they? And why do you think Lori was having an affair?'

Jess clears her throat. 'He admitted it. The other day. He doesn't know who it was with, though. But after I told him about the picture then maybe he assumed it must have been Nathaniel?'

Carolina stares at her. 'This is a bit of a shock to me. He never once mentioned that when we were together.'

'And that's a bit strange, isnt' it?'

'I don't know. He's a very private man. Maybe he didn't want me to know.'

Jess concedes this could be true. 'But why was he so adamant that I stay away from Nathaniel after he approached me in the street? Why didn't he want to know why he'd tracked me down?' As she poses this question, something occurs to Jess. 'Unless... it was both of them?'

'What do you mean?'

'What if Dad and Nathaniel did it together?' Even to her own ears it sounds far-fetched, but what was it they said? Often the truth is stranger than fiction.

'Woah, Jess, slow down a minute. That sounds preposterous! Look, I understand, love. You're hurt and angry, and you just want answers. But your dad didn't know that man.'

'He did, though.' Jess tells Carolina about meeting Nathaniel's ex, Elsbeth, and what she revealed about seeing her dad at their flat.

Carolina falls silent for a moment. 'I never knew that,' she says, shaking her head. 'Well, it seems I'm learning a lot about your father tonight. I wish I hadn't driven now – I could do with a drink for the shock. Are you sure about this, Jess? Can you trust that woman?'

'I can't trust anyone,' Jess replies. 'But I can't think of any reason she'd lie. She's put Nathaniel well and truly out of her mind. She's even moved to Spain now. Far away from it all.'

Carolina shakes her head. 'It would kill your dad to know that you're even considering this.' Tears glisten in her eyes.

'I just need to know the truth.'

Carolina pats her hand. 'I know, sweetheart. I do understand. That's all any of us ever want.' She sighs. 'So, what are you going to do?'

'I need to go to the police. They could reopen the case?' She's about to tell Carolina that she needs to get some evidence about where her dad was the night Nathaniel was killed, but one look at Carolina's pale complexion, the tears rolling down her cheeks, tells Jess the poor woman has heard about all she can handle for now. 'I know I don't have evidence but it might be enough that Nathaniel was killed within days of finding me. Right before he was going to tell me what he knew. Surely the police will want to go over it all again? A lot must have changed since the nineties – they must have updated the way they investigate cases.'

'I hate to say it, but you're doing the right thing. I won't stand in your way. In fact, I'll be there to support you. We can do it together.'

'Really?'

Carolina nods. 'I have to take Rocket to the groomer at nine thirty tomorrow morning, but shouldn't be too long. Shall we meet at my place at eleven?'

Jess throws her arms around her. 'Thank you.'

'Will you be okay tonight on your own? You can come home with me? I would stay here but I'm not sure I filled his water bowl this evening.'

'I'll be okay.' It's only a few hours until morning. Jess can get through the night. Besides, she wants to write notes to take to the police. Dates, times. Everything she's learnt. They'll need it all.

On the doorstep, she watches Carolina drive away. She heads inside, fully aware of the devastating impact this will have on Carolina's and Zara's lives.

She's about to close the door when another car pulls up outside, and Harrison jumps out and walks towards her.

FORTY-ONE

NOW

Jess

'You didn't get back to me. I was worried,' Harrison says as he approaches Jess. 'I've been trying to call you. Why aren't you answering? Was that Carolina I just saw leaving?'

'I told Zara about Gabriel and she sent Carolina to check on me.'

'I don't like the sound of that. What happened?'

Jess pulls him inside and locks the door.

'What's going on, Jess?'

She tells him what she found out and prepares for him to gloat. But she should know him better than this, and all he does is take her hand and tells her he's sorry. 'He's a piece of scum. You were right not to trust him. You know, even when I was setting up the cameras, I didn't really think he'd be up to anything.' He pauses.

'I thought you'd be pleased that I didn't trust him.'

'Don't you know me by now? Of course it hurts seeing you with someone else, but that doesn't mean I don't want you to find happiness.'

Jess smiles. His words should be comforting, but at the moment they're lost in a maze. She heads towards the kitchen. 'I need water.' She turns back to Harrison. 'The funny thing is, I'm not upset about the relationship not being what I thought it was. I'd hardly known him long. It's the way he used my mum that makes me angry.' She explains her plan to go to the police in the morning. 'Carolina offered to come with me. I told her I was worried Dad might have been involved somehow.'

Harrison gets two glasses from the cupboard and fills them with water, handing one to Jess. 'That must have been difficult for her to hear.'

'It was,' Jess agrees. 'But she actually listened and took it quite well. I could tell she was devastated, though, that I'd even think that.'

Harrison nods. 'You're the strongest person I know,' he says. 'Many people would have been a wreck if this had happened to them – but you just keep going, even though it must be terrifying not to have any answers. And thinking someone out there believes you know something.'

'I am a bit like a bloodhound, aren't I?' she admits. 'I can't let things rest. Not until they're finished, or I have answers. That's what keeps me going.'

Harrison sips his water. 'I'm staying here tonight, Jess. On the sofa. I hope you understand that it's something I have to do.'

She nods. Not only is she too exhausted to protest, but she'll sleep easier knowing that Harrison is downstairs. 'Don't expect me to make breakfast in the morning.' She forces a smile.

'How do you do that?' he asks.

'What?'

'Keep your sense of humour with all of this going on.'

'Because it feels like it's coming to an end,' she says. 'Once the police know, then I won't have to shoulder this burden on my own. They'll know what to do. I'll tell them about Dad.

About Uncle Neil. My aunt. All of the lies my family have been telling for my whole life.'

'Just remember your dad had an alibi, Jess. You can't fake being in hospital, can you?'

She tells him her theory about her dad working with Nathaniel. 'What if they did it together? What if Mum hadn't told Nathaniel about my dad and vice versa, and they were both angry with her?' Jess is aware of how this sounds, though.

'That's a bit far-fetched, isn't it? Harrison says. 'Anyway, I thought you believed Nathaniel was innocent?'

'I do. It's just... something isn't making sense here. I'm missing something huge.'

'Then you're doing the right thing going to the police.'

'Do you know what's strange?' Jess says. 'When I talk to my dad, he's just, well, my dad, and I can't believe I even think any of this stuff. But as soon as I'm away from him, doubts set in and it all seems to make sense.'

Harrison shrugs. 'Maybe it's denial. Or maybe your dad is just innocent. We need to know, don't we? I have to say, though, Jess, I work with the man every day, and I just can't see it.'

'Tomorrow can't come soon enough.' Jess checks the time on her phone, and is surprised to see it's nearly two a.m. 'Let me get you some sheets and a pillow,' she tells Harrison.

When she comes back, he's lying on the sofa. He sits up to make space and pats the seat beside him. 'Will you sit with me for a bit? I know it's late, but—'

Jess's phone rings. It's Zara. 'I'll call my sister back later,' she tells Harrison, sitting beside him. There are some things she needs to say to him first.

'I'm sorry for the way things ended with us,' she says. 'I did love you.'

He smiles sadly. 'I know. You were just being honest about what you wanted. Or what you didn't want. I can't hold that against you. I've had time to reflect on it now, and I blame myself for a lot of it.'

Jess stares at him. 'What do you mean? It's not your fault I don't want to have a family.'

'No, but it's my fault that I was trying to make you do all the compromising. I couldn't see past my own wishes. But I've realised that I don't have to be so set on being a father. Not if it means losing the only woman I've ever loved.' He looks away.

Stunned into silence, Jess can't find any words within her. 'No. You shouldn't have to compromise on something so important.'

'It's not a compromise. It's about me realising what the most important thing is.'

There are tears in her eyes as she turns to him and reaches for his hands. 'Can you give me some time? With all of this going on, and with all that happened with Gabriel, I just can't rush into any decision. About anything.'

He winks. 'Take as long as you need.' He folds his arms. 'By the way, why is it so cold in here?'

Jess hasn't had a chance to call anyone about the boiler; it's been the last thing on her mind. 'Boiler broke,' she explains. 'I need to call someone.'

'I'll take a look at it,' Harrison offers, pulling himself up.

She thanks him, even though she's sure he won't be able to fix it. She knows it's important to him to try, to do something to help her.

Upstairs, she gets ready for bed before remembering she needs to return Zara's call. There's a favour she needs to ask her sister, and she only hopes Zara doesn't ask any questions. Jess won't throw the bomb that will explode her sister's life. Not until she knows for sure.

Her head sinks back into the pillow as she waits for her sister to answer.

'Sis!' Zara exclaims. 'Didn't you get my messages? Are you

okay? All I got from Mum just now is that you're okay and she's too tired to talk tonight. She promised to call me back in the morning. She did sound exhausted. Not herself.'

Jess hates doing this to her sister. 'I think it was probably just all the worry about me. And traipsing over here at midnight. It's taken its toll on her.'

'Yeah,' Zara agrees. 'She was sick with worry when I messaged her, but I couldn't come myself – I've been looking after Audrey's kids. Anyway, are you okay? I can't believe Gabriel. I've blocked him on my phone and all social media. Ryan has too. What a scumbag. He shouldn't be allowed to do that. Isn't it illegal or something?'

'I suppose he was just doing what he thought would advance his career.'

'No excuse,' Zara snorts. 'I feel terrible. I'm the one who suggested you two would hit it off.'

'It's nobody's fault but his.'

'Can you forgive me?'

'You don't even have to ask me that.' Jess pauses. 'But actually, I do have a favour to ask. And I need you just to trust me. Please don't ask any questions. Not yet. I'll explain everything when I can.'

Zara hesitates. 'That sounds worrying. But I trust you know what you're doing. So what do you need?'

'I need to know what Dad's plans are in the morning. Well, for the whole day. And it can't come from me. Can you call him early and find out?'

'Is that it? But why do—'

'No questions, remember?'

'Ugh. Okay.'

Jess assures her again that she will explain everything as soon as she can, and they end the call with Zara promising to send her their father's itinerary first thing in the morning.

As she pulls the duvet up to her chin and closes her eyes,

she feels strangely at peace. Harrison is downstairs, and she's sure she can feel warmth coming from the radiator. Tonight she will be safe. And tomorrow, if the police listen to her, this will all be over.

FORTY-TWO

NOW

Jess

This is it. Whatever happens this morning, whether she uncovers anything or not, something will change today. Something which will lead to justice for her mother. Jess can't bear to think about her dad. The ramifications of this will spread far and wide, the name he's worked so hard to build for himself will be sullied. Despite this, Jess is more determined than ever to see it through. Everything has changed now, but she needs to tread carefully. Still, in her heart she hopes she is wrong.

Zara's message came at seven o'clock. Their dad will be at a conference in Moorgate this morning, and is unlikely to be back in the office until after lunch. This gives Jess plenty of time, and she cancels the photoshoots she has planned today, something she's never done before. A nasty bug, she explains to the clients she's had to let down. To make up for the inconvenience – not to mention the lie – Jess offers to reschedule them all at half price.

And now she's in Chiswick, letting herself in to her father's house. What she's doing makes her the worst kind of daughter.

It's eight-thirty and she's not due at Carolina's for another two and a half hours. Plenty of time to root through her dad's things before driving to Kingston.

This house wasn't the place Jess grew up in; she might not feel like such an intruder if it had been. And on top of that, she doesn't even know what she's looking for. There's a home office upstairs, as good a place as any to begin. If Jess has learnt anything from Gabriel, and even Nathaniel, it's that people with something to hide always leave a trace somewhere.

It's tidy in here, and more homely than the rest of the house; no surprise given how important work is to Danny. *Like father, like daughter.* She glances at the large square framed photo hanging on the wall – their dad with his arms around young Jess and Zara. Ten and five years old they would have been. It's always been Jess's favourite photo. She looks away, forcing her attention back to what she's doing here.

Jess makes her way towards the black filing cabinet in the corner of the room. It's bound to be more work files, but she can't leave before checking. She pulls open the top drawer, and flicks through all the files. Among them are mortgage documents, folders for various property information. Nothing that provides Jess with any answers.

Her phone rings and she ignores it. It's probably Harrison; she'll call him when she's finished here. There's more of the same in the middle drawer, but she carefully checks every document.

She's expecting more of the same when she opens the third drawer, but unlike the other two, it's locked. Why would her father lock anything up here when he lives alone? When there's nobody to hide things from?

Frantically, she searches his desk drawer again, this time looking for a key. There's no key small enough but when she tips out his pen holder, along with the pens and scissors, a silver key drops onto the desk. The right size. Her heart races. 'Please let this be it,' she whispers.

She rushes back to the filing cabinet and pushes the key into the lock, taking a deep breath as it glides inside and turns.

There's only one file inside and it's labelled '*Personal*' in her father's handwriting. She pulls it out and checks the contents. His passport is in there, along with his birth certificate. Despite what she's doing, Jess smiles to think of her dad as a baby. Babies are innocent, and that's what she wants to believe her dad is. She pulls it out and studies it. That's when she notices the piece of paper stuck behind it. She peels it off and reads the words, staring at them in the hope that given enough time, they will make sense.

But the enormity of what she's looking at shatters her existence.

FORTY-THREE

NOW

Jess

By ten thirty, Jess is sitting in her car outside Carolina's building. There were several choices she could have made as she left her father's house, the piece of paper folded neatly in her pocket. Going straight to the police, for one. Not wasting another second. But she will stick to the plan; Carolina needs to be told what Jess has found, no matter the consequences. And there was nobody else Jess would want to go to first.

With no warning, nausea erupts inside her and Jess only just flings the car door open in time to lean out and avoid throwing up all over herself. There's an old bottle of water in the glove compartment – who knows how long it's been there – but Jess grabs it and gulps it down, swirling some around her mouth to wash away the vile, bitter taste.

She's screwing the lid back on when Carolina's Volvo appears, her stepmum waving to her as she passes Jess's car. Jess manages to smile as she opens her door, ready to face what's to come.

I only have to do this once. And never again will I have to experience this horrific pain. And fear for the future.

Carolina carries Rocket from the back seat and clips his lead onto his collar. 'Are you okay, love? I bet you didn't get any sleep, did you?'

'A little. I'm okay. Just ready for what today will bring.' Jess takes in Carolina's appearance: the dark rings under her eyes, the heavily applied mask of foundation. Her make-up does little to revive her fatigued skin. 'I'm sorry you didn't get any rest.'

'We'll get through this together,' Carolina says. 'Okay? Just come in for a minute while I get Rocket some food. Then we can get going. We're doing all right for time, aren't we?'

Jess nods. 'Have you heard from Dad?'

'Not since I called him when he was at your place. Look, I know you're scared, but you're doing the right thing. And the police will clear this all up, I know it. And then everything will be okay. Well, as okay as it can be.'

Carolina opens the door and lets Rocket off the lead. He trots in and heads straight for the kitchen, sniffing around in search of food. 'I'll just sort him out, love.' She gestures to her walking boots and old jeans. 'And change out of these old things. I can't turn up at the police station dressed like this, can I? Why don't you wait in there?'

Jess senses someone is in the living room before she sees him. Her father. He's sitting in Carolina's armchair staring at Jess, leaning forwards with his elbows resting on his legs.

'I'm sure you can understand why Carolina had to call me?' he says.

She should have foreseen this. 'Are you here to tell me what you did, then?'

'I did nothing, Jess. How can you think so low of me?' He thumps his chest. 'It hurts right here that you could believe I'd do anything like that. I know I'm not perfect, but murder? Especially your mum. I loved her. It wasn't always easy between us, but what relationship is perfect? Look at you and Harrison.'

Jess's legs are shaking, so she reaches for the arm of the sofa and sits opposite her father. She wants to wait for Carolina to come back – her stepmum needs to be here to hear what Jess has found. She glances at the door, but there's no sign of her yet.

'You've got to stop all this, Jess,' her father says. 'What good does it do? None of us can change the past, can we? What we need to do, as a family, is put it all behind us.'

Does her dad really believe this is possible? He thinks there's a solution to every problem and he won't see that this time there isn't one. At least not one that leaves their family intact. She shakes her head. 'It's not as simple as that, though, is it, Dad? So many lies have been told in this family, lies masquerading as the truth. It's got to stop.'

Danny stands, walks towards the window. 'And you think going to the police is the answer? To tell them what? That your father killed your mother twenty-eight years ago?'

'Did you?' This is what she wants to know above all else. 'Please, just tell me the truth, Dad.'

He's silent for a moment, giving Jess time to imagine the words flowing from his mouth. *I did it. I'm sorry. I killed your mother, Jess.*

'How could I have done it?' Danny objects. 'I was in hospital. I developed a hernia and had to have surgery. You know all this, Jess.'

'It was planned surgery, wasn't it? You knew the dates and times you'd be in hospital.' The perfect alibi.

'What's that got to do with anything?'

'It means... you could have got someone else...'

'Don't even say it, Jess. Words can't be taken back once they're spoken. Have you thought about that? You go to the police and make them investigate me and then what? Even if they do – which is doubtful given the lack of evidence – they won't find anything. Because I *didn't* do it. And you'll have broken our relationship. Irreparably. There's no way back if you do this.'

The weight of his words lies heavily on her, crushing her chest. She reaches into her bag, feels for the paper.

Carolina appears, Rocket wagging his tail behind her. 'I'm sorry, Jess. I really am. But I had to talk to your dad. How could I not? I couldn't have you thinking that he'd done that to your mum. I couldn't sleep at all last night worrying about it. It's just... so awful.'

'I trusted you,' Jess says. She can't look at Carolina.

'Please, just hear him out. Do it for me.'

Jess can barely take in her words. Inside her, darkness is descending and she's beginning to wonder how she'll play this now. 'I've heard everything I need to hear,' she says. She turns to her father. 'You told Zara you'd be at a work conference in Moorgate this morning. Another lie.'

'I didn't want to worry her. If I'd said I was coming to talk to Carolina, then she would have known something was wrong. The two of you have always been close. She would have told you and—'

'You were worried I'd go to straight to the police without picking up Carolina first.'

Danny stares at his shoes. Jess knows he loves her; if she can just wear him down, make guilt gnaw away at him, then surely he'll do the right thing and confess? 'Did you plan this with Nathaniel?'

'What? No! I swear to you – I didn't know who he was until he was arrested. I'd never seen him in my life.'

'Where were you last Monday night?' Jess demands.

'What? Why?'

'Just tell me!'

Danny pulls out his phone and scrolls through his calendar. 'I was... at a work meeting. Hold on, that was the night

Nathaniel was killed, wasn't it?' He thrusts out his phone. 'See. Look what that says.'

It proves nothing. 'How can I believe you, Dad, when you've already lied to me?'

'It's called trust, love,' Carolina says. 'It's called knowing your dad inside and out, because you do. I do too. He's always been there for you, hasn't he?'

Jess nods. Despite what he's done, and all the lies, he was always there for her. She can't even recall him ever losing his temper with her or Zara.

'Then please just trust him,' Carolina urges. 'Let this go, Jess. Too many people will get hurt otherwise.'

Jess turns to her stepmum and notices Carolina's pallid complexion is even more ghostly, the dark crescents under her eyes larger than they were when she arrived.

'Okay,' Jess says. It's time to end this. It's breaking all of them. 'So, you're promising me that there are no more lies? There's nothing else about Mum's death I don't know about?'

Danny crosses to the sofa and perches on the edge of the seat. 'No, I swear. Now, please, Jess, can we just put an end to this?'

It's time. Jess reaches into her pocket and pulls out the folded sheet of paper. A yellowing marriage certificate, confirmation of the union between Daniel Richard Moore and Marion Carolina Hughes.

'What's that?' her father asks. His face crumples in on itself, because Jess is certain he recognises what she holds in her hand. It's been in his possession for long enough.

Behind her, Carolina moves closer, her eyes wide with horror as she registers what Jess has found.

'This is your marriage certificate,' she says, looking at each of them in turn. 'Only the strange thing is, it's dated April 1988. Not 1996 when you both claimed you got married.'

Carolina lunges forwards, swiping at the paper, but Jess is too fast, pulling it out of her reach and darting towards the door.

Her father stands, walks towards her. 'I... I can explain, Jess. I'm sorry. It was... I made a mistake not telling you. Please just let me explain.'

Jess has never heard her father begging for anything.

Carolina pushes him backwards and he stumbles onto the sofa. 'Don't say a word, Danny. I'm warning you. You need to keep your mouth shut.'

'He doesn't have to say anything,' Jess says. 'I have all I need to know. And all the police will need to know to open up the case again.' She sounds confident, but a tsunami of nausea swirls inside her, and she doesn't know how much longer she'll be able to hold it back.

'I can explain, Jess,' her father begs again.

'Go on then, Danny, the great charismatic entrepreneur. What have you got to say for yourself? How will you worm your way out of this one?'

He's a shrunken man, and in spite of everything, sadness swells inside Jess. 'I won't even try,' he says. 'I'm going to tell you the truth.'

'Stop!' Carolina screams and lunges at him.

He grabs hold of her arms and grips them tightly. 'I need to do this, Carolina. There have been too many lies. It's time. We've been hiding for too long. Didn't we know that one day it would catch up with us?'

'No!' she screams again. 'Don't do this, Danny.' She sinks to the floor, grabbing his legs. 'Please don't do this. You don't have to say anything. What about Zara?'

Her father's face is twisted in anguish. 'Jess is our daughter too,' he cries.

Jess knows what he's about to tell her, and she shrinks back against the wall, letting it take her weight. 'Jess deserves to know the truth,' Danny continues, letting go of Carolina's arms. 'I should have found a way to tell her years ago. I should never have let it come to this.'

While Carolina drops to the floor and curls up in a ball, sobbing, Danny begins to speak. 'I never told Lori this, but I was married to Carolina when I met her. We'd been married for five years at that point. Then Lori was sent by an agency to do some temping at my office, and I couldn't keep my eyes off her.' He glances at Carolina before turning back to Jess. 'I know it was wrong. I was happily married. I loved my wife, but...'

On the floor, Carolina wails.

'We couldn't have children,' Danny continues. 'We were trying from the moment we got married, and month after month, nothing happened. It destroyed us. I know there's lots of help nowadays for people struggling to conceive, but in the late eighties and early nineties, IVF wasn't as common. And Carolina was ashamed. She didn't want to talk to any doctors, or get any help. She just kept hoping it would happen. She pushed me away for a long time. But it's no excuse.'

Carolina's moans continue to mingle with Danny's words. 'Meanwhile, I did something terrible, and I started having an affair with your mum. I was torn. I really fell for her, even though I loved my wife. I should have told her I was married, but I kept putting it off and then it was too late. We were having a relationship. A proper one.' He stares at Jess. 'It's possible. To love two people at the same time. People don't want to believe that, because it shatters everything we believe about morality, and society, but it's the truth. You can love different things about them both. You can need them both.'

Jess shakes her head. These words are coming from a stranger, not the loving father who raised her.

'I should have told your mum that I was married. She would have put a stop to it then and there because that's the kind of person Lori was. She never would have carried on with me if she'd known, no matter how strong her feelings grew as time went on. But I was a coward and I kept my mouth shut. To her and to Carolina. And then—'

'I came along,' Jess mutters.

Danny nods. 'Yes. It was a complete shock. Lori had been on the pill. It wasn't meant to happen. A terrible irony when Carolina was trying so hard every month. But as guilty as I felt, I was so happy. I wanted you desperately from the second she told me. But it made my life more... complicated. I struggled with what I was doing, but threw myself into work and... tried to block it out. I'm good at doing that. I knew it would destroy Carolina if she ever found out about you. I had to be careful.' He glances at Carolina, who's staring into space, her wails subsiding.

'But then Lori found out. She followed me one night and saw me go home to Carolina. Before that she'd believed I lived in the flat I rented to keep the two parts of my life separate.' There are tears in his eyes now. 'She wanted nothing more to do with me. It was over. In a way, it was good, a decision had been made for me so I didn't have to make it myself. Only it came with a price. Lori wouldn't let me see you.'

Jess gasps. 'So that's why you did it? You wanted to get her out of your life so you could keep me?'

He shakes his head. 'No!'

'She wasn't having an affair, was she? Because you weren't even together. That's why she was free to be with Nathaniel French, or whoever she wanted to be with. Another lie!'

'I know. But you have to believe me when I say I didn't want to hurt Lori to get custody of you. I was ready to take her to court. To do things properly. I admit I tried to see you and I turned up at her mum's house one time. I was angry. I thought scaring her would make her see sense.' Danny grips his hair, pulls at it. 'She had it in her head that I was some kind of monster. That I wasn't a fit father to you. But she was wrong. I'd just done something stupid. Unforgiveable, I know. It had no bearing on my love for you. I'd found out she was planning to take you away from London. Move across the country. A friend of mine was a solicitor and she explained that the best chance of getting custody of you was if I was in a stable and loving relationship. And I was. I had Carolina. But it meant I had to confess to her. And break her heart.'

Danny stops and turns to Carolina, reaching down for her hand. She snatches it away and even through her waterfall of tears, Jess can see she's glaring at him. 'That was the worst night of my life,' he says. 'And yours too, love. I told you that there was a way we could be a family, and I'll never forget how your eyes shone, just for a moment, before I told you what that would mean. That I was already a father.'

And now it is Danny's turn to shed tears. 'You said you forgave me. You said we could make it work. Me, you and little Jess. You would be the mother you'd longed to be. I told you we would take Lori to court, to prove that we would be more stable parents for Jess, that we'd give her everything she needed. And you agreed. But you had a different plan, didn't you, love? A different way to have Jess in our lives.'

Although Jess has known since her father started talking, maybe even before that, she's crushed by the weight of her world collapsing around her. She stares at Carolina and no longer sees the woman who raised her, who made sure she had all the love she'd ever need. The woman who sat patiently with her for hours at a time when Jess had meltdowns because she couldn't handle what had happened. Carolina was the one who wiped away her tears, and told her that everything would be okay.

Danny continues speaking, turning to Jess now. 'She... waited until I was in hospital. She knew I'd never let her confront Lori. You have to believe me, Jess. I could have had no idea what would happen. What she would do... to your mother.'

Jess sinks to the floor, her tears soaking her coat. 'When did you know?'

'It was a few days after I got home.' He glares at Carolina. 'Tell her!' he shouts. 'It's time to end this now. And face the consequences.'

Finally, Carolina looks across at Jess. 'I... I just wanted to see her, that's all. To have a look at the woman my husband had spent five years of his life with, while he was married to me. Can you imagine how that feels? How it eats away at you until you have nothing left to like about yourself. You feel like *nothing*.'

'She didn't know!' Jess screams. 'None of it was Mum's fault!' She turns to her dad. 'It was *yours*!'

Carolina hangs her head. 'I know that. I've had years to let that sink in. To live with my actions.'

'What did you do to her?' Jess demands. 'Tell me!'

Carolina is silent for so long that Jess fears she will never speak again.

'Go on,' Danny urges. 'You need to tell her. It's Jess. She deserves to know.

When she finally speaks, her voice is barely above a whisper. 'I found out that Lori was staying at her mum's house. Danny had told me she was planning to leave London and take you away. I went there early the day after your dad's operation, while he was still in hospital. I saw her leaving with you in your buggy. I can't tell you what that did to me. It made me feel dead inside. I was used to my friends all having babies before me, and yes it hurt, but I was okay at dealing with that. But seeing Lori with you, my husband's child... You won't know this but Danny and I met at school. *School,* Jess. We were fifteen. There was never anyone else, for either of us. It was just the two of us, he was my *family*.' She wipes her eyes with her sleeve.

'I don't care!' Jess yells. 'Just tell me what you did!

'She walked around the park, and I kept my distance, but I

followed her. When she started singing to you, I couldn't take it any more. This rage took over me. I wanted to hurt her. It was as if I wasn't me... someone else had taken over my body. I swear to you, Jess, I wasn't in my right mind. I happened to spot a pile of rocks and rubble someone had discarded. I grabbed a large rock...'

'That's enough,' Danny demands.

'No. I want to hear it.' For the first time in her life, Jess needs to know all the details.

Carolina sobs. 'I threw it at her. I didn't plan to. Like I said, it felt like it wasn't even me doing it. There was blood dripping from her face, and... she didn't care about herself, she just rushed around to check you were okay in your buggy.' Carolina hangs her head. 'When I witnessed that... that pure love she had for you... I lost control. I grabbed the brick...'

'Stop!' Jess cries. She is done. She can't listen to another word.

But Carolina ignores her. 'Lori saw me. She knew who I was. And all she cared about was that you would be okay.'

Silence falls upon them as the three of them sit; all of them know this is the beginning of the end.

Jess is the first one to break it. She turns to her dad. 'You *knew* this. And you didn't tell the police.'

Danny hangs his head. 'I was stuck, Jess. Ravaged with guilt, because my actions had caused Carolina to do this. The infertility... it all messed with her head. And my affair. Not even just a brief fling, but a five-year-long life I had with another woman. *I* was responsible for what happened.' He looks at Carolina. 'We both were. So, we were bound together by this terrible secret.'

There are so many questions vying for attention in Jess's mind. 'How did the police not find out you were married?'

'I've often wondered that. My best guess is that they were overstretched, and not as thorough as they could have been.

But I had an alibi, remember? They weren't looking at me at all.'

Jess lets this sink in. 'You took me to Portugal. We were on our own, Carolina wasn't there. I'd remember that.'

'Carolina left me,' Danny says. 'Straight after that morning in the park. And not long after that I took you abroad.' He glances at Carolina. 'But a few years later we found our way back to each other. We supported each other through it all. That's how we managed to work. And how could either of us have ever been with other people when we carried... all of this wherever we went?'

'Zara,' Jess says. 'How did—'

'An unexpected twist of fate,' Danny explains. 'Somehow, Carolina fell pregnant, and then we had even more of a reason to hide the truth. From everyone. Please don't think it was easy, Jess. It's tormented us both for years. All we could do was try to be the best parents we could to you both.'

While keeping the worst kind of lie. Jess is suffocating in this room, in this house. If she doesn't get some air soon, she won't survive this. 'Nathaniel French,' she says. 'You were going to let him go to prison for something he didn't do.'

'No,' Danny insists. It would never have come to that. The police couldn't find evidence because there wasn't any.'

Jess stares at her father. 'He found out, didn't he? And you...' She can't bring herself to say the words.

Danny nods. 'After he approached you, I had to find him. To see what he knew. He told me that he'd found out I was married, and that he was going to tell you everything. He said the police wouldn't listen to him if he went himself, that it would be better coming from you.'

'You killed him to stop him talking to me.'

'No. Not myself, at least. But having a bit of money can buy you anything. And it wasn't hard to find a couple of thugs who would scare him off for us. They weren't supposed to kill him,

Jess. I didn't want any more bloodshed. I think he fought back and got a good look at their faces so they panicked. They'd already done time in prison and didn't want to go back there.'

Somehow Jess finds the strength to pull herself up. 'I thought there was nothing you could say that would make me think any worse of you. Of both of you. And what about that black car that nearly ploughed into me? That was you too, wasn't it?'

'I was never going to hurt you,' Carolina says. 'I never would. You're my daughter. That was just meant to scare you, to stop you wanting to pursue this. But you smashed into that taxi. I didn't want that to happen.'

'I am *not* your daughter.' Jess fumbles in her pocket for her phone.

'What are you doing?' Carolina says, wildness replacing the sadness in her eyes.

'Calling the police. I've heard enough.'

'No, you can't! Please, Jess. It will tear Zara apart. Please don't do that to your sister. To your dad. He was just protecting me.' Carolina pulls herself up and swipes at Jess's phone, snatching it from her hand. 'I can't let you do this, Jess!' she shrieks. 'I can't go to prison!'

Before Jess can react, Danny grabs Carolina and pulls the phone from her grasp. 'It's over,' he tells her. 'Let Jess make the call. It's what we deserve.'

'It's what *you* deserve,' Carolina screams. 'This is *your* fault! I'm not going to prison because of what you did to me.' And then she runs, faster than Jess would have believed possible, through the living room and hall and out into the communal car park in front of the building.

Jess sprints after her, and she can hear Danny following her, but he's not in the fittest of health and he lags behind.

She sees and hears the scene play out before it actually happens. The busy road outside. The lorry making it's way too quickly along the road. Carolina's body being dragged underneath it. The squeal of the tires as the lorry driver makes an emergency stop.

Her dad's scream as he takes in what's just happened. As he is forced to confront the devastating cost of all his lies.

FORTY-FOUR

NOW

Belle

Belle walks along the beachfront, her footsteps slowed by the wind. They've warned that a storm will hit Cornwall's shores before lunchtime, but she needs to get her steps in. She checks her Fitbit and rolls her eyes. Four hundred and ninety-seven. At least ten thousand, the GP had insisted. Most days she manages it, on others she falls far short.

Still, she tries not to let it get to her. In her twenties, she'd never been one to panic about small things. Or big things. Laid-back Belle, her friends had called her. 'Ha,' she says aloud to the rolling sea. How they'd laugh at her now if they could see how she'd turned out. Most of her friendships fizzled out long ago, though, so who is left from her past?

She approaches the newsagents and heads inside for the morning paper. She knows it's old fashioned to read a newspaper, rather than catching up with the news on her phone. That's what you're supposed to do nowadays, isn't it? To be relevant. But phones give Belle a headache and she'll be damned if she cares what anyone thinks of her. That's something, at least, which hasn't changed about her. She loathes computers too. Anything to do with technology. It's not about her age, or the fact that she was in her thirties before mobile phones were a thing. And she's not even *that* old. No, it's just who she is. What she prefers.

The smiling man is behind the counter again today. Belle knows he's the manager, yet he doesn't think it's below him to serve behind the till. She admires that. Plus, he always has a cheerful word, no matter what time of day she comes in. She should at least ask him his name. That's what most people would do, isn't it?

'Hi,' he calls, waving at her. 'You're braving it, then? You do know there's a storm fast approaching?'

'I like to live dangerously,' she says, smiling. 'Just the paper today.' Her eyes flick to the bars of chocolate strategically arranged below the till. She grabs a Twix. 'And maybe one of these. To keep me going when the storm hits.' She chuckles, then reaches over to the newspapers.

That's when she sees the name. Lori Gray. She grabs the paper and scrutinises the words, scanning the article until she's taken in the important details. Finally there are answers to the Lori Gray murder case. Her ex-partner's wife. Carolina Moore.

Belle throws some change on the counter and rushes out.

'Are you okay?' the shop manager asks, calling after her, but Belle ignores him.

She sits on the beach, the wind blustering around her, and reads the whole article. 'Poor Jess,' she whispers to the sea. How horrific for Lori's daughter to find out like that. And equally as bad is that her father knew all about it. For all these years. Twenty-eight – Belle knows, because she's kept track of every one of them. Lori's murder hit her hard, and she's never been the same since.

Belle closes her eyes and remembers sitting in the Block-buster staffroom, comforting Lori as she opened her heart and revealed everything. But she'd never said a word about being worried about Danny or his wife. She'd barely mentioned them. Belle would have gone to the police otherwise. Yes, she definitely would have.

She should have anyway. The guilt of it is something she's lived with for most of her adult life. Lori was her friend and Belle let her down. She should have reported to them what Lori had been doing, how she'd tried to rid the world – or at least some of London – of adulterous men. If Belle had only done this, the police might not have been so set on the idea that it was Nathaniel French. Their enquiries might have led them to find out about Carolina.

Anyway, Belle had thought nothing of that because everyone knew it was Nathaniel, didn't they?

And now Belle has learnt that Lori and Nathaniel French had been in a relationship. Why didn't her friend tell her? She just has to trust that Lori had her reasons.

Belle looks up and watches the sea hammer against the shore. How strange that nature can be so beautiful yet so destructive and dangerous, she thinks.

'I'm a stupid fool,' she says. 'I let you down, Lori. Your Jess should have had answers years ago, and it's my fault that she didn't.'

But Belle was keeping Lori's secret, as she'd promised her friend she would. *'I can't have another person on this earth knowing what I did. I can't risk Jess ever finding out when she's older.'*

This is what's kept Belle silent for all these years. How could she ever go back on a promise she made to her friend? Lori would never have gone back on her word. She was a decent person. Someone with a pure heart. She just took the wrong path sometimes.

Waves crash down and smother the sand by Belle's feet. She needs to get going. It won't be long before debris is flying everywhere and trees are uprooted. Danger to life, they say this storm will cause. Just like Danny and Carolina were a danger to Lori's life.

She pictures her friend – small and pretty. Innocent in so many ways. Full of hope for the future. And all of it wiped out. It had taken Belle years to come to terms with it. She'd tried everything not to have to deal with it: drink, men, even experimenting with drugs. None of it could erase the pain, or fill the gaping void that Lori had left in her life. Belle should have turned up at that bar that night. Instead, she'd been with that waste-of-time jerk she'd been a bit obsessed with. If she'd only told him to take a hike. Then the outcome for Lori would surely have been different.

Belle's willing to bet that a lot of men out there were grateful that they'd only known her friend as Lizzi. That way when it was all over the news, they could ignore it, even though Lori's face was plastered all over every newspaper for months. Every television screen in the London area. Probably all over the country too. What kind of people inhabit this world? Those men would have all breathed a sigh of relief when the police arrested Nathaniel French. Now they could all stay silent.

Belle needs to find Lori's daughter. She will drive to London. Explain to her what Lori revealed to her that night. Sometimes promises need to be broken for the greater good.

She begins to fold the paper but her eyes fix on the picture of Jess Moore. The spitting image of her beautiful mother. And Lori's words speak to her as if she's standing right here on this windswept beach.

'I can't risk Jess ever finding out when she's older.'

With tears in her eyes, Belle folds the paper under her arm and heads back to the newsagent to ask the manager his name.

It's what Lori would want her to do. Live her life. Seize whatever happiness and beauty she can in this cold, cruel world.

And then she will go home, eat her Twix, and get stuck into the new romance novel she bought the other day.

EPILOGUE

TWO YEARS LATER

Jess

Jess stares out of her bedroom window, watching the children in the playground across the road. It's quiet here, and some days she misses the bustle of Camden. The streets teeming with bodies, everyone with somewhere urgent to be. But she left that behind because what she wanted – needed – was peace, serenity. A park minutes from her doorstep. And she wasn't willing to go outside of London to get it. She is a Londoner, just like her mother was, and this is where she'll stay. Chingford is nice. Lori would have liked it, Jess is sure of that.

'Are you ready to go?'

Jess turns and smiles at Harrison. 'Yep. I'm ready.'

It's still difficult for her to face walks around the park, but with his help she's managed it every day for a few months now. With the help of her counsellor, Jess realised that she needed to face her fears, not run from them. What she's learnt to do is confront them, and fight them with every inch of her being. It helps that Lori loved walking her around the park. It was her happy place. And Jess wants to carry on this legacy. It's one of the few things that can bring her closer to her mother.

It also helps Jess to know that it wasn't a random attack by a stranger, and that Lori wasn't just in the wrong place at the wrong time. That's what has haunted Jess all these years. But now she knows that it wouldn't have happened to anyone else that morning. It was meant only for Lori.

Of course, Jess hasn't been able to do this without Harrison. Not yet. That will come with time. Every journey begins with one step, she reminds herself on those days she feels defeated.

They reach the park, and Harrison squeezes her hand. 'What shall we have for dinner tonight?' he asks, and Jess knows this is his way of distracting her.

'I fancy curry,' she says, gripping his hand more tightly.

He nods. 'Mmm, sounds good to me. 'I'll drive and pick it up. Remember last time – we had to wait nearly two hours! We weren't even hungry by the time it finally arrived.'

'Good point,' Jess agrees.

'And we've still got that bottle of red in the cupboard, haven't we?'

'Yeah, but...' Jess stops herself. She's not ready to tell Harrison yet. It's too early. She wants to give it a few more weeks, until her twelve-week scan, and then she can show him the photo. It has to be special; this is a huge moment for them.

'But what?' he asks.

'Nothing, I was about to say I'd prefer Prosecco, but red is fine.' She'll make an excuse not to have any later. Hopefully he won't notice what she's doing.

They walk a bit further until Jess stops by a bench opposite the lake. 'Can we... sit here for a while?'

Harrison raises his eyebrows. 'Really? Yeah, of course. Let's do it. Are you sure you'll be okay?'

She nods. They've never done this before; usually it's a hasty walk, with Jess practically pulling him along. 'I'll be just fine now.' They sit down and she watches a dad sailing a remote-controlled boat with his young son. They look so content, and Jess wonders if, overlying all the difficulty, the tantrums, sleepless nights, early mornings, this is what parenthood means. 'I feel like everything's changed' she explains. 'Everything feels... better.'

Harrison smiles. 'Does that mean you'll—'

'No. I'm not ready to talk to my father. Or visit him in that place.' As much as she won't set foot inside her father's prison, she would never try to stop Harrison going. Jess accepts that he has to.

At her father's request, Harrison took over the company when her father was handed his sentence. She knows why Danny offered it to him, and gave away the most important thing in his life. It was his way of trying to make things up to Jess in some way. And Jess has come to realise that no matter how much Danny thought he loved her and Zara, his business always came first. She believes that, ultimately, this is the main reason he protected Carolina. He didn't want his life to unravel, to lose it all.

'Are Zara and Ryan still coming for dinner tomorrow?' Harrison asks.

'Yes. I said I'd attempt a roast dinner,' Jess says.

'I'm glad you two are okay.'

Jess had feared that in the aftermath of all the revelations, and the role Jess had in bringing them to light, Zara would turn against her. That she'd shut Jess out of her life. And her sister *had* found it difficult, her life shattered in a way that Jess is only too familiar with. But in time she'd let Jess back in, and they had supported each other through the worst days and nights. Jess is aware that Zara visits both her parents in prison, but they never discuss when she does, or what Zara talks to them about. It is nothing to do with Jess. They are now their own separate family.

'I meant to tell you, I bumped into your uncle the other day.'

'Oh?' When she'd first learnt the truth, Jess's aunt had rushed round with offers to help in any way she could. They'd had no idea, she'd insisted. Jess had nodded and smiled, but simmering away was resentment that they'd treated Lori so badly, made her last years alive hell.

'Yeah, it was interesting. He said he was leaving Mionie. That he finally had the guts to walk away from his sham of a marriage. His words, not mine.' Harrison smiles. 'I think in a way, Lori has inspired us all to be better people. To live more meaningful lives.'

Jess nestles against him. 'I like that. My mum would have liked that.'

They sit quietly, letting the sun soak their skin. And Jess feels lighter, more free, than she's ever felt.

'Me and you, just us two,' Harrison says, wrapping his arm around her.

Jess giggles. 'Did you just quote *Sex and the City*?'

'Well, you made me watch it enough, didn't you? Anyway, I thought it would make you laugh. But those words are true for us, aren't they? And we'll have an amazing future, just you and me, kid.'

Jess punches his arm. 'Why don't you just quit while you're ahead!'

She nestles back into his arms, smiling. *Just us three.*

Harrison

They sit on the park bench, basking in the rays of the sun, and peace floats over him. He's been worried about Jess, wondering whether living so close to a park was a good idea after all, but she was adamant that it's what she wanted. Lori had loved living in Clapham opposite the park, and he knows

Jess is doing this to feel close to her mother in some small way.

And to his surprise, today she seems to have really turned a corner. It's hard to believe they're actually sitting in this beautiful park, and that it happened at Jess's request. Usually her aim is to walk as quickly as she can to complete the circuit before heading straight home. Not today, though.

Everything will be okay. For both of them.

And Harrison means every word he says to Jess. He's made his peace with not being a father. Yes, it's been difficult to turn his back on that dream, but it's more important to him that he has Jess in his life, that he can support her through everything. He will never let her down. Not that she needs his help – Jess is the strongest, most independent woman he knows, despite what she's been through. And it only makes him love her even more.

He kisses the top of her head, breathes in the scent of her shampoo. Grapefruit, he thinks, and it makes his stomach rumble. He wishes he could scrape Jess's pain away, remove it so that it can't touch her again.

A lump forms in his throat. The guilt threatening to floor him. *Not now*, he prays. *Don't ruin this moment. This is about Jess, not me.*

But even as he listens to her talking about the film they can watch on Netflix with their curry tonight, some comedy he's not heard of – Jess refuses to watch or read thrillers – his mind plays over the conversation he had with Danny, just after Nathaniel French had approached Jess. The deal Harrison made with the devil. He can even picture the khaki green jumper Jess's father was wearing that day Harrison confronted him at his house, and told him he knew that he and Carolina had been married before Danny met Lori.

Danny's face had become translucent, and he'd had to sit down at the kitchen table. 'How did you know?' he'd demanded.

But Harrison had refused to tell him. How would it look

that he'd hired a private detective at an astronomical price, in the hopes of finding some answers for Jess? He hadn't even cared that it wouldn't change Jess's mind about their relationship. In fact, since Gabriel had shown up that had looked unlikely anyway, but he'd only wanted Jess to find peace.

But the moment Harrison had found out about the secret Danny and Carolina had been hiding, he no longer cared what Jess's father thought of him. All that mattered was Jess. And Harrison's job. Danny had been making cuts at the company, and Harrison wanted to keep his position. He'd worked too hard to have it snatched away, and this would ensure that Danny could never get rid of him.

'What do you want?' Danny had demanded. 'Because everyone has a price, don't they? So, what is it? What's yours?'

'Why have you been lying all these years? What have you got to hide? Because it seems like there's an obvious answer to that.'

Danny had refused to answer, drumming his fingers on the table, and again demanding to know what Harrison wanted.

'I want you to tell Jess. Yourself. It needs to come from you. The whole truth. And quickly. She's suffered enough.'

Danny shook his head. 'Oh, come on. There must be something. I know you want my daughter back in your life, but that's beyond my control, isn't it?'

'I just want Jess to know the truth,' Harrison had assured him. 'From your mouth.'

There had been a long pause before Danny had spoken again. The tapping on the table had grated on Harrison. 'You'll climb the ladder quickly here, son,' Danny said. 'You're one of the best. Do you understand what I'm saying?' He'd narrowed his eyes. 'And then one day, not soon, but one day, when I'm ready to retire, this company will belong to you. I'll put it in writing.'

And with those words, everything changed. Harrison had

made a split-second decision. Was it based on ambition and greed? Jess would find out, he'd convinced himself. Maybe he could even steer her in the right direction. As long as Danny never suspected he was doing it. But Harrison hadn't had to in the end. Jess had found her own way to the truth.

It was a decision Harrison has regretted ever since.

And every time he thinks about this, Harrison tries to convince himself that he didn't know Danny and Carolina were involved in Lori's murder. That the lie they told didn't have to mean something more sinister.

But every so often, in his nightmares, the truth comes out.

A LETTER FROM KATHRYN

Thank you so much for taking the time to read my sixth psychological thriller, *The Suspect* – I really hope you got involved with the characters and were taken by surprise at the end! If you did enjoy it, and want to keep up-to-date with all my latest releases, just sign up at the following link. Your email address will never be shared and you can unsubscribe at any time.

www.bookouture.com/kathryn-croft

I always thoroughly enjoy plotting and writing my books and I hope you enjoyed the ride this one took you on.

Whether you've just discovered my books or have enjoyed any of my previous novels, I'm extremely grateful for your support. Reviews are so important to authors, so if you did enjoy it then I'd be extremely grateful if you could spare a moment to post a quick review to let others know your thoughts. As always, any recommendations to family and friends would also be greatly appreciated!

It's always wonderful to hear from readers so please feel free to contact me via Twitter, my Facebook page or directly through my website.

Thank you again for all your support!

Kathryn x

KEEP IN TOUCH WITH KATHRYN

www.kathryncroft.com

 facebook.com/authorkathryncroft

twitter.com/katcroft

instagram.com/authorkathryncroft

ACKNOWLEDGEMENTS

This is my tenth book and it wouldn't be in anyone's hands without the help of many people.

Thank you to my agent, Hannah Todd, for all your hard work, passion and determination. You're always there to talk to and offer advice, and I'm privileged to have you as my agent. Also, a huge thanks to everyone at the Madeleine Milburn Literary, Film and TV Agency for being such a fantastic team, tirelessly championing your authors.

I couldn't be happier to once again be published by Bookouture, and I owe a tremendous thank you to my brilliant editor Lydia Vassar-Smith for taking me on and for making this book as strong as it can be with your incredible editorial insight. It's such a pleasure to work with you and thank you for 'getting' my books. Thank you also to Kim Nash and Noelle Holten and the whole Bookouture team – it's amazing to be back!

The biggest thank you to every single person who has read or reviewed this book – without you I wouldn't be able to do the job that I love so much, so I really appreciate that you've taken the time to read my words.

I think the pandemic has taught us all just how much we value our family and friends, and how important human interaction is. Thank you to everyone who is in my life – I'm grateful to all of you for your support, your kindness and your company. A writer's life can be very solitary, so I'm especially grateful to my husband and children for the noise, chaos, laughter and love you fill the house with every day (just not when I'm trying to write, please!).

Thank you to all the other authors out there for making sure we never run out of books to read. I can't imagine a world without books – I always say that, if I had to, I could give up anything except books (and tea of course!).

Made in the USA
Middletown, DE
14 May 2023

30585917R00196